The Waiter

Bradleigh Collins

To Charity
for inspiring me to finish this book

And to Dana
for being there for all of it

To Charity
for inspiring me to finish this book

And to Dana
for being there for all of it

One belongs to New York instantly,
one belongs to it as much in five minutes as in five
years.

- TOM WOLFE

1. What Happens in Central Park

God, I don't want to go home.

It was my first thought when I awoke to the sound of the hotel's radio alarm clock. "This is 1010WINS. You give us twenty-two minutes, we'll give you the world."

According to the newscast, it was seventy-seven degrees and going up to a high of eighty-eight on this Saturday, the twenty-eighth day of August. And, at the sound of the tone, it would be nine o'clock.

I rolled over to turn down the volume. Then I grabbed the phone and called my cousin Josh. He answered with a groan.

"Is it that bad?" I asked.

"Like you're not hungover too."

Actually, I wasn't. I had paced myself throughout

the previous night's pub crawl. The evening started with margaritas and Mexican food at Mama Mexico. It ended about five hours later with tequila shots at Bourbon Street.

"I just need a really big iced coffee and a cinnamon raisin bagel. Meet me at Zabar's at ten."

"Ten-thirty," he mumbled before hanging up.

I laid there, thinking about how much I was going to miss the feel of these crisp white sheets. After a few minutes, I climbed out of bed and opened the drapes. The rooftops and water towers dotting the skyline of the Upper West Side looked like disjointed puzzle pieces. I loved waking up to this view of the city every day. I wanted to move to New York more than anything, and now was the perfect time to do so. I'd just turned thirty, it was the last year of the nineties, and a new millennium was approaching. I was also recovering from an apocalyptic breakup with someone I'd been dating for almost ten years. Now, more than ever, I needed a new start.

But first, I would need a new job. That was the primary reason for my trip. Hoping for a transfer, I'd interviewed at the Manhattan headquarters of the advertising firm I worked for in Atlanta. The interview had gone well, and I was cautiously optimistic.

I took a nice long shower and wrapped myself in the hotel's comfy bath robe before rifling through my suitcase to find something to wear. I settled on a cute Old Navy denim mini-dress with spaghetti straps. It would be perfect for spending the day in Central Park. A little makeup, a lot of sunscreen, a high ponytail, and I was ready. I left a tip for the hotel maid, grabbed my Coach backpack, and headed out the door.

The sun was blinding and people scurried past me as I stopped to put on my sunglasses. New Yorkers are always in a hurry to get somewhere, anywhere. I, being a tourist for now, was taking my time and taking it all in.

The brightness of the day made everything appear in technicolor. Trees along Broadway seemed greener than the ones on Peachtree Street. A gold spire atop the Apthorp gate glistened in the sunlight as though it were winking at me. In the distance, the orange and white Zabar's sign stood as a beacon, drawing me closer and closer to my morning caffeine fix.

When I walked in, the scent of fresh baked bread consumed me. I grabbed a shopping basket for bottled waters and Gatorades to take back to my hotel room.

"My god, it smells like an orgasm feels in here!" Either the other shoppers didn't hear what Josh said, or they didn't care because nobody reacted.

"How's the hangover?" I said with a hug.

"Better. I had some Alka-Seltzer earlier and now I'm just starving."

We walked up and down the narrow aisles gathering everything we thought we'd need for the day. I found my water and Gatorade while Josh grabbed a bag of Milano cookies and some potato chips. Then we got coffee and cinnamon raisin bagels and headed to the checkout.

"My friend Darryl thinks you're hot," Josh said as we paid for our food. "He has a thing for redheads."

"Your friend Darryl is an alcoholic. I thought he was gonna throw up on the sidewalk in front of Jake's Dilemma last night."

"Yeah, he's a bad drunk."

We walked out of Zabar's and started heading back towards the hotel.

"Why would you wanna fix me up with a bad drunk? Besides, I'm never dating again."

"Don't worry, I told him he didn't have a chance. Dalton would kill him."

Just hearing his name made me wince.

"Dalton's a jackass," I said with a mouthful of bagel and warm butter dripping down my chin. "I'm not taking him back this time."

I wanted to mean it, and I was trying hard to mean it. I'd been keeping a running tally on my FranklinCovey Day Planner of how many days I had gone without speaking to him. It was up to thirty-five.

"Yeah, right," Josh said. I could understand his skepticism. Dalton and I had broken up and gotten back together about a hundred times over the last decade. It was never a healthy relationship. If you asked any of my friends or family members to describe Dalton in one word, they would all use the same one. Toxic.

We dropped off the waters and Gatorades in my hotel room. Then we headed east on 77th Street towards the park.

"I can't believe you wore those shoes again." Josh looked down at my feet. "That clip-clop sound makes me insane. Every girl in the city is wearing those freaking shoes."

"Don't talk about my Stevies that way. They're the most comfortable shoes I own." They were black Steve Madden platform slides with stretchy fabric across the top. The style went with everything and gave me the extra boost in height that my five-foot-five frame needed.

We continued walking towards the park while discussing the previous night's antics. A drunken Josh made his karaoke debut at The Parlour singing Rick Astley's "Never Gonna Give You Up." His performance was a hit, resulting in a rousing response from everyone in the bar and a couple of phone numbers for Josh. I laughed so hard that my abs were still hurting.

"Jimmy's nice," I said. Darryl's brother Jimmy was a bouncer at The Parlour. "What's his story?"

"His story is that Darryl drives him crazy. Why, are you interested in Jimmy?"

"I'm not interested in anybody."

We walked past the Museum of Natural History and crossed over into the park. Throngs of New Yorkers, tourists, and Upper West Side nannies pushing double-wide strollers were all descending upon the great green Mecca of Manhattan.

As we approached the bottom of the hill, something - or rather someone - caught my eye. Over to the right in the grassy area was an incredibly attractive man doing some type of strange workout. Shirtless. He would drop and do several pushups. Then he would pop back up and do a series of high knee jumps. It was exhausting just watching him. And very erotic. He had dark brown hair with spiky bangs that fell over his forehead. He was wearing a pair of Adidas track pants that hung low on his hips and exposed what I like to call his "Ken doll handles." But I couldn't stop staring at his perfect shoulders.

"Hello, Mr. Deltoids," I said under my breath as we passed by.

Josh turned and looked. "I thought you weren't interested in anybody."

"I'm interested in that body." It was the first time I'd found someone attractive since Dalton and I broke up.

"Jesus, stop ogling the poor guy, Sam. You're such a perv."

I continued ogling as we turned left onto West Drive. Mr. Deltoids must have sensed me looking. He stopped his workout long enough to look over his sculpted shoulder and smile at me. I couldn't help but smile back. I also couldn't help bumping right into Josh because I wasn't watching where I was going.

"Really Sam?"

"Oh god. He just smiled at me."

"Go talk to him, doofus."

"I can't."

"Why not? What have you got to lose?"

"My dignity."

"So you'd skip the chance to meet a guy that's attracted to you because you might embarrass yourself?"

Josh had a point. What was keeping me from turning around and walking over there and introducing myself? Oh, I remember. It was that number Dalton did on my self-esteem. Yeah, no.

"I'm flying back to Atlanta tomorrow. Besides, if he looks that good, he must be a jerk."

We continued walking along the path, coming into full view of a horde of runners, cyclists and roller-bladers. It was a perennial parade of men. And I was willing to bet that not all of them were emotional sadists like Dalton.

We made our way onto the Great Lawn. Josh pulled out a blanket from his backpack and laid it down.

"Are you planning on calling either of those girls from last night?"

"I can't remember what they look like."

"They were both cute. Especially the blonde. Katie, I think."

Josh reached into his backpack and pulled out a napkin.

"Yeah, Katie." He handed the napkin to me. There, written in black ink next to the Parlour's logo, were the digits of a girl that was probably wondering if the cute karaoke guy with the amazing voice was going to call.

"Call her. See if she wants to meet us out tonight."

"I'm not calling her today. It's too soon. She'll think I'm a psycho."

"Oh god! What is it with you guys and your two-day rule?"

"Hey, it works." He made a makeshift pillow with his backpack and laid down.

"Give me your *Time Out New York*. I wanna find a place to go for dinner tonight."

He pulled the magazine out of his backpack and handed it to me. I began thumbing through page after page of restaurants, clubs, Broadway shows, art galleries, and more. I could live here my entire life and still not have enough time to experience everything this city had to offer.

Josh was already asleep. His snoring was muted slightly by the ambient sounds of the park. We had plans to meet his friends later tonight at The Bubble Lounge, so we'd decided to do an early dinner. I flipped to the restaurant guide and perused the recommendations for our area. I grabbed a pen from my backpack and circled a few places. Then I laid back on the blanket, looking up at the sky. Under no circumstances could I fall asleep. I was afraid I'd end up snoring, drooling, or contorting myself into a position that exposed my ass.

We stayed in the park for hours and then we were starving. I showed Josh my potential choices for dinner.

"Pomodoro is fantastic," he said. "I've been there before."

"Are we dressed appropriately?" I gestured to my mini dress and Maddens and his khaki shorts and CBGB shirt.

"I don't think they even have a dress code at Pomodoro. Besides, they have outdoor seating, which is great for people watching."

"Great for girl watching, you mean."

"Girls are people."

We packed everything up and headed out. The restaurants and bars lining Columbus Avenue were already buzzing with early diners and drinkers.

"I have to pee," I said as we entered the restaurant.

"Okay, I'll get us a table outside. What do you want to drink?"

"Apple martini and a glass of ice water."

As I walked to the back, the smell of Italian food made me ravenous. I hadn't eaten anything since my morning bagel, and I was now looking forward to devouring the breadbasket.

I freshened up and headed back to the front of the restaurant. I joined Josh, who was already sitting outside drinking a beer and looking at the menu. Just as I sat down, a glorious green apple martini appeared in front of me. I reached for the glass and took a sip.

"Hey, didn't I just see you guys in the park this morning?"

I looked up at our waiter. I saw the dark hair falling across his forehead. It was Mr. Deltoids. Mr. Deltoids was our fucking waiter.

2. The Waiter

The Waiter stood there, smiling at me.

"Yeah, I remember you," Josh said. "I told my cousin to stop leering at you this morning." I could feel my face turning red.

"Your cousin?"

"Yeah, my totally single cousin Sammy here." He emphasized the word "single." Josh and The Waiter both laughed. I wanted to crawl under the table. I couldn't bring myself to look at either of them, so I buried my face in the menu.

"I'm just gonna climb over the railing here and step in front of a bus," I said without looking up.

"Please don't," The Waiter said. "I'll be right back with some bread and I'll tell you guys about our specials." He walked away. I glared at Josh, who was sitting across the table from me grinning like a Happy Buddha statue.

"What?" Josh asked, "This is fucking fantastic!"

"I am mortified."

"Why? He obviously likes you. Every guy likes you. Come on. You're hot and you know it."

"That is so not true. And he's our waiter. It's his job to be nice to us. Which makes this even more humiliating."

I really had no idea if he was flirting with me in particular or if he was this friendly because it resulted in big tips. And even if he was flirting with me, I was leaving tomorrow. And even if I weren't leaving tomorrow, I was still gun-shy about getting back into the dating world. The pain from my breakup with Dalton was too fresh. I gulped my martini. I was going to need some liquid courage to get me through this dinner.

And then it appeared. The breadbasket I'd been craving. Only now, my stomach was filled with butterflies and alcohol.

"So Sammy," The Waiter said, "That's kind of a guy's name, isn't it?"

"Yeah." I summoned enough courage to look up and make eye contact with him. He was even better looking up close. He had beautiful brown eyes, sexy full lips and cheekbones that were made for precision glass cutting.

"Is that short for Samantha?"

"No. Just Sammy. It was my grandfather's name. Well, his name was Samuel, but everybody called him Sammy."

"You spell it with an 'i'?"

"Nope. With a 'y' like a guy."

"Interesting." His smile lingered a bit, causing me to wonder if Josh was right. Maybe he was flirting with me. Or maybe I have something in my teeth.

"So, here's what we've got going on menu-wise tonight."

As he rattled off the specials, all I could think about was how I felt like Drew Barrymore's character in *Never Been Kissed*, a movie that my best friend Dana and I had been to see a few months ago. I felt like a total geek. I had been with Dalton for so long that I had no clue how to date, or flirt, or even know if someone was flirting with me. I had zero game.

"I'll give you guys a few minutes to decide," The Waiter said as he walked away.

"Sam, you should see if he wants to meet us out tonight," Josh said mockingly, looking down at his menu.

"God no! And I swear, if you ask him or embarrass me any further, I will call that girl Katie from last night and tell her to meet us out too. I still have the napkin."

"Touché."

I studied the menu, then glanced over to see The Waiter laughing with the bartender as he loaded a tray of drinks for another table. I looked around the restaurant. All the waiters and waitresses were wearing the same thing. Black pants with a white button-down shirt. I'd seen my waiter without the shirt. My face felt flush again. And just like that, he was back.

"Have you guys decided?"

Josh ordered first. Spaghetti and meatballs.

The Waiter turned to me. "How about you, Red?"

"I'll have the fettuccine with basil."

"Excellent choice. It's my favorite dish." He winked and disappeared.

"I think you're his favorite dish," Josh mumbled.

"Stop."

"Dude, he's totally flirting with you."

"Dude, I've totally got no game. I have completely forgotten how to do this."

"There's nothing to do, Sam," Josh said reassuringly. "Just be yourself. You're funny. You're gorgeous. You're related to me. It's all good."

Josh always knew how to make me feel better. Growing up, we were inseparable. We were also the black sheep of our ultra-conservative southern families. As kids in the 1970s, we bonded over roller-skating, disco dancing, and *Star Wars*. Our teenage years were spent driving around our tiny hometown of Douglasville, Georgia, listening to Cheap Trick and Motley Crue. We went to different high schools and colleges, but we still managed to hang out together all the time and were always fixing each other up with our friends.

Josh was working as a C.P.A. for Ernst & Young when I was hired at the ad agency in 1994. One of our clients was the Atlanta Olympic Committee. I was constantly scoring invitations and tickets to all the cool happenings in Atlanta during the mid-90s. Josh was frequently my plus-one.

For about a year, he dated my co-worker Julie. She liked the fact that he looked like David Arquette, and he liked the fact that she had huge tits. Obviously, their relationship didn't last. A couple of years ago, Josh was offered a big promotion at the Ernst & Young headquarters in New York. He took it. Now he lives in a small one-bedroom apartment near Riverside Park.

"What time are we meeting your friends tonight?" I slathered butter on a piece of bread. The martini was working its magic and I was starting to relax a bit.

"Around nine or ten," Josh said, finishing off his beer.

The Waiter was back with our food.

"Be careful, darlin'," he said as he placed the dish in front of me. "This plate is really hot."

Darlin'. Okay, he's flirting with me.

"You guys ready for another round?"

Josh signaled yes.

"Oh, not for me, thanks," I said. "I'm pacing myself."

"Hot date tonight?" The Waiter asked.

"No. We're just meeting some friends out later."

"At the Bubble Lounge," Josh interjected. I cut my eyes to look at him. "Sam's leaving tomorrow, so we're gonna do it up right tonight."

"Oh, really? Where are you running off to?"

"Atlanta," I replied. "Home."

"Ah, I thought I detected a southern accent."

"He has one too." I pointed at Josh.

"Yeah, but his isn't sexy," The Waiter replied smiling at me. "I'll be right back with that beer."

Josh laughed. I sprinkled some fresh parmesan onto my fettuccini and took a bite. It was so good and I was so hungry that I didn't even care if The Waiter saw me scarfing it down. After a few minutes, he came back with Josh's beer and some more ice water for me.

"How is everything?"

"I love the spaghetti and meatballs here," Josh replied. "I get it every time."

"This is so good," I said. "I think I need to take it back to my hotel so I can be alone with it." Both Josh and The Waiter laughed.

"Where are you staying?"

"On the Ave Hotel. Broadway and 77th."

"Oh, the one by Fishs Eddy?"

"Yeah. I love that store!"

"Have you been to the GreenFlea at Columbus?"

"No, I haven't."

"Oh man, you gotta go before you leave. What time is your flight?"

"Six-thirty tomorrow night."

"Wanna meet me there in the morning around ten?"

"Sure." I could feel Josh smiling at me from across the table.

"Great!" The Waiter scooped up my empty glass. "It's a date."

He disappeared to the back of the restaurant again. My heart was racing. I looked across the table at Happy Buddha.

"What were you saying about having no game?" Josh asked.

"I can't believe that just happened. No games. No wait two days. Just, 'Hey, wanna hang out with me?' Who does that?"

"Not me," Josh said. "I've got game. But not that kinda game. That was smooth."

I sat there stunned and discombobulated as we finished our meal. What are the odds that some random stranger I'd been lusting after this morning would be asking me out a few hours later? What are the odds that I would pick the very restaurant he worked at from a list in a magazine?

"Dinner is on me," Josh said as he reached for his wallet. "I owe it to you for humiliating you."

"Yes, you do. But I got the tip. And it's gonna be a big one."

"I'll bet," he laughed. "I'm going to the bathroom and then we'll head out."

Josh walked towards the back and handed The Waiter his credit card. I sat there at the table trying to calm myself as I watched the cabs whizzing down Columbus Avenue, stopping to pick up people and deliver them to their next New York minute. The sun was starting to set and another Saturday night was just getting started.

The Waiter was back. He placed the folio with Josh's credit card on the table. Then he kneeled down beside me. We were face to face. I felt weak.

"So, Sammy." God, even his voice was sexy. Very

deep. Very New York. "Why don't you write down your phone number in case I need to call you tomorrow?"

I somehow managed to form words. "I'll give you my business card. It has my cell number on it."

I reached into my backpack and pulled out a card. As I handed it over to him, my cell phone began to ring.

"Great," The Waiter said. He put his hand on my bare knee as he started to stand up and leaned in closer.

"I'm really looking forward to seeing you tomorrow, Red."

"Me too," I smiled. He stood up and disappeared once again. I placed a few twenty-dollar bills in the folio.

My phone was still ringing. I retrieved it from the bottom of my backpack and looked down at the number on the screen. My heart stopped. It was Dalton.

3. Dalton

Why the fuck is he calling me?

It's all I could think about as Josh and I walked back to the hotel. I didn't answer the phone. I turned it off and shoved it back into my bag as we left the restaurant. The restaurant where I'd just had my first New York minute. A minute I couldn't even enjoy now because why the fuck is he calling me?

I didn't tell Josh that Dalton called. I wanted to pretend like it didn't happen. No way was I going to let him spoil my last night in the city. Dalton had a knack - an almost psychic ability - to insert himself back into my life right at the very moment I was ready to move on.

"You're awfully quiet," Josh said as we waited to cross the street. "Are you thinking about your new lover?"

"No, I'm thinking about what to wear tonight."

"Yeah, Tribeca's a bit more upscale. I'm actually gonna have to find a clean shirt with a collar."

We walked up Broadway until we reached 77th Street.

"I'm gonna grab the one train uptown," Josh said. "I'll meet you back here around nine and we'll take a cab."

I hugged him goodbye and headed up to my room. As soon as I got inside, I sat down on the bed and took out my phone. I turned it on and waited. The screen lit up. And there it was. A new voicemail message from Dalton. I felt sick. My hands started to shake. I'd experienced this fight-or-flight feeling before.

A couple of months ago on a Sunday afternoon, my sister Wendy called to tell me that our dad had been rushed to the hospital. He'd recently had heart surgery and was now having trouble breathing. My dad's health had been deteriorating for years, thanks to a pack-a-day smoking habit he had no intention of breaking.

Dalton and I immediately drove to Douglasville, which is about a half-hour west of Atlanta. I was a nervous wreck. When we walked into the waiting room, my entire extended family was there. They were all crying. I saw my sister walking towards me. I could tell by the look on her face that my dad had just died. My knees buckled and Dalton caught me right before I hit the ground. I buried my face in his chest to muffle my scream.

My sisters and I went into my dad's hospital room. I looked at him lying there in the bed. My mother was standing next to him, holding his hand. I ran and hugged her and cried so hard I couldn't breathe. She told me it was just his time to go and that he was no longer in any pain. My mother was the strongest person I knew, and even now, after just losing the love of her life, she was determined to be strong for her three girls. I leaned down and kissed him on the forehead. I told him I loved him. In one week, it would be my thirtieth birthday. And my dad wouldn't be there.

I was still in shock as we all walked out of the hospital. Dalton turned to me. "So like, what do we have to do here?" he said coldly. "I've gotta get back to work tomorrow."

I let go of his hand, which up until that point, had been the only thing keeping me steady on my feet. I started to walk towards my mom, who was a few steps in front of me with my sisters. I kept thinking if I could just make it to her, if I could just grab her hand, I would never look back at Dalton again. He grabbed me by the arm.

"I'm sorry," he said, pulling me back to him. "I didn't mean it like that."

I wanted to tell him to fuck off right then and there, but I was emotionally gutted. I didn't have the strength to go through another breakup with Dalton while also trying to deal with the death of my father.

Funeral arrangements were made for Thursday.

Dalton worked as an IT consultant and traveled extensively. His current assignment was in Miami. I told him to just fly out on Monday as usual and come back Thursday for the funeral. I had taken the week off and was surrounded by friends and family, including Josh.

Dalton was late for the funeral, of course. He blamed it on Atlanta traffic. My entire family would have preferred that he not even show up. They weren't fans. Especially my father, who thought Dalton was "the most arrogant son-of-a-bitch I've ever met in my life."

I should have left him a long time ago, but I loved him. More than anything in the world. I'd loved him since the first time I laid eyes on him. I was majoring in English and minoring in Theatre at Georgia Tech. I'd been cast as Jill in a local production of *Equus*. Dalton was a friend of the director who had recruited him to play the part of Nugget - the Stallion horse. The horses had no lines in the play, but they were an integral part of the story. The person playing Nugget had to be physically imposing and incredibly sexy. Dalton fit the bill on both accounts.

The first day of rehearsal, the entire cast was gathering on the stage for a read-thru. I took a seat at the table, facing out into the audience. The doors in the back of the auditorium opened up and this huge hunk of a man came walking down the aisle. I remember thinking that he looked like some kind of superhero. He jumped up on the stage and we immediately made eye-contact.

He was the tallest, most beautiful man I had ever seen. Six-foot-four with broad shoulders and long dark curly hair. He was a cross between Michael Hutchence of the band INXS and the lead character from that TV show "Renegade," which was quite popular at the time.

He walked around the table and sat down right next to me. Then he scooted his chair even closer. The smell of him was intoxicating. He was wearing Calvin Klein Eternity for Men.

"Hi! I'm Dalton."

He had green eyes that were almost as light as mine.

"Sammy," I smiled.

After the read-thru, the cast went out for drinks in Buckhead. Dalton never left my side, chatting me up the entire night. I learned he was ten years older than me and graduated Georgia Tech with a degree in computer science. He also had a black belt in karate and worked part-time as a bouncer at a couple of bars in Atlanta. He asked me if I wanted to go see *Bram Stoker's Dracula* the following night. Then he walked me to my car and kissed me. We were together ever since.

Dalton was my first true love. In the beginning, things were perfect. He was the smartest person I'd ever met and everything I thought a man should be at that stage of my life. The ultimate alpha male - protective, encouraging, and genuinely concerned about my well-being. I would soon find out that he was possessive, manipulating, and cared only about himself.

But he did love me. And he had no trouble telling me. He told everyone, especially when he was drunk. Our sex life had become the talk-of-the-town, especially on guys' nights out. That's one of the main reasons I stayed with him. The sex. It was addictive. For years we repeated a viciously unhealthy cycle of co-dependency. We would break up. He would show up. We'd have sex. And then we would make up.

We definitely loved each other. The problem was that Dalton was emotionally abusive. And apparently I was an emotional masochist because I put up with it. He never physically assaulted me. But he regularly beat the shit out of me with his words and with his actions.

A week after my father's death, on my birthday, I confronted Dalton about his cruel behavior that day. His excuse was that he just wasn't good at dealing with death. He didn't know how to help me. I should probably see a psychiatrist. He said all of these things to me before he'd even wished me a happy birthday.

We had plans to go out to dinner that night with Dana and a few of my other friends. Dalton didn't have to work the next day because it was a holiday weekend. He remembered it was July 4th, yet somehow forgot it was my birthday.

All day, I kept thinking he was going to surprise me. That maybe he had something really special planned because it was my thirtieth and because I'd just lost my dad. But I soon realized he didn't.

Around five o'clock, I went into the living room of his house where he was at his desk working.

"So, I'm gonna get ready to go out and celebrate my birthday. Are you planning on coming?"

"Oh, yeah, right," he looked up from his computer. "Happy Birthday. You want a cake or something?"

It got worse.

A few weeks later, Dalton and I were supposed to attend his co-worker's wedding on Sunday. I spent all of Saturday shopping for the perfect wedding present, finding the perfect card, and getting everything perfectly wrapped. I barely knew the guy that was getting married.

When I arrived at Dalton's house that night around eight, he wasn't there. I called his cell phone.

"I'm at Rhonda's watching a movie," he said. Rhonda was one of his so-called platonic friends that always wanted to hang out with Dalton, but never with me. It was obvious she didn't like me. But that never stopped Dalton from spending time with her. I always wondered how Rhonda would feel if I started hanging out with her boyfriend. Of course, she didn't have one. I was convinced she wanted mine.

"Okay," I responded, a bit confused. "Well, I'm here. I thought we were going to Café Intermezzo."

"I'm leaving soon," he replied. Four hours went by without a word from Dalton. At midnight, I left, taking with me the two-hundred-dollar wedding gift that I'd be returning the next day. I changed my access code on the entry to my apartment complex. The next day, I would get my locks replaced. I was done. And this time, I meant it.

I awoke the next morning to a series of voice-mail messages from Dalton. I deleted them all. And I avoided him like the plague. I hadn't seen him, spoken to him, or heard from him until now.

I looked down at my phone again. Then I pressed a couple of buttons. I was prompted by the screen.

"Are you sure you want to delete this message?"

Fuck yeah I'm sure.

4. Last Night

The Bubble Lounge was crowded and the music was loud. Women in little black dresses bounced up and down to Will Smith's "Wild Wild West" as Wall Street wannabes circled them like sharks. Josh and I navigated our way through the feeding frenzy to the downstairs bar where his friends already had a table. He introduced me.

"Sammy, this is Kyle and Lucy."

Kyle was Josh's co-worker at Ernst & Young, and Lucy was his fiancé. They were a stunning couple. Kyle was a dead ringer for Mario van Peebles. Lucy had jet black hair and porcelain skin. They looked like they'd stepped right out of a Benetton commercial.

"I love your maxi-dress," Lucy said as Kyle and Josh headed for the bar. "Ralph Lauren, right?"

"It is, actually." I was surprised she could so accurately identify my dress in such a dimly lit bar. "How did you know?"

"I recognized it from the Bridget Hall ad. I work for *Vogue*."

"And now you're my new best friend." I sat down next to her. "What do you do at *Vogue*?"

"Advertising. I'm an account manager. Ralph Lauren is one of our biggest clients."

"Really? I work for an ad agency in Atlanta. I just interviewed for a position here in the New York office."

"That's fantastic! I hope you get it. If not, let me know. We're always hiring at *Vogue*."

"Wow, thank you! That would be a dream. Can I send you my resume?"

"Of course. Josh has my contact info. Feel free."

"You're amazing! Thank you so much."

The guys were back from the bar. Josh handed me a glass of champagne.

"Did Sam tell you about her hot date tomorrow?"

I smiled just thinking about it. I told Lucy and Kyle the story of my chance meeting with The Waiter and how it had turned into a day-date for tomorrow.

"Cheers to that!" Lucy said as she held up her glass. "That's destiny."

The four of us toasted. I wondered if it was destiny. Or just a coincidence. I took a sip of champagne. Then I turned to Josh.

"By the way, I called that girl Katie and told her

to meet us here."

"You what?"

"Yeah, after you name-dropped 'Bubble Lounge' to The Waiter, I went back to the hotel and called her up."

"Who is Katie?" Kyle asked.

As if on cue, Katie appeared in the doorway by the stairs.

"That's Katie." I waved and motioned her over. She had a big smile and blonde hair styled in a chin-length bob. She reminded me of a very petite Cameron Diaz.

"Damn, she's hotter than I remembered," Josh said.

"You're welcome." I smiled at Josh. Then I hugged Katie and introduced her to Kyle and Lucy.

"Let's get you a drink," Josh said to her. They disappeared to the bar.

"We love Josh," Lucy said. "I'm surprised some woman hasn't snagged him up by now."

"I don't think he wants to be snagged."

The three of us sat there discussing Lucy and Kyle's upcoming wedding. It was happening on New Year's Eve at the Marriott Marquis overlooking Times Square.

"Where did you guys meet?

"Madison Square Garden," Lucy said. "At a Billy Joel concert."

"How romantic."

We stayed at The Bubble Lounge for another hour. Then Josh decided he'd had enough champagne. He suggested we all go across the street to the Tribeca Tavern to shoot pool and drink "respectable beers." I was really starting to feel like a fifth wheel. I thought about calling it a night. But it was my last night in the city, and I wanted to spend as much time with Josh as I could before leaving. So I went.

When we got to the Tavern, Katie excused herself to the bathroom. Josh and I went to the bar to get drinks.

"You did good, cuz. Katie's really cool. And since you called her and I didn't, it's not like I broke the two-day rule."

"You are such a freak. And speaking of freaks."

"What?"

"Dalton called me today." I don't know why I felt the need to tell him. Maybe I was tipsy from the champagne. Maybe I just needed his advice. Maybe it was because I couldn't stop thinking about Dalton no matter how hard I tried.

"Holy shit," Josh said. "Well, you know you guys will end up back together. What did he say?"

"I don't know. I deleted the message without listening to it."

"Why?"

"Because I don't want to be back in that place. Emotionally, you know. I don't know if I'll ever be able to forgive him."

"Fuck him, Sam. He doesn't deserve you. Besides, you're gonna move up here. Once you're out of his sight, he'll be out of your mind."

"God, I love you."

"I love you, too. I'd offer to beat him up for you, but you know, he's Thor and I'm more of a Groot."

"I have absolutely no idea what you're talking about."

"That's because you don't read comic books."

Katie was back. We got our drinks and Josh got quarters for the pool table.

"Give me some of those," I said. "I wanna play something on the jukebox." I was still feeling like the odd-man out and just needed a minute to collect my thoughts.

Josh handed me a few quarters. I walked over to the jukebox as he, Katie, Kyle and Lucy commandeered the pool table. I stood there, pushing the button and flipping through various songs. I was starting to get really sad. This weekend had been a welcome retreat from my depression. Josh was my comic relief, and I was going to miss him terribly. And even though I was excited about seeing The Waiter tomorrow, I knew that once our day date had ended, I'd be flying back to Atlanta and back to a life I was dead set on escaping.

I stood there at the jukebox, perusing song after song. Suddenly, there was someone right next to me.

"Hello, Red." I looked up, hoping it was The Waiter. But it wasn't. It was Drunk Darryl.

"Hi Darryl," I said, managing a smile. "Everybody's back there playing pool."

He leaned in closer. "You know, you look just like

the Little Mermaid."

"Huh?"

"You know, Ariel. The Little Mermaid. With your red hair and big eyes and all." Darryl did not understand the concept of personal space.

"Um, that's sweet, but weird, Darryl. Why don't you grab a beer and I'll meet you back there with the others."

I just wanted to get rid of him. I continued flipping through the musical selections. Then I found it. I laughed out loud as I fed quarters into the slot and selected the song. I couldn't think of a happier way to end my last night in New York.

I wandered back to the pool table and grabbed a stool next to Katie. I found out she was originally from Connecticut and worked as an ER nurse at Columbia Presbyterian. She lived not too far from Josh on the Upper West Side. I told her the story about meeting The Waiter and confessed that I was getting a bit nervous about seeing him.

"What's there to be nervous about?"

"I don't know. What if he doesn't show up?" I was starting to believe that our chance encounter and mutual attraction were too good to be true.

"He'll show. And if he doesn't, he's a loser," Katie said.

Lucy chimed in. "The good thing is that it's a day date in a public place. It's not like you're waiting by yourself in a restaurant or bar."

The conversation then turned to Josh and Katie. "So how did you and Josh meet?" Lucy asked.

"He impressed me with his karaoke skills last night at The Parlour."

"Oh, if you think that was good, just wait until my song comes on," I said.

"Why?" Katie asked.

"It's a flashback. To our childhood."

"What do you mean?"

"The only thing there was to do in our hick town was go to the roller-skating rink. This song was our anthem. Josh and I spent weeks learning all the words so we could sing along."

The three of us sat there, sipping our martinis and watching Josh and Kyle play pool while Darryl annoyingly narrated every shot. It was almost one o'clock in the morning and I needed to head back to the hotel soon. I didn't want to look like a total zombie the next day in case The Waiter actually showed up. I also wanted to take a shower before going to bed so I wouldn't wake up smelling like smoke.

Then it happened. A cowbell, a conga drum and a high-hat cymbal. The thumping bass line of a familiar song crawled through the speakers. Josh immediately looked at me.

"Oh, no you didn't!" An enormous smile spread across his face.

"Rapper's Delight?" Katie asked. I nodded.

Suddenly Josh and I were eleven years old again. The pool stick became his microphone. He still knew all the words.

It wasn't long before everyone joined the sing-along, which quickly turned into a dance party. I didn't want the song to end. I didn't want the night to end. I did, however, want to make my escape from Drunk Darryl who had somehow managed to make me his dancing partner.

Afterwards I said my goodbyes to everyone, promising Katie and Lucy I'd keep them updated on The Waiter and my potential move to the big city.

Josh walked me outside. "Call me after your big date tomorrow. We'll grab lunch before you leave for the airport."

"Will do," I hugged him. "Love you."

"Love you, too." A cab pulled up. I hopped in and waved goodbye.

"Where to?" the driver asked.

"Broadway and 77th, please."

To my next New York minute.

5. The M7 Takes Forever

I woke up early and, as they say in the south, nervous as all get-out. I wanted to give myself plenty of time to get ready for my date with The Waiter. That is, if he actually showed up. I also had to pack. I chugged a Gatorade and threw all my clothes onto the bed.

What if he does show up? That thought scared me more than if he didn't. I hadn't been on a date since I broke up with Dalton, and I wasn't sure if I was ready to see someone again. I wasn't sure about anything. Except that I had to get dressed.

I decided to wear my new Jean Paul Gaultier halter top and maxi skirt. I bought it at a sample sale after my job interview on Thursday. It was comfortable and classic and just the right amount of sexy. And today I would wear flat sandals. I was afraid the clip-clop sound of my Maddens would be just as annoying to The Waiter as it was to Josh.

I finished packing and jumped in the shower. Afterwards, I spent a bit more time on my makeup than usual and pinned my hair up into a messy bun. It was now nine-thirty. I checked out of the hotel and left my luggage with the bellhop. I wanted to take one last stroll around the neighborhood. Plus, I didn't want to arrive at the flea market too early and appear too eager. *God, I sound like Josh.*

The more I walked, the more I convinced myself that The Waiter wasn't going to show. I figured I would just go to the market and enjoy it by myself, and then I'd meet Josh for a late lunch. I was already prepping myself for disappointment.

I turned back onto 77th Street and paused to look at all the quirky dishes in the window at Fishs Eddy. I wanted to go in and buy some to take home with me, but I had no room in my suitcase and I was afraid they would break, so I continued walking.

As I crossed Amsterdam, I heard laughter coming from the corner playground, which was already filled with neighborhood children. The flea market was just one block away, and I was beyond apprehensive. I took a deep breath and tried to distract myself by gazing at the beautiful brownstones lining the street. I imagined how wonderful it would be to live in one of them. But as each step brought me closer and closer to my destination, my legs turned to jello and my hands began to shake.

Then I saw him. He was leaning against the fence by the entrance. He was wearing a gray t-shirt, black track pants, and sneakers. A large backpack was hanging off his shoulder. He looked up and saw me coming.

"Hey, Red!" he yelled.

"Hi!" I smiled and waved as I walked towards him. He met me half-way.

"Morning beautiful." He gave me a quick hug. He was taller than I remembered. Not as tall as Dalton, but close. His hair was still wet. It smelled like my Aveda candle. "You're tiny," he said, looking down at me.

"No, you're just really tall and I'm wearing flats. Okay, I'm short."

He laughed. "Come on, shorty. I'll show you around."

The market was behind a school and covered almost half the block. Hundreds of tents were lined up side-by-side with vendors selling everything from hand-carved soaps to vintage clothing to Persian rugs. There was also every type of food you could imagine. Baklava. Grilled corn. Mozzareppas. Egg rolls.

My senses were on overload from the smell of exotic food and incense. The sight of colorful silk pashminas and gilded antique mirrors that looked heavier than most cars. The sound of Sinatra singing "Fly Me To the Moon" on a vintage record player as a beautiful elderly couple danced inside the tent. And the touch of The Waiter's hand on my back as he guided me through the market gave me chills.

"What do you think?"

"This place is amazing!" I said. "I'm not leaving

here without one of those pashminas. Or a mozza-reppa. Or four."

The Waiter laughed. I was no longer nervous and felt relaxed. I picked up a light blue pashmina from one of the tables.

"So, you're a writer," he said.

"How did you know that?"

"Your business card."

"Oh, yeah."

"Have you written any books?"

"Not yet. I definitely want to in the future. Right now I just write ad copy and content for various clients. And some freelance articles. I was in town interviewing for a position here in our corporate office."

"You're moving here?"

"If I get the job."

"So there's a chance I might see you again?"

"If I get the job," I repeated.

"You'll get it. Wait here. You have to try something. I'll be right back."

I was still holding the pashmina. I wrapped it around my shoulders. It was so soft. I had to have it. And I got one for Dana, too. I paid the vendor and stepped across to the mozzareppa stand.

"Two please."

A few minutes later, The Waiter returned with two paper cups. "This is my favorite thing about the GreenFlea. Fresh grape juice. And it's ice cold."

I took a sip. It reminded me of taking communion as a kid in church and how I always wanted more because it tasted so sweet. But this was even better.

"Okay. That's it. I'm never leaving. I will just live here at the flea market and drink grape juice and eat mozzareppas for the rest of my life."

"You're adorable," he said. I handed him one of the mozzareppas and we continued to explore the market. He told me he grew up in Brooklyn and was from a large Italian family. His father was a doctor. His mom a history teacher. He was in the process of getting his MBA at Columbia. That's why he was working at Pomodoro. The schedule was flexible and the money was great.

"Basically, I go to work, to school, and to the gym. That's my life."

"Where do you live?"

"The Ansonia. Broadway and 74th."

"Do you have to work today?"

"Yea, but not until three. I wanna get to the gym around one and get a workout in, but I've got a couple of hours. What are your plans?"

"I'm meeting Josh later for lunch and then off to the airport."

"Wanna go for a walk with me?"

"Sure. I just wanna pick up some of those soaps on the way out."

I purchased four bars of mint soap as we were leaving. Then we walked over to Central Park. We took the exact same path that Josh and I had the day before.

"The scene of the crime," I said, as we passed the

spot where I first saw him.

"It's my favorite place in the park," he said. "It's so peaceful."

"Aside from the tacky tourists leering at you?"

"I was leering back."

"Seriously?"

"I noticed your red hair. And then your legs. I assumed Josh was your boyfriend. I'm glad he wasn't. He's a funny guy."

"I adore him. We've always been really close."

We walked over to a nearby bench and sat down. I told him how Josh ended up in New York and how he'd been trying to get me to move here. The Waiter told me about growing up in Brooklyn with three brothers and one sister and how his five-hundred square foot studio now felt like a mansion because he had it all to himself.

The two of us sat there on the bench talking for what seemed like forever. Then my phone rang. I felt a familiar panic and assumed it was Dalton. That he somehow sensed I was happy at this very moment and felt the need to fuck it up. I pulled the phone out of my backpack and was relieved to see it was Josh.

"How's it going with lover boy?"

"Fine," I replied, hoping The Waiter didn't hear him. "We're in Central Park. What time do you wanna meet?"

"Half hour? At Big Nick's?"

I looked down at my watch and realized it was half past noon. "Okay. See you there." I hung up and looked at The Waiter.

"I'll walk you back," he said. "I need to catch the M7 bus at Amsterdam and head up to the gym."

We got up and began walking out of the park.

"So, is there a boyfriend waiting for you back home?"

"God, no!"

He laughed. "You just said that like you have the plague or something. Like nobody would ever date you."

"I did have the plague. I broke up with him."

"Ouch," he said as we walked up to Central Park West. The traffic light was about to change. He grabbed my hand. "Come on, we can make this light."

We ran across the street just in time. When we reached the other side, I expected him to let go of my hand. He didn't. We were just slowly strolling hand-in-hand past the Museum of Natural History. But not slow enough. I knew I only had two more blocks to enjoy that rare sensation of holding hands with someone you like for the first time. Especially someone you knew you wouldn't see again for a long time.

"When will you find out about the job?" he asked as we crossed over Columbus.

"Within a couple of weeks I think." We passed the entrance to the market. "Thanks for turning me on to the GreenFlea."

"I love this place," he said. "I'm here every Sunday."

We continued walking until we got to Amsterdam, stopping right in front of Vermouth Lounge. "Wait with me until the bus comes? If you can, I mean. The M7 takes forever."

"Sure," I replied. He was still holding my hand. "I can't believe I just met you and now you're leaving me." He leaned against the one-way signpost.

"I know. I still can't get over the fact that you were our waiter last night. That's crazy."

"Yeah, what are the odds?" There was a nervous silence. Then he looked down at me. "God, you have the most amazing eyes."

"Thank you." I looked up at him.

He put his arms around my waist and pulled me in to him. *Oh my god, he's going to kiss me! He's totally going to kiss me!* And then he did. Right there on the corner, right underneath the crosswalk sign, he kissed me. His lips were full and soft and he tasted like grape juice. I could hear the children playing in the background. Then I heard the sound of the bus approaching.

"Fuck!" he screamed and threw his head back. "The one time I want the bus to be late it's on time."

He kissed my forehead. "I'll call you this week, okay?" I nodded. Then he ran across the street toward the bus stop. He turned around and yelled at me. "Later Sammy with a 'y' like a guy!"

I laughed and waved. He smiled. Then he disappeared into the bus.

As I crossed over Amsterdam, I giggled. I actually giggled. I was still sad to be leaving New York, especially now, but I knew I'd be re-living this moment over and over until I saw him again.

And I was determined to see him again.

6. Shadowboxing

"**D**etails," Dana said as I got in the car. "I want every goddamn detail."

I was back in Atlanta. Dana and I were leaving the airport en route to El Azteca, our favorite Mexican restaurant on Ponce, which just happened to be stumbling distance from my apartment.

"Dana, I swear, I felt like I was in a Norah Ephron movie. It was so spontaneous and romantic and he was just so...so, I don't know...matter of fact. Hey, I like you. Hey, let's hang out. Hey, I'm gonna kiss you now."

"How was the kiss? Was there tongue?"

"There was until the bus came."

Dana had been my best friend since grammar school and we still did everything together. Everybody loved her. She was one of the most driven and authentic people I knew and was great at her job. Dana worked as a public relations manager and had a natural ability for putting people at ease. She was also the spitting image of a young Jodie Foster, with piercing blue eyes and skin I'd been jealous of since the day I met her.

"How is my buddy Josh doing?" Dana and Josh dated briefly in high school, but they soon became more like brother and sister.

"Same old Josh. We had a blast. I hooked him up with a girl. Katie. You'd like her."

"I love Josh."

"Everybody loves Josh. He was in rare form this weekend."

We merged onto the interstate. The Atlanta skyline glared at me. I felt guilty. I had been cheating on her after all.

"What's Simon up to tonight?" Dana and Simon had been dating for the last three years and living together for the last two. Simon was one of the good guys. He was a handsome graphic designer and avid runner. He was crazy about Dana.

"He's home watching the Cowboys-Broncos game."

"Oh, I'm taping *Sex & the City* tonight," I said. "Wanna come over tomorrow and watch it?"

"Isn't this week's the one with Jon Bon Jovi?"

"Yep."

"Then yes, definitely."

"Thanks for picking me up at the airport."

"Of course! I couldn't wait to hear about your

weekend."

"Well, I have something else to tell you, but I need a margarita first."

"Oh god. This has to involve Dalton." She knew him way too well. She knew us way too well. Dana had been there from the very beginning of our relationship. She never once had a problem telling Dalton what a dick he was to his face and, oddly enough, he adored her for that. When things were good between Dalton and me, Dana loved him like a brother. When they were bad, she despised him. But she also knew how much I loved him, and she was always rooting for our relationship to work.

We arrived at the restaurant around ten and grabbed a table outside. Soon our regular order of frozen margaritas and cheese dip appeared. I told her about the phone call.

"He's so fucking predictable." She stirred her margarita with a straw. "He always does this."

I nodded. "It's the only thing I can depend on him for."

"What do you mean?"

"Well, how many times has he left me stranded at the airport? I mean, I could never even count on him to pick me up, which is why I always ask you. But anytime I'm experiencing a little happiness that doesn't involve him, he shows up like clockwork."

"Yep, every time," Dana agreed. "And orgasms."

"What?"

"That's the other thing you could always depend

on him for. Mind-blowing orgasms."

"Like I needed that reminder."

"Hey, maybe the hot waiter can help you out with that," she laughed. "Aren't you the least bit curious what the voicemail said?"

"Of course. I mean, I hope it's not something bad and that everyone in his family is okay. I would feel terrible if something happened."

"Michelle would have called you if it was an emergency." Michelle was Dalton's sister. We were good friends. She always took my side over his and would regularly apologize for her brother "being such an asshole."

"Why can't he just leave me alone?"

"Because you always take him back."

"Not this time."

"Why do you always take him back? You always say never, and then you let him right back in."

"Because I don't want to be alone. I hate being the odd man out. Party of three. Party of five. Plus, I keep thinking he'll change. That we'll change together. Grow together."

"You really think Dalton's capable of change?"

"Why not? I'm constantly rearranging my life for him."

"And there you have it," Dana said.

"What?"

"Think about what you just said. Your life revolves around Dalton. His needs. His schedule. His ego. Sam, I know you love him, but sometimes you just have to let go of someone you love for your own good."

As usual, she was right. I had no response. No defense. So I ordered another margarita.

After dinner, we headed back to my apartment. Dana wanted to borrow a dress to wear to a work function later that week, so she came upstairs. My apartment was on the third floor of an old Ford factory where they used to make Model T cars. It was built in 1915 and converted to lofts in the mideighties. The building shared a parking lot with a grocery store that was known as "Murder Kroger" after a girl was shot and killed there. There was also a nearby liquor store and several retail shops underneath, including a nail salon, Chinese restaurant, and the infamous Model T Drag Bar. It was an incredibly cool place to live, and despite the Murder Kroger moniker, I always felt safe.

My apartment, however, was anything but cool. I opened the door and was assaulted by the heat.

"And I'm officially in hell."

I sat my suitcase down and turned on the air conditioner. Dana made a beeline for my closet.

"Oh, I have something for you!" I shouted at her in the next room. I opened my backpack and took out the pashmina and a couple of bars of the mint soap. The smell took me right back to the flea market and right back to The Waiter. I smiled. Dana walked back in with the dress and hung it on the doorknob. I handed her the goodies.

"Oh this is beautiful!" She wrapped the black pashmina around her shoulders. "It's so soft. And these smell amazing! Thank you! Okay, I gotta pee and then I gotta go."

She sat the soaps down on the table and disappeared into the bathroom, still wearing the pashmina. I unzipped my suitcase. Right on top was my pashmina. Underneath was the denim dress I wore the day I met The Waiter. Every piece of clothing was now a piece of history. I took out my Steve Maddens. I thought of Josh and laughed. And there was the black pantsuit I'd worn to my job interview. If I got this job, I would be moving to Manhattan in a matter of weeks.

Dana came back in the living room. "Okay babe, I'm outta here."

"Thanks again for the pickup!" I hugged her.

"Thanks for the dress! I'll get it back to you this weekend. Love you."

"Love you too. Tomorrow night, *Sex & the City.*"

Dana gave me the thumbs up as she headed to the elevator. I closed the door. I walked over to my entertainment center and turned on the CD player. Fiona Apple began to sing. She would keep me company as I finished unpacking. But first, I needed some iced tea. That's one thing you can't get in New York. Sweet tea was like water in the south, and I hadn't had any in four days. I went to the kitchen and poured myself a glass.

As I walked back into the living room, I saw that Dana had forgotten her soaps and left them on the table. I was just about to call her cell phone to tell her when the downstairs buzzer rang. I immediately buzzed her back up. And then I went back to unpacking.

A few minutes later, Dana knocked. I opened the door. It wasn't Dana. It was Dalton.

"So what," he said as he stood there towering over me, "you were just never going to talk to me again?" His hair was longer than the last time I saw him. He was wearing a black t-shirt, jeans and Doc Marten boots.

"What are you doing here Dalton?"

"I need to talk to you." He walked right in and sat down at the table.

"You've got five minutes." I closed the door and leaned against it, my arms folded tightly in front of me as some sort of subconscious shield. What I really needed was a bulletproof vest.

Dalton looked at my suitcase. "Where have you been?"

"New York."

He picked up a bar of soap from the table and sniffed it. Then he stared at me, saying nothing. Fiona continued to sing about shadow-boxing in the background, which seemed eerily appropriate for the current situation.

"Talk," I said.

"I'm in Atlanta," he replied.

"I see that."

"No, I mean, I'm working on a project here in the Atlanta office for a while. I'm not traveling."

"So?"

"So I just wanted to see you."

"You've seen me."

"And tell you that I was sorry."

"Okay then."

I opened the door and motioned for him to leave. He sat there for a minute. Then he stood up and walked over to me. I couldn't look at him. He put his hand on the back of my neck. I froze. He leaned down and kissed my forehead.

"I'm sorry baby," he said. Then he left.

I shut the door. The smell of his cologne lingered in the apartment. That same fucking cologne he was wearing the day I met him. I stood there, trying to process what had just happened. And then I started to cry.

In a matter of minutes, Dalton had dredged up all the feelings I'd been trying so hard to suppress over the last month. And I hated him for it. Part of me wanted to believe that he was actually sorry, and for that, I hated myself.

It was now midnight and I was exhausted. I changed into my pajamas and sat down at the computer to check my email before going to bed, a bad habit I'd developed that I couldn't seem to shake. In any case, I figured it would take my mind off Dalton and give me a head start on my work week. I grabbed my day planner and opened it, pen in hand. There, for the month of August, were twenty-eight consecutive days of hand-drawn smiley faces representing every day I hadn't spoken to Dalton. If I were an alcoholic, I would have a 36-day chip. But tonight, I was thrown off the wagon.

I logged in to my work email. Most of the messages were junk that I deleted immediately. A couple were from Brenda, the bitchy account manager that hated me because I refused to flirt with sales managers at company outings and happy hours. "They pay your salary," she would say. "The least you could do is show them some attention." Her emails could definitely wait until tomorrow. Then I noticed an email from an address I didn't recognize. The subject line simply said, "Hi!" I opened it.

Hey Red! Hope you had a safe flight. How's Hotlanta? Let me know if you hear about the job. (You're going to get it.) Enjoyed our morning stroll. We'll talk soon.

P.S. Your lips taste like grape juice.

I read it again. And again. And then again. Then I got up and walked over to my suitcase. I picked up the pashmina and wrapped it around me. My morning moment had found me again.

I crawled right into bed and turned out the light.

7. Bitchy Brenda

riday afternoon at the office. It had been one week since my job interview and I still hadn't heard anything. I would have been completely depressed if it weren't for the nightly ICQ chats I'd been having with The Waiter.

It started with a phone call on Monday. After talking for over an hour, The Waiter suggested ICQ messaging to avoid the inevitable long-distance charges we were about to rack up. We exchanged usernames and our bedtime chats began, usually after he had gotten home from work.

During our Wednesday night chat, a message from Dalton popped up. It simply said, "Hi." I simply ignored it and changed the settings so he couldn't see when I was online. I was still pissed about him ambushing me. Plus, I wasn't going to let him interrupt my catching up with The Waiter every night.

I had also managed to catch up with Josh. He and

Katie had gone out again. Things were going well and they both couldn't wait until I "got my ass back up there." I couldn't either. I was craving New York. And I was really craving The Waiter.

When I first heard his voice on the phone, I got that same giddy feeling as the day he kissed me. I hadn't even known him for an entire week, but I liked him. I really liked him. I had learned more about The Waiter in five days than I learned about Dalton the entire first year we were together.

Around three o'clock, Bitchy Brenda stopped by my cubicle. "Still haven't heard from corporate?" Brenda was in her early fifties. She was five-foot-ten with frizzy blonde hair. People in the office called her "Big Bird." It was common knowledge that she was sleeping with half the sales team.

"No, nothing yet."

"Maybe you're just not cut out for New York." She smirked and walked away.

My office phone rang. I picked it up.

"She's a cunt."

I laughed audibly. It was my co-worker Deb who sat directly across from me. I swiveled in my chair to look at her.

"Well, I couldn't just yell it out, but she is a see-you-next-Tuesday," she said quietly into the phone. "She probably sabotaged your interview. She knows everybody up there in corporate."

It was true. Brenda made frequent trips to the home office in New York. And even though I didn't report to her, she could certainly hold sway with the powers that be.

"You may be right. She does hate me." My other line rang. "I gotta get this." I hung up with Deb and took the other call. It was corporate. I didn't get the job. They hired someone that already lived in New York. But they would keep me in mind for any open positions in the future, blah, blah, blah.

I knew exactly why I didn't get the job. It was Bitchy Brenda. She had probably just heard from one of her contacts and - after not speaking to me all week - made it a point to stroll by my desk just now and drop a little condescension. I felt defeated. And I wanted to cry.

I turned back to Deb. "I didn't get it. You were right."

She got up and walked over to my desk. "Fuck that bitch. Let's get outta here."

It was pretty common for staff to leave early on Friday afternoons, especially in the summer. There were client events or happy hours or having to "drop off some artwork" for a customer. Most of these were excuses to hit the bar, which is exactly what we were doing. Plus, it was Labor Day weekend.

We decided to go to Manny's Tavern. It was just ten minutes from the NationsBank Plaza where our office was located. When Deb and I arrived around four, it was already crowded. Manny's was the closest thing to Cheers you could find in the south. Everybody knew everybody, and we were all regulars. The drinks were cheap but stout and the crowd was friendly but sometimes obnoxious.

I called Dana before I left the office and told her about the job. She said she'd meet us here after work. I needed all the moral support I could get. I knew that even if Bitchy Brenda had nothing to do with it, which I wholeheartedly believed she did, there was still a chance that I wouldn't get the job. But I was so hopeful. Now I just wanted to drink myself into oblivion.

Dana arrived about an hour later. I was already on my second apple martini. "I'm so sorry, babe." She gave me an extended hug. "You'll get the next one. A better one."

"And Brenda will get herpes." Deb clinked my glass with hers.

"She's probably already got it. Maybe that's why she's in such a bad mood all the time."

"I think this calls for a girls' night out," Dana said.

Deb was in.

"I'm gonna need a nap first. I'm pretty tipsy as it is."

"Give me your keys. Let's finish this round and we'll go pick up Simon. He can drive your car back. Then I'm picking you up around nine and we're going out. I'm not going to let you sit home and mope."

But of course, that's exactly what I wanted to do. Instead, I took a two-hour nap and a long hot bath. I decided to channel my anger and disappointment into determination. I would blow off steam tonight and spend the rest of the long weekend scouring

Monster.com and the New York Times classifieds for jobs. I would get back up on that work horse. I would get my ass back to New York.

Our night began with dinner at Ru San's. It continued with stops at Leopard Lounge and Nomenclature Museum, two clubs in midtown that were within walking distance of each other. Leopard Lounge was the place to be seen drinking expensive cocktails, and Nomenclature was the place to listen to alternative music with alternative people. Around midnight, we headed to the Clermont Lounge.

The Clermont is an iconic Atlanta club that's been around since the sixties. It's referred to as the place "where strippers go to die." That's part of its charm. A strip club located in the basement of a rundown hotel on Ponce, and not even a five-minute walk from my apartment, the Clermont was known for two things. One, it had the best DJs in Atlanta, and two, Blondie - the legendary stripper that was so famous she had her own comic book. Blondie was also famous for crushing beer cans between her enormous breasts. But I suppose the real reason everyone clamored to the Clermont was because it was the one place in Atlanta where you could just be yourself. And enjoy everyone else being themselves. At the Clermont, the freaks were the beautiful people. And we were all freaks.

The music inside was pounding and everybody on the tiny dance floor - including the three of us - was dripping with sweat. But every time a song would fade out and we would think about taking a break, an even better song would come on that kept us dancing.

We saw Simon and his friend Sean walk in. Dana motioned that we'd meet them over at the bar. They had gone to the Braves game earlier and then to a few sports bars downtown. I'd met Sean once before. He was cute in a preppy sort of way. Not my type at all, but completely Deb's.

"Alright, one more drink and I'm going home," I said. "My feet are killing me."

"That's because you wore those heels," Deb replied. "I don't know how you walk in those things, much less dance in them."

I leaned down to adjust the strap on my sandal. When I looked up, I saw Dalton standing by the entrance staring at me. He was talking to Dave, the bouncer.

"Fuck!"

"What's the matter?" Dana asked.

"Look who's here." I motioned towards the door.

"What the hell is he doing here?" she asked as he walked over to us. "What the hell are you doing here?"

"I've missed you too, Dana," Dalton said. He and Simon exchanged their usual "hey man, how's it going" greeting. "I need to talk to Sam."

Dana looked at me. "Are you okay?"

"Yeah, I'm fine."

"We'll give you guys a minute. I'll be right over there." She pointed to an area by the dance floor where Sean and Deb were chatting.

I took a sip of my martini.

"How many of those have you had?"

"Not enough to make me forget you're an asshole."

"I know I'm an asshole. I'm trying not to be."

The female bartender smiled at Dalton. "Whatcha drinking gorgeous?"

"Scotch."

"Why are you even here? Shouldn't you be watching a movie with Rhonda or something?"

"Sam, I'm sorry. I don't know how many times I have to say it." He grabbed my hand and held it. "I miss you, babe."

I missed him too, but I wasn't about to tell him that. I just stood there, sipping my cocktail, holding his hand.

The bar was getting crowded. Dana and Simon and Deb and Sean were out on the dance floor. A table opened up right next to us and Dalton quickly grabbed it. He sat down and pulled me onto his lap. I could feel Dana looking at me from the dance floor. I looked up just as she mouthed the words "What the fuck?" I shrugged and threw my hands up in the air. She shook her head.

"So, are you gonna give me another chance or what?"

"I'm speaking to you, Dalton. That's the best I can do right now."

"And you're sitting on my lap."

"Only because my feet are hurting."

Dana and Simon were back.

"I'm gonna take your drunk friend home now," Simon said.

Dana leaned down and hugged me. "Do you want us to take you home?"

"No, I'm okay," I said. "We're just talking."

Dana got in Dalton's face. "Don't be a dick," she said, poking him in the chest with each syllable. "Don't. Be. A. Dick."

He laughed. "Goodnight, Dana."

"Love you, Sam. I'll call you tomorrow."

They left, with Dana taking one last chance to turn around and point her finger at Dalton before walking out the door.

"You never answered my question," I said to him. "Why are you here?"

"It's Friday night. I saw Dana's car at Murder Kroger. I figured you guys would be here."

"You figured I'd be drunk."

"I figured correctly. Why are you so drunk?"

"Because Bitchy Brenda sabotaged my dream job in New York."

"You interviewed for a job in New York?"

"Yeah, but I didn't get it. So Deb and Dana took me out to make me feel better."

"Do you feel better?"

Just then I saw Blondie making her way through the crowd. I jumped up. "I'm gonna get you a Blondie lap dance! She can crush your head between her boobs. That will definitely make me feel better." I started to walk over to her. Dalton stood up and pulled me back.

"You are not getting me a lap dance."

I made a square around his face with my index fingers. "You know what this is? This is you not being fun." He laughed. Then I yelled out for Blondie.

"Okay, time to go." He picked me up and slung me over his shoulder and started carrying me through the bar.

Deb and Sean were still on the dance floor. "Deb, I'm taking her home!"

"Sam, call me tomorrow!" I wanted to wave at her, but I was using both hands to hold my little black dress down so I wasn't flashing anyone my thong. Not that anyone there would have cared or even noticed.

"Later man," I heard Dalton say to Dave as we left.

"Bye, Dave," I said. I could see his shoes but not his face. Everybody knew Dave and Dave knew everybody. If anyone but Dalton was hauling my drunk ass out of the Clermont over their shoulder, Dave would have stopped them in their tracks.

"Put me down, Dalton! I'm still mad at you." He was carrying me up the hill to the street where his car was parked.

"You can still be mad at me in the car, Sam."

When we got to the car, he put me down. Slowly. My body slid down his until my feet were on the ground and my arms around his neck. He leaned me up against the passenger side door. I looked up at him. I knew exactly what was about to happen. And

I had no intention of stopping it.

Dalton leaned down and kissed me. It lasted forever. And I still wanted more.

8. Thirty-Six Days

I woke up with a pounding headache and a regretful recollection of the night before. *Oh god. I kissed Dalton.* I immediately checked to see if my clothes were still on. They were. I had slept in the same dress I'd worn out last night. My hair and my pillow smelled like smoke. Someone had taken my shoes off, and I didn't remember that someone being me.

I rolled over. No Dalton. *Okay, I didn't sleep with him.* I think I would have remembered if I had. At least I hope I would, given the fact that I haven't had sex in over a month. And sex with Dalton was certainly not something you forget.

I got up and headed for the kitchen to get some aspirin. There in the living room, asleep on my couch, was Dalton. He was laying there wearing nothing but his white Calvin Klein boxer briefs, looking like some kind of Greek statue or anatomy drawing that belonged in a museum. I just stood there in the doorway, staring at him. I had been in love with this man for most of my adult life. My heart ached for him even though he was right there in front of me. That was the essence of our relationship. I really wanted to believe he was sorry, but I'd been here too many times before. I could see the writing on the wall. Hell, I wrote the writing on the wall.

I went to the kitchen and took a couple of aspirin. Then I started the coffeepot. When I walked back into the living room, Dalton was awake.

"How are you feeling?" he asked.

"Like a loser that needs a shower." I walked towards the bathroom.

"Want some company?"

"Nah, I'm good." I went into the bathroom and locked the door. The last thing I needed was him joining me in the shower. Sex was the slippery slope that always got us back together and always got me another soul crushing.

After I finished my shower, I put on my robe and blow-dried my hair. Then I walked back into the living room.

"Wanna go to Majestic?" Dalton asked.

"Fuck yeah, I do." The Majestic had the best breakfast in town and I was starving. Plus, I needed to extricate Dalton from my apartment so I could get to work lining up my next job interview.

"I'm gonna jump in the shower first." He got up and walked past me, stopping to lean down and kiss me on top of my head. "You're still funny as hell when you're drunk."

"You're still a jerk when I'm drunk."

"Yeah, but you love me anyway." He closed the bathroom door.

Asshole. He was right. I did love him anyway. It felt good being out with him last night. Slipping back into our usual couple banter. Sitting on his lap. Having his arms around me. And that kiss. Goddamn that kiss. I kept thinking about it as I got dressed. The greatest thing about my relationship with Dalton was the passion. The spark was always there. But the explosion and the shrapnel that follows was never far behind.

As soon as I finished getting dressed, the bathroom door opened. Dalton stood there with a towel wrapped around his hips, water dripping down his chest from his long wet hair. His chiseled oblique muscles were fully exposed. God, what I wanted to do to that body. What I had done to that body. He caught me staring and smiled vindictively.

"I'm using your toothbrush," he said.

I wanted him so badly. I missed him so badly. And I knew that all I had to do was walk over to him and give him a look. The towel would drop. He would lift me up onto the sink like he had done so many times before. I would wrap my legs around him and he'd walk me into the bedroom where we'd spend the entire day making up for lost time. And then I'd be right back where I started. I quickly snapped out of it.

"I'll meet you downstairs. I need to get something at Kroger." I grabbed my purse and ran out of the apartment. I walked over to Kroger even though I didn't actually need anything. I bought some Alka-Seltzer and tampons just to cover my hasty exit. I could always use Alka-Seltzer and tampons.

I left the grocery store and walked over to Dalton's car. It was a fancy red sports car that was way too fast and way too flashy. I used to refer to it as the extension. Not that he needed one.

We arrived at The Majestic around ten and were seated at a booth near the back. I ordered a grilled cheese and fries and he ordered steak and eggs. I was already on my second cup of coffee.

"So, tell me about this New York thing," he said.

"Not much to tell. I interviewed for a job in corporate last week and I didn't get it because Bitchy Brenda hates me."

"You were just going to move to New York and not tell me?"

"I wasn't speaking to you at the time. I hadn't been speaking to you for thirty-six days to be exact."

"Sam, about that night," he said.

"Yeah, about that night."

"I fell asleep. Rhonda didn't wake me up."

The sound of her name made my jaws clench. "Of course she didn't."

"I swear to god nothing happened."

"Okay." I didn't know if I believed him or not.

"Does that mean you forgive me? That I get another chance?"

"You get the chance to have breakfast with me right now."

"Fair enough."

We sat there eating our Majestic breakfast like two civilized people. It was nice, actually. He was going to his office afterwards, and I was grateful for that. I needed to get my head back on straight and focus on New York. The sooner I could find a job, the sooner I could escape what was certain to be another round with Dalton.

When I got back to the apartment, I sat down at my desk and logged onto Monster.com. I started submitting for every single writing job I saw based in Manhattan. I figured if I got any interest, I could do another long weekend in the city and schedule a few interviews in one day. I had plenty of vacation saved up and I knew my boss would approve the time off.

Just as I hit the submit button on my third job application, an ICQ message popped up from The Waiter. "Whatcha doing Red?"

All of the sudden, I felt guilty. Like I had somehow tainted our budding relationship by hanging out with Dalton. The Waiter and I weren't really seeing each other. But we were doing something. I typed out a response.

"I'm recovering from a girls' night out in which I attempted to drown my sorrow. I didn't get the job."

My phone rang. It was The Waiter.

"I can't believe you didn't get it. I'm so sorry

hon."

"Thanks. I'm pretty bummed. But now I'm just sitting here blasting Monster with my resume."

"Good. So that means you'll be back up here soon."

"I hope so."

"Me too. I can't wait to see you again."

I wondered if he could hear me smiling through the phone.

"So, what were you wearing last night while you were drowning your sorrow?" I immediately thought about holding my mini-dress down to cover my ass while Dalton was carrying me out of the Clermont.

"Oh, the usual. Little black dress.

"How little? Bring it the next time you come up."

"I will."

"Okay babe, I'm going to head to the gym before work. Talk later?"

"Of course."

After we hung up, I called Josh.

"I did a bad, bad thing."

"You had sex with Dalton, didn't you?"

"No, but I did kiss him. Because I was drunk. And I was drunk because I didn't get the job."

"Get the fuck out. Really? That sucks!"

I gave Josh the rundown of why I thought I didn't get the job as well as an overview of the previous night's antics. Then I remembered Lucy had mentioned that *Vogue* was always hiring.

"Hey, can you email me Lucy's contact info? I

wanna send her my resume. She said she might be able to find something for me at *Vogue*."

"Sure," he replied. "I'll go do it right now."

"Thanks Josh. I'll talk to you later."

I sat there for a minute, just picturing myself working at *Vogue*. What are the odds? I figured they were better for me than for most, since I had an inside contact. In any case, I was feeling a lot better about myself and my prospects today than I did yesterday. And how great would it be to tell Bitchy Brenda that I was moving to New York to work for *Vogue*?

In less than a minute, Josh had sent me Lucy's info. I quickly fired off an email message to her and attached my resume along with a few writing samples. I thanked her profusely for offering to help.

The downstairs buzzer rang. I went over to answer it. "Yes?"

"Delivery for Sammy St. Clair."

"Come on up." I pressed the buzzer. Deliveries were pretty common on Saturdays, even though I couldn't remember ordering anything. In a few minutes there was a knock at my door. I opened it to see an enormous bouquet of peach-colored roses. I was stunned.

"Sign here, please." The delivery guy handed me a pen and I signed.

"Thank you." I closed the door and set the flowers down on the table. They smelled like perfume. I counted them one-by-one. There were thirty-six in total. Three-dozen roses from Dalton. I smiled as I read the card.

I'm sorry about the job. I'm sorry I'm a dick. I'm sorry you didn't talk to me for 36 days. But I'm not sorry about that kiss.

9. The Guilt Trip

I spent the rest of Saturday and all day Sunday applying for jobs. On Monday I went to a Labor Day barbecue at Dana and Simon's. We sat outside drinking margaritas and analyzing the Dalton situation. Dana was impressed that I hadn't slept with him. I was impressed that I hadn't slept with him. I told her about the flowers. It wasn't the first time Dalton had sent me flowers, but Dana and I were both taken aback at the seeming sincerity of the card. I could feel him reeling me back in. If I stayed in Atlanta, I knew I'd end up back with him. Dana agreed.

Tuesday I got an email from Lucy about a job at her friend Jackie's start-up. Jackie had worked at *Vogue* for several years before launching a fashion site called e-Styled.com. It brought together stylists, designers, clothing brands and all kinds of fashion industry people and allowed consumers and subscribers the ability to style outfits and build wardrobes online. It was an incredibly creative concept, and the company was well-funded. They were looking for an Online Editor to write web content, newsletters, ad copy, and fashion related articles. Lucy asked if I would be interested. Of course I said yes.

It was now Wednesday afternoon. Deb and I had just returned from a cardio funk class at the frog pond. Okay, the Australian Body Works gym wasn't actually in a frog pond. It was in The Rio Mall, which was two blocks from the office. It's where we spent most of our lunch hours. The inner courtyard had this strange water fountain with hundreds of gold frogs lined up in a foosball formation. That's why we called it the frog pond.

Just as I sat down at my desk, the phone rang. I answered. "Hi Sammy, this is Victoria Neal. I'm the Human Resources Manager at e-Styled. We'd love to have you come in for an interview next week. Are you available Monday?"

"Yes, of course. I'd love to."

"Great! How about two o'clock?"

"That works for me."

"Okay then. I'll send you an email with all the details and we'll look forward to seeing you on Monday."

"Thank you so much," I said as I hung up the phone. I was so excited my entire body was shaking. I immediately put in a vacation day request for Monday. My boss was off this week, but I knew he would approve it. Then I called our in-house travel agency to arrange my flight and hotel. I would fly to New York Saturday morning and fly back Monday night. And I'd be staying at On the Ave Hotel again.

After securing my travel plans, I sent Lucy an email telling her about the interview and thanking her for putting in a good word for me. I told her I'd love to take her out to lunch or dinner this weekend if she had time.

Then I called Josh. "Guess who's gonna be in the city this weekend?"

"Seriously?" he responded. "Why? What happened?"

"Lucy," I said. "She got me an interview on Monday. I am so taking her out to dinner."

"This is great," he said. "We can all hang out again."

As soon as I hung up with Josh, I called Dana. "You're gonna get laid this weekend," she said. Suddenly I felt nervous. The Waiter didn't even know I was coming yet. Doubt quickly set in. *Would he still want to see me? What if he already had plans? What if he was seeing somebody else? Why wouldn't he be seeing somebody else? Of course he's seeing somebody else.*

After talking to Dana, I logged on to ICQ to see if The Waiter just happened to be online in the middle of the day. He was. *Was he chatting with somebody else?* I messaged him.

"Hey! I have another job interview on Monday. I'm coming back to the city this Saturday."

"Are you serious?" he responded instantly. "That's perfect! What are you doing Saturday night?"

"I don't know yet. Hanging out with Josh and Katie and Lucy and Kyle at some point, I'm sure."

"I want to take you to this really cool show. My friend is in it. Josh and everyone can come. I'll get comp tickets for all of us."

"Okay. That sounds like fun. Thanks."

"Chat tonight? Regular time?"

"Absolutely."

I could not remember the last time I'd been this excited. In just the last hour, I had scheduled another job interview in New York, booked my trip, and landed a second date with The Waiter.

I left work right at five o'clock and headed home to start packing. Around six-thirty, Dalton called.

"Hey babe. Wanna go get something to eat?"

"I can't. I'm packing."

"Packing for what?"

"I'm going back to New York this weekend. I have another job interview on Monday."

"That's great babe. Congrats."

"Thanks. I'm excited. And nervous."

"Want some company?"

"If you come over here, I won't get any packing done. I won't get anything done."

"I meant do you want some company in New York this weekend," he said. "I'll go with you."

I was taken aback. "No! It's gonna be a quick trip. I'm leaving Saturday and coming back Monday."

"So? I'm up for a quick trip with you. I can visit the New York office Monday. Show my face up there.

Maybe I'll get a better assignment." Dalton's company was also headquartered in New York.

"No, Dalton. This is something I need to do on my own."

"Why? Have you got a boy-toy in New York you don't want me to know about?"

Oh my god. He knows. How the hell does he know? I wasn't sure if I should tell him about The Waiter or not. I was afraid if I told him, he would get mad and show up in New York and ruin my entire weekend. If I lied, I would be doing the same thing to him that I begged him not to do to me. So I went with a neutral answer that was kind of the truth.

"No. No boy-toy." I certainly didn't think of The Waiter as a boy-toy. "I just need to focus on this job interview, and if you're there, I'll be focused on you."

"Okay. Suit yourself. Where are you staying?"

"I don't know yet." I had to lie this time. I didn't want to tell him the name of my hotel because I was certain he would "surprise" me.

"Listen Dalton, I have to go pack. I'll call you when I get back from New York, okay?" At this point, I just wanted to get off the phone with him before he asked more questions that I would have to answer with more lies.

"Want me to pick you up at the airport on Monday?"

I laughed out loud. "Are you kidding me? You suck at airport pickups."

"I'll be there this time. I promise."

"Okay Dalton, if I need an airport pickup, I'll call you." Yet another lie. But it finally got me off the phone with him.

As I hung up, I glanced over at the enormous bouquet of peach roses on my dining room table. Guilt crept into my weekend plans like an army of ants invading a peaceful picnic. *Do men ever feel this much guilt? Of course they don't.*

I felt guilty that I had just lied to Dalton about The Waiter. When I was talking to The Waiter on Saturday, I felt guilty that I had kissed Dalton the night before. The truth was, I wasn't in a relationship with either of these men. Dalton was my past, and I was trying keep it that way. The Waiter could be my future. But I didn't owe either of them anything.

Later that night, I was having my usual ICQ chat session with The Waiter.

"You have to dress casual Saturday night," he said. "Jeans, sneakers. Nothing fancy. Something you wouldn't mind getting messed up."

"Are we going to a mud-wrestling bar or something?"

"Not even close. Trust me, you will be blown away."

"I'm excited," I said. "And a little scared."

"The show starts at ten. I'm working until seven. Why don't you guys meet me at Luna Park in Union Square around nine?"

"Okay. That sounds great."

"I can't wait to see you again," he said.

"Me either."

After our conversation, I was too excited to go to sleep. I stayed up until two in the morning obsessing over what outfits to pack for a three-day trip. Of course, these weren't just any outfits. One might help me land my dream job. Another might end up on the floor next to The Waiter. Dana was right. There was an actual chance I could get laid. For the first time in a very long time, I might actually have sex with someone that wasn't Dalton.

In just three short days, I'd be back in the city again. And face-to-face with The Waiter. Maybe this time, a little more than face-to-face.

10. Worst Case Scenarios

My flight landed at La Guardia at ten. I landed in Manhattan around noon. I checked into the hotel and immediately headed to Big Nick's for a slice of pesto pizza, which I planned on eating in Central Park. I was so happy to be back in what was starting to feel like "my neighborhood."

I got the pizza to go. Then I took a walk down 77th Street. I walked past Fishs Eddy. Past the fire-house with its big red arched doors, one of which was open, exposing the big red fire engine inside. A firefighter waved. I smiled and waved back. Soon I was on Amsterdam, right at the very spot where The Waiter kissed me. I wanted to hug the one-way sign he was leaning against but, thankfully, I didn't. Instead I continued walking, passing the brown-stones I wanted to live in one day. Then on to the GreenFlea. It was only open on Sundays, so the gates were locked. But I couldn't help gliding my hand along the fence where The Waiter was standing when I first saw him that day.

I continued on until I was in Central Park and sitting on the bench where we'd had our conversation. I couldn't believe I was going to be seeing him again tonight. Once again, I was giddy. But then it hit me. This was exactly the same way I felt about Dalton when I first met him. And look how that turned out. It only took one bite of my pesto pizza to determine that my stomach wasn't having it. My self-doubt had officially kicked in. Worst-case scenarios began playing out in my head, and in a matter of seconds, I had already ruined my entire weekend. The Waiter wasn't going to show up. I would be humiliated in front of Josh and his super-chic New York friends. I would probably blow my job interview on Monday. And I would head back to Atlanta demoralized and depressed. Bitchy Brenda was right. Maybe I wasn't cut out for New York.

I threw my pizza in the garbage and started back to the hotel. As I crossed Central Park West, I wasn't thinking, "this is the spot where he held my hand for the first time." Instead, I was thinking, "what if he doesn't show up tonight?"

Nothing that The Waiter had said or done had given me any inclination that he would do something like that. In fact, the last thing he said in our chat last night was, "I can't wait to see you tomorrow." But yet, somehow, doubt and fear had already cemented themselves deep inside my brain.

Josh had made dinner reservations for all of us at seven-thirty at Blue Water Grill. It was right across the street from where we were meeting The Waiter. I figured I would just go to the hotel, unpack, take a nap, and give myself plenty of time to get ready.

When I woke up around five, I was feeling a little better. I couldn't wait to see Josh, Katie, Lucy and Kyle. Lucy and I already had plans to get together for brunch tomorrow to discuss the job interview. I decided I would just try to change my focus from The Waiter to The Job. I was here in the city for an interview, and to hang out with some truly amazing people. If The Waiter showed up tonight, that would just be a bonus.

I had told everyone what The Waiter said about dressing casually. Josh hinted that he knew where we were going but wouldn't tell me anything specific. After agonizing for days over what to wear, I settled on a pair of light-washed Levi's, a black tank-top, a pearl choker necklace, and a comfortable pair of ankle boots. I also wore a black light-weight cardigan to dress up the look enough for dinner and drinks. The makeup was flawless, and I piled my hair into what was quickly becoming my signature look - the messy bun. I was ready.

Josh and Katie met me in front of the hotel. Soon we were all in a cab headed down the West Side Highway. It was so great to see both of them. I could tell that Josh really liked Katie, and I already knew she was smitten with him.

"I can't believe you're already back," Katie said. "It's like you never left."

"I know. I can't wait to give Lucy a big hug. She's

the reason I'm back so soon."

"Well, that and your new boy toy," Josh laughed. I immediately thought about Dalton and how I had lied to him about The Waiter. I didn't want Dalton coming to New York with me this weekend, yet here he was, seated comfortably in my head.

When we arrived at the restaurant, Lucy and Kyle were already at the bar. I hugged both of them while Josh checked us in, and then we all followed the hostess back to our table.

"Josh thinks he knows what show we're going to tonight, but he won't tell me."

"Oh, we all know," Kyle said. "Josh told us not to tell you so it would be a surprise."

"How do you guys know?"

"By the way you told us to dress."

"Yeah," Josh chimed in. "We've all heard about this show, but none of us have seen it yet. It sounds really cool."

"It was so nice of your friend to get us tickets," Katie said. "I can't wait to meet him."

Yeah, if he shows up. "I'm just so happy to be back in the city. It's been an interesting couple of weeks."

"We need drinks," Josh said. And god, did I.

After dinner, we headed over to Luna Park. It was a restaurant and bar located in an open-air pavilion at the north end of Union Square. I'd already had a martini and was feeling a bit more relaxed, but I was still nervous about seeing - or not seeing - The Waiter.

As we were walking down the steps into the bar,

I looked at the multiple strands of lights hanging above us. They looked like fireflies hovering in the air. I got the feeling that I had been here before. "This place looks familiar."

"Yeah, it was in an episode of *Sex & the City*," Lucy said. "That's why it's so freaking crowded now."

And crowded it was. I had no idea how I would find The Waiter in here. It was a little after nine and I didn't see him anywhere. We maneuvered through the crowd towards the bar. I scanned the entire place. No Waiter.

"I don't see him," I said to Josh.

"He'll be here, Sam."

I felt my phone vibrate. I pulled it out to see that I had a message from The Waiter. My heart sank. I knew he was calling to tell me he couldn't make it. I walked away from our group to listen to the message, but it was too loud inside the bar to hear. I walked out into the park. Deep down, I knew he wasn't coming. I figured I had two choices. Give in to the humiliation and let this ruin my night, or hide my heartbreak, laugh it off, and try to make the best of it. I decided on the latter. I wasn't about to waste a Saturday night in New York City.

Suddenly, I felt an arm around my waist, warm breath on the back of my neck, and sensed a familiar scent.

"Hey baby," a voice said.

I turned around. There he stood. He leaned down and gave me a quick kiss on the lips followed by an extra-long hug.

"I can't believe you're here," I said, looking up at him.

"Me either," he replied.

"I was just trying to listen to your voicemail."

"Oh, yeah," The Waiter responded. "I just wanted to let you know I was running a little late. Where's Josh?"

"Over there," I pointed. He grabbed my hand and led me back down the steps and through the crowd. My doubt and fear quickly disintegrated.

When we got to the bar, Josh introduced him to everyone. Then he handed me an apple martini and looked at The Waiter. "What are you drinking?"

"Old Fashioned. I see you all got the memo about the dress code."

"Sam's the only one that doesn't know where we're going," Josh said. "We figured it out when she told us what to wear."

"Have you guys seen the show?" The Waiter asked.

"No, but we've all heard about it," Kyle said. "It sounds interesting. I've never been to a show where you stand up the whole time."

"What?" I said. "There are no seats?"

"That's why I told you to wear comfortable shoes, Red. I've seen it twice. My friend Nick is in it. They're having an after-party in the theater tonight if you guys want to hang out when it's over."

"That sounds great," Katie replied. "I'm so excited." Then she grabbed my arm and leaned into my ear. "Your man is so handsome."

"Yes, he is."

"Oh, and I hope you guys don't mind getting wet," The Waiter said.

"Wait, wet?" I was confused. "What do you mean?"

"You'll see."

"Well, I'm glad I wore a black tank top and not a white one."

"I'm not." The Waiter smiled. Josh handed him his drink.

"Okay, I have to propose a toast," Josh said, raising his glass into the air. "To Sam being back in the city!"

"Thanks to Lucy," I said.

"To Sam getting that fucking job," Lucy replied.

"Wait, I have to get a picture!" I pulled out a disposable camera I'd bought for the trip and asked a girl standing next to us if she would take our photo. She obliged. Then we all clinked our glasses together. I had a new tribe. A Manhattan tribe. We stood there in the park sipping our cocktails under the hanging lights. The Waiter held his drink in one hand and me in the other. Being this close to him and smelling the scent of his hair again was intoxicating. I couldn't remember the last time I was this turned on.

"Are you ready to get wet?" he whispered softly in my ear.

I already was.

11. Come Fly With Me

The show was called *De La Guarda Villa Villa*. It was performed in an old bank building that had been converted to the Daryl Roth Theatre.

After getting our tickets, we were ushered into a bar area where everyone was hanging out before the doors opened. The audience was an eclectic mix of people mostly our age or younger.

"You want another drink, Red?"

"No, I'll wait for the after party." It was getting a bit warm inside with so many people packing in, so I took off my cardigan and tied it around my waist.

Soon the doors opened and everyone began filing into the theater. It was a huge black-box style space with a concrete floor.

"Where's the stage?" I asked.

The Waiter pointed up to the ceiling. I looked up. Josh, Katie, Lucy, and Kyle were all looking up. The low ceiling was covered with some type of white paper. A catwalk platform was set up with drums, microphones and other musical instruments. Other than that, it was just an empty square that was quickly filled with a sold-out audience.

"Come stand right here," The Waiter said, pulling me over to a spot in front of a large speaker. "This is the best place to see everything."

The lights went out and the theater was completely dark. A hush fell over the crowd. The Waiter was standing behind me with his arms around my waist. "You're going to love this," he said. I rested my head on his chest as I looked up.

Stars began to appear on the ceiling, slowly, one-by-one until it was completely covered. Soft music started to play. Then a flash of light, followed quickly by the shadow of a performer flying through the air, suspended from a cable. I was mesmerized. I'd never seen anything like this before.

Then it started to rain. Drops of water fell onto the paper ceiling as the sound of drumming got louder and louder. Music blared. Strobe lights flashed. The crowd was whipped into a frenzy until suddenly one of the aerialists busted through the paper ceiling. Then another. And another. This kept happening until there was no more ceiling.

Balloons and confetti and water fell from the sky, covering the entire audience. The performers were bouncing down to the floor and then flying back up to the rafters. Then I noticed one of them place a safety harness on an audience member and quickly scoop her up into the rafters with him. I looked to my left. Another performer was harnessing Josh, who had the biggest smile on his face. "This is fucking awesome!" I heard him yell, and then he went flying.

I was laughing uncontrollably as I watched Josh fly over us. All of the sudden, one of the performers dropped down right in front of me. "Hi Sammy!" I turned and looked at The Waiter.

"Sam, this is my friend Nick. He's going to take you for a ride."

"Oh my god!" I screamed, as Nick wrapped the harness around me. I was absolutely terrified. But everything was happening so fast that my fear didn't have time to stop me.

"Hold on to me!" Nick said. And then up to the rafters I went. At first, I closed my eyes. Then I opened them to see Josh flying past me. I was laughing and screaming at the same time. I was also holding on to Nick for dear life. There I was, flying high above a crowd of people down below as confetti and balloons and water rained down on all of us. It was exquisite. And then I was right back down on the ground in front of The Waiter. Nick unhooked me from the harness. "She's a natural!"

"I knew it!" The Waiter said, grabbing me and pulling me back into him. My heart was pounding.

"That was amazing!" I yelled at the top of my lungs, hugging him while simultaneously jumping up and down.

The show went on for another hour or so and

was filled with dancing and stomping and chanting and what I can only describe as aerial art. It was like watching the circus and being part of the circus at the same time.

When it was over, the majority of the audience exited out onto the street while we followed The Waiter back to the bar for the after-party. I was wet and sweaty, as were all of us, and I didn't even care because I was still so high from the adrenaline rush.

"Now I need a drink," I said to The Waiter.

"Coming up." He led me over to the bar. The DJ started playing Terrence Trent D'Arby's "Dance Little Sister."

"Oh my god! I worship this song!" I immediately started dancing.

"Who is this?" The Waiter asked. I looked at him like he had two heads.

"Seriously? I don't know if I can know you anymore if you're not down with the sheer perfection that is *Introducing the Hardline According to Terrence Trent D'Arby*. It's one of the best albums ever made."

"I thought he was dead," The Waiter said. I fake fainted into his arms. He laughed. I continued dancing.

"Dude, that was insane!" Josh said as he and the others bellied up to the bar. "Thank you so much!"

"Yes! Thank you!" Lucy said.

"Of course. I knew you guys would love it. Nick will be out in a few minutes. I'll introduce you to him."

"He's probably got bruises from where I dug my

fingers into him." I stopped dancing long enough to take a sip of my martini. "What if I was afraid of heights?"

"I don't think you're afraid of anything." *If he only knew.*

He sat down on a bar stool. Then he grabbed me by the waist with both hands and pulled me over to him. Instinctively, I placed my hand on his face, tracing the outline of his perfect cheekbone.

"That was so much fun," I said. "This has officially been one of the greatest nights of my life."

"We're just getting started baby." He gave me a long kiss and then ran his thumb slowly back and forth across my mouth.

"These lips are gonna be the death of me," he said.

"People made fun of me in grammar school because I had big lips. They called me Mick Jagger."

"Seriously?"

"Yep. Now those bitches pay big money to get lips like this."

"They're beautiful. You're beautiful."

Now the DJ was playing Christina Aguilera's "Genie in a Bottle." The Waiter buried his face in my neck, moving his lips randomly across my skin.

"You smell so good. What is that?"

"Gucci Rush."

"It's sexy."

Everything about this night was sexy. The show was sexy. This song was sexy. The Waiter was definitely sexy. And for the first time in months, I actually felt sexy too.

"There he is," The Waiter said as Nick walked over to us.

"Oh my god, thank you so much!" I said to him.

"Did you have fun?"

"It was amazing! I can't believe you guys get to do this every single night."

"Did he tell you we're going into business together?" Nick asked.

I looked at The Waiter. "No, he didn't."

"Yeah," The Waiter said. "We're opening a new concept gym. Aerialist training, boxing, martial arts, that kind of stuff."

"That's incredible," I responded. "Where?"

"Not sure yet. We're scouting places now," Nick responded. "Mr. MBA here is the brains. I'm the brawn."

The Waiter laughed. "I've been taking boxing lessons from this guy for the last two years. He's the best."

We stayed at the after-party for another hour drinking and dancing and chatting with the cast. We left around one-thirty. Kyle and Lucy headed downtown to their apartment on the Lower East Side while Josh, Katie, The Waiter and I shared a cab uptown.

"Two stops," Josh said, as he hopped into the front seat of the cab with the driver. "Seventy-seventh and Broadway then Riverside and Tiemann."

I sat in the middle between Katie and The Waiter. I knew that if Josh and Katie weren't in the cab, The Waiter and I would be making out like crazy. The sexual tension was palpable.

"What are you guys doing tomorrow?" Josh turned around and asked.

"I'm working from noon until six," The Waiter responded. "But then I can meet you guys wherever after that."

"I'm meeting Lucy at one for brunch. Then I wanna go scout out the place I'm interviewing on Monday."

"Where is it?" Josh asked.

"On 60th Street, between Broadway and Columbus."

"Oh, that's right at Columbus Circle. We can meet you there."

The cab stopped on the corner of Broadway in front of Fishs Eddy. The Waiter reached for his wallet.

"I got this," Josh said immediately. "We'll see you guys tomorrow."

"Thanks, man," The Waiter said. He got out and extended his hand to me. I hugged Katie goodbye and exited the cab. Josh got out to join Katie in the back. I hugged him.

"Have fun tonight, cuz," he said smiling. I gave him a look.

The Waiter and I walked inside the lobby of the hotel right into an open elevator. I pressed the button. When the doors closed, he kissed me. The kiss lasted all nine floors. The doors opened and I stepped out into the corridor, taking him by the hand and leading him down the narrow hallway to my room. The anticipation was glorious. When we got to the door, I fumbled through my bag for the key. The Waiter kissed my neck as he unhooked my choker necklace. The touch of his fingertips on my skin made me tremble. I finally found the room key and opened the door.

The moonlight coming through the hotel window cast a perfect glow across the bed. I didn't even bother to turn on the light. I did bother to put the "Do Not Disturb" sign out. As soon as we stepped inside, The Waiter grabbed me and kissed me. I dropped my bag and the room key. He dropped my choker necklace. Finally, I was able to kiss him the way I wanted to. Full-on, passionately and without worry about being in public. I ran my fingers through his hair. He lifted my tank top over my head and tossed it. Then he unbuckled my belt. I stepped out of my boots and took off my jeans. He took off his shirt. I couldn't help running my hands up and over his abs, chest and shoulders. The very same shoulders I couldn't stop staring at in Central Park were now in my possession.

I ran my hands back down his body and slowly unbuckled his belt. He picked me up and walked over to the bed. He laid me down and took off his jeans. Then he was on top of me.

"You are so fucking sexy," he said, kissing my face and neck and slowly working his way down my body. He kissed my stomach.

"That tickles," I said. He looked up at me and smiled. "How about here?" He slid my panties down and gently planted a kiss above my right hipbone.

"There too," I said.

He moved over to my left side and planted another kiss. "And what about here?"

He continued down. I had been fantasizing about this moment since the day I met him. Now it was happening. And it was better than I could have ever imagined.

"Please tell me you have a condom," I said. "Of course I do." He grabbed his jeans and pulled one out of the pocket. He tossed it on the bed and I immediately opened it. I wanted to scream "hurry" because I couldn't wait, but I didn't.

He laid back on top of me, propping himself on his left forearm, causing his bicep to flex hard. It wasn't the only thing that was flexing hard. His mouth covered mine. His body covered mine. And then it happened.

For the first time in years, I was having sex with someone that wasn't Dalton. And I didn't feel the least bit guilty inside.

The only thing I felt inside of me was The Waiter.

12. Busted

I woke up with The Waiter's arms around me. I could feel his breath on the back of my neck as he slept. My initial instinct was to try to get up without waking him, brush my teeth, freshen my makeup, and sneak back into bed. But I didn't dare move. I wanted this moment to last as long as possible.

My cell phone began to ring. *Goddammit!* It was in my bag on the floor, along with my room key, my necklace, and all of my clothes. All of his clothes too. I knew it was Dana calling to see if I had gotten laid. She'd made me promise to call her first thing Sunday morning. I had no intention of getting up to answer the phone. I knew she'd understand.

The sound of the phone ringing woke The Waiter up. "What time is it?"

I leaned over and looked at the clock. "It's almost eight."

"Good," he groaned and stretched, reaching over

and pulling me back. "We can stay in bed for a while." He turned me over and kissed my forehead. Then the tip of my nose. "How did you sleep?"

"Like the dead. You wore me out last night with the flying circus and the after-party and then the after-after-party."

"I'm about to do it all over again," he said, rolling over on top of me.

"Right now? You're taking me to the flying circus again?"

"Something like that."

Two hours later, The Waiter had to go home and get ready for work. He got up and got dressed while I watched from the bed like a pervert in a peep box with a pocketful of quarters.

"Leave a message on my cell where you guys are gonna be tonight and I'll meet you when I get off."

"Okay."

He leaned down and kissed me. "Later, Red."

As soon as he left, I got up and put on the hotel robe. I needed to take a shower, but I wasn't quite ready to lose the scent of him all over my body. I wanted to just lie in bed and replay every single minute. My phone started ringing again. I laughed out loud. I knew Dana couldn't wait to hear about my night with The Waiter, and I couldn't wait to tell her.

"I'm sorry, Dana," I said as I answered the phone. "I've been kinda busy."

"It's Dalton." *Oh fuck*. It was Dalton.

"Oh, hey. Dana's been calling me all morning, so I

thought it was her."

"Just exactly who was keeping you so busy this morning?" His voice was ominous.

There was a knock at the door. I figured the "Do Not Disturb" sign had fallen off and the maid was here to clean the room. It was a welcome interruption to this phone call.

"Hang on Dalton, the maid is here." I opened the door.

"Hey babe, I left my wallet," The Waiter said as he walked back inside.

"Who the fuck is that?" Dalton yelled into the phone. I knew they had both heard each other.

"None of your fucking business. I have to go." I hung up.

The Waiter stood there looking at me. "Are you okay? Who was that?"

I had already lied to Dalton about The Waiter. But I wasn't about to lie now.

"That was the plague."

He looked confused. "Are you back together with him?"

"God, no!" I responded. "It's a long, ugly story. I can tell you tonight if you want to hear it. But no, I am definitely not back with him."

"Good." He wrapped his arms around me. "Because I'm kinda crazy about you."

I looked up at him and smiled. "I'm kinda crazy about you, too."

"Maybe we're both just crazy." He leaned in and gave me a long kiss. "I'll see you tonight."

As soon as he left, I knew I had to call Dalton back and tell him the truth. I had just come clean with The Waiter - well, somewhat clean. The rest of the cleansing would come tonight. Now I had to be honest with Dalton. I called him.

"What the fuck?" he answered.

"I'm sorry, I shouldn't have hung up on you like that."

"So you're fucking some guy in New York now? That's why you didn't want me to come with you this weekend!" He was livid.

"Dalton, I'm sorry I lied to you. But you and I are not together anymore."

"That's pretty fucking obvious, Sam." He hung up on me. I was sick to my stomach. I called Dana crying.

"Sam, you know I've always loved Dalton like a brother, but fuck him. Seriously, fuck him! You don't owe him any explanation after all the shit he's put you through."

"I know. I just still feel so bad."

"Forget about Dalton. Focus on your man there. And focus on getting that job."

"You're right." Dana was always right.

"By the way, how was the sex?"

"It was incredible. I don't even know how to describe it. I mean, it was weird at first, being with someone that wasn't Dalton."

"I'm so glad The Waiter popped your Dalton cherry."

"That's lovely, Dana."

"Well, now it'll be easier for you to move on. Move on Sammy, seriously."

Dana's pep-talk motivated me just enough to get in the shower, get dressed, and head down to Balthazar to meet Lucy for brunch. I wanted to focus on the job interview and learn as much as I could about her friend Jackie, who would hopefully become my new boss.

"You are going to love her," Lucy said as we sat down. "She's one of the nicest people I've ever met. She's incredibly smart. And funny as hell."

"Lucy, I can't thank you enough for getting me this interview."

"Girl, you got it yourself. Jackie was really impressed with your writing samples."

Soon we were sipping mimosas, and I was diving into a bowl of French Onion Soup. "I've been researching the website and am totally in love with the concept. I never know what to wear."

"You've got incredible style," Lucy said. "Jackie will love that about you."

"I saw her picture on the site. She's intimidatingly attractive."

"She's a goofball. Seriously, she's really down to earth. And she's a redhead, like you."

"I noticed that. How old is she?"

"She just turned 50."

"Get the fuck out. Are you kidding me? She looks a lot younger than that."

"Yeah, she does. She's my icon."

"Well now I'm really nervous about what to

wear tomorrow. I brought a pantsuit and a dress, but now I don't like either of them."

"Don't wear anything conservative," Lucy said emphatically. "It's a startup. Find something edgy. Bonus points if it's a throwback to the seventies. That's Jackie's favorite fashion decade."

"Good to know," I responded.

"We'll go to Scoop. It's right across the street. You'll find something perfect there."

"I know I said this the night I met you, but I'm saying it again. I love you." She laughed.

We finished brunch and headed across the street. Scoop was an adorable boutique that sold a mix of designer and indie clothing brands. The entire store was organized by color, and everything was out of my price range. But that didn't stop me from trying on several bohemian style dresses that fit the seventies vibe I was looking for. I ended up purchasing a Missoni wrap dress that was the most money I'd ever paid for a single item in my life. But it came with a really cute reusable Scoop tote bag that Lucy said was as much of a status symbol in Manhattan as a Gucci or Chanel.

I said goodbye to Lucy, promising to call her right after my interview, and hailed a cab up to Columbus Circle. I wanted to explore what I hoped would become my new work neighborhood. There was a Starbucks on the corner directly across from Central Park and a subway stop, both incredibly convenient if this were to be my daily commute. I pictured myself coming out of the subway every morning, stopping off for a latte before heading into the office. I walked up the street until I found the address. It was a 12-story building with a gray facade situated between a post office and a courtyard. I took out my camera and snapped a photo. *This is going to be my new office.* I wanted this job so badly. I was determined to do everything I could to get it. Hence the hefty credit card charge for the designer dress I was carrying in my designer Scoop bag.

It was almost five o'clock. I called Josh to see where he and Katie wanted to meet.

"Let's go to P.J. Clarke's. It's on the corner of Columbus and 63rd. Give us thirty-minutes."

I left a message on The Waiter's cell phone telling him where to meet us, and then I walked three blocks uptown. I had some time to kill, so I headed over to the fountain at Lincoln Center to take more photos. I knew I looked like a tourist, but I wanted to document the entire weekend. And hell, I was a tourist. At least for now.

Josh and Katie were already at the bar when I walked in.

"So I totally fucked up my life this morning," I announced and then promptly ordered a drink.

"What happened?" Josh asked.

I proceeded to tell him and Katie the details of my morning mix-up and how The Waiter and Dalton were now fully aware of each other.

"Damn Sammy," Josh said. "That's fucked up. Dalton's gonna hunt him down and kill him."

"Who's Dalton?" Katie asked.

"My ex."

"He's a dick," Josh said. "He's also six-four and a black belt in karate, so I would never say that to his face."

"Why do you even care what he thinks if he's your ex?" Katie said.

"It's a long story." I realized I had the perfect opportunity to rehearse my confession for The Waiter. I told Katie everything about Dalton while Josh filled in a few of the more painful memories I'd chosen to leave out. The more I talked, the angrier I got. At myself. For putting up with it for so many years.

After listening to the entire saga, Katie was adamant in her response. "You have to stop enabling him. Why would you let him mess up the good thing you've got going on here?"

Josh motioned to the door. "Speaking of the good thing you've got going on here."

The Waiter had just walked in. He was wearing jeans and a black t-shirt that showcased every muscle I'd spent the previous night and most of the morning getting to know intimately. He walked over and gave me a big hug.

We finished a round of drinks at the bar and then grabbed a table for dinner. I ordered a salad. My stomach was still a bit queasy from the earlier conversation. The Waiter didn't seem the least bit phased by what had happened this morning. He repeatedly held my hand and kissed it throughout dinner, prompting an approving smile from Josh.

After dinner, Katie and Josh headed for the subway while The Waiter and I decided to walk back to my hotel.

"Call me after the interview tomorrow and let me know how it goes," Josh said. "What time is your flight?"

"Eight-thirty." I hugged him and Katie goodbye. I missed them already. New York was starting to feel more like home than Atlanta. And I didn't want to leave. I especially didn't want to leave The Waiter.

We started our stroll up Broadway hand-in-hand. The sun was just starting to set and the weather was perfect. Definitely still summer, but with the slightest hint of fall in the air.

"We've got about fifteen blocks, Red," The Waiter stated. "Plenty of time to tell me how you managed to contract the plague again."

I took a deep breath. And then I told him everything. How we met. How he was my first real love. How we would break up and get back together. How he made me feel like everything was my fault. How he acted the day of my dad's death. And on and on and on.

The Waiter listened intently the entire time. When we got back to the hotel room, he hugged me.

"I'm so sorry about your dad," he said. "I'm sorry you had to go through all of that."

I almost started crying. I hugged him even tighter.

"You know the worst part about all of this?" he asked.

"What?" I looked up at him.

"You said you always get back with him."

"Not this time. I'm moving on. Literally. To New York. And he would never in a million years move to New York."

"Good. Now we don't have to talk about him anymore."

"We don't have to talk about anything," I said. I untucked his t-shirt from his jeans. He smiled and took it off. I kissed his neck, then his chest, then all six of his perfectly defined ab muscles, slowly working my way down until I was on my knees. I started unbuckling his belt.

"I could really, really, get used to this," he said, looking down at me and running his fingers through my hair. I looked up at him and smiled.

"No more talking."

13. Because it's New York

"I'll wait for you here at Starbucks," The Waiter said. He was off today, so he accompanied me to my job interview.

"Okay," I replied.

"You're going to get it. And did I mention how hot you look in that dress?"

"About a million times since I put it on."

"Go." He let go of me and kissed my hand. "Go get it, Red."

I walked away but couldn't resist the temptation to turn and look back. He smiled, looking me up and down, and then blew a kiss. I laughed and kept walking. If ever I needed to walk into a job interview with a shitload of confidence, this was the day. I was strutting down 60th Street in my four-and-a-half-inch wooden Chloe sandals. I had purchased them on major sale a while back at Jeffrey in Phipps Plaza.

They were a modern version of Candies and another nod to the seventies I hoped Jackie would notice. I was glad I had packed them for my weekend trip.

I entered the building and stepped into the tiny elevator. I pressed the button. It was the slowest elevator ride of my life. With each approaching floor, I became more nervous. I took a deep breath. *You got this, Sammy.*

The doors opened and I walked out into a huge open loft. It was filled with modular workstations and racks and racks of clothing. There was a kitchen with a full-size cappuccino bar in the back corner and a photo studio set up right next to it. I walked over to the reception area, which contained a white lacquered desk and a large neon "e-Styled" sign. It was by far the coolest office space I'd ever seen.

There was a woman leaning over the reception desk finishing up a phone call, so I waited off to the side before approaching. She hung up the phone and looked up. It was Jackie. And I was instantly intimidated. She was even more attractive in person.

"Hey! You have to be Sammy," she said with a big friendly smile.

"Yes," I responded.

"I have so been looking forward to meeting you. I'm Jackie." She walked around the desk and shook my hand. She was wearing a perfect white pantsuit that reminded me of Bianca Jagger in the Studio 54 days. Her red hair was parted down the center and slicked back into a bun.

"Our receptionist George is out right now, so I

was filling in for him. Come back to my office and we'll have a chat."

I was taken aback not only by the fact she had a male receptionist - how modern, but also that she, the owner and CEO of the company, was just casually filling in for him like it was nothing.

"Ann Marie," she said to someone as we walked by, "can you keep an eye on the reception area until George gets back?"

"Sure," she nodded. Jackie was wearing sky-high red-bottomed Christian Louboutin heels that made her seem almost six-feet tall. Without them, she was probably closer to my height, give or take a few inches.

Scattered throughout the office along with clothing racks were foam board website mockups, stacks of fashion magazines, and tables full of shoes and accessories. The whole loft was one big fashion closet. My heart began to palpitate at the thought of this being my workplace.

There were no enclosed offices in the loft aside from Jackie's, which was in the back left corner. There was one glass-enclosed conference room opposite her where people were gathered watching a slide presentation.

"Have a seat," Jackie said. Her office was modest but stylish. She sat in a silver Herman Miller Aeron chair behind a white lacquer desk, similar to the one in the reception area but smaller. I expected the exposed brick walls to be covered with photos of her with Anna Wintour and other fashion industry people, but it wasn't. There was just one large framed photo of the entire e-Styled staff. A beautiful bouquet of fresh flowers in a round glass bowl sat prominently on her desk.

"Those flowers are beautiful," I said.

"Aren't they? I stop every Monday morning at the bodega on the corner and pick up fresh flowers for myself. I've been doing it for years."

"That's a lovely habit," I remarked.

"The fact that you use the word 'lovely' is a lovely habit," she said.

I laughed.

"I have to say, I really loved your writing samples. You have a very distinct voice. Southern chic, I'd call it. Funny, clever, but real and honest."

"I have a full portfolio for you." I took it out of my bag and handed it to her. "Do you need another copy of my resume?"

"Nope!" she said as she thumbed through the pages. "This is impressive. And the recommendation letter from your boss was very heartfelt."

"I adore him," I replied. "He's retiring soon. He'll be greatly missed in that office."

She started the interview by telling me about the company. There were eighteen full-time employees, and they also worked with several freelancers. The company was well-funded, having just received another round of financing, and was now in the pre-IPO stage. She was currently in the process of hiring five additional full-time employees which would include two sales managers, another programmer, a marketing assistant and my position.

"So, Sammy. Tell me. Why do you want to move to New York?"

"Because it's New York," I said immediately. "Every time I visit, I don't want to leave. It's starting to feel more like home than Atlanta."

She looked at me and smiled. "Well, you certainly have the New York look down. I love that Missoni on you."

"Thank you. I picked it up yesterday at Scoop."

"They're one of our clients," she said.

"Really? I was panicking about what to wear, which makes me your target audience. I packed several outfits, but I hated them all. Lucy turned me on to Scoop."

"Lucy is the best ad rep they've got at *Vogue*. I tried to poach her, but she's out of my price range."

We continued the standard interview back and forth. I told her about my experience at the ad agency. She told me about how she came up with the idea for the company when she couldn't figure out what to wear to a wedding in the Hamptons. She envisioned a website where she could just type in "what do I wear to a Hamptons wedding?" and get different outfit options and advice from legitimate stylists and industry insiders. Our conversation flowed effortlessly. I felt more like I was chatting with a friend than being interviewed by an icon.

She finished flipping through my portfolio. "So I have one more question that has absolutely nothing to do with your writing skills. And I hope you won't think I'm completely shallow."

"Okay," I said nervously.

"Is that your natural hair color? Because if it is, you're coming to the salon with me right now."

"This is so not my natural color! This is Joshua at Van Michael Salon in Atlanta."

"What's your natural color?" she asked.

"Blonde."

"Why did you change it?"

"Spite."

She looked confused. "What do you mean?"

"Long story short. I was in a play in college where I had to wear a red wig. My boyfriend at the time loved it and was always trying to get me to dye my hair red. The day he broke up with me, I dyed it. And I've been a redhead ever since."

Jackie laughed loudly and without the least bit of self-consciousness. I wanted to be that confident in my own skin.

"I love it!" she said. "Lucy was right. You're perfect for this job. I always hire people on instinct. And I want you to come work for me. Can you start next month?"

I wanted to stand up and scream, but I tried to keep my composure. "Seriously?"

"Let's see," she looked at the calendar on her desk. "How about Tuesday the 12th? Monday is Columbus Day and we're closed."

I had absolutely no idea how I was going to find an apartment and get moved in such a short time frame. But I didn't care. I would make it happen no matter what it took.

"Yes, that works for me. Oh my god, I'm so excited!"

"Well, there's just one thing," she added.

I braced myself. I knew this was too good to be true.

"We don't pay for relocation expenses, but I will pay your freelance rate if you can write your first piece over the next month."

"Of course! I'd love to."

"I want you to write about what to wear for a job interview, using your own personal experience and how you ended up with that dress. Scoop will love it."

"I can do that. Great!" She stood up.

"Okay, I'll have Victoria send out your offer letter and all the other paperwork. And here's my business card. If you have questions about anything, anything at all, call me."

"Oh my god, thank you so much." I stood up and extended my hand. She walked over and hugged me instead.

"Welcome to the family. I think you're going to fit in well here, Sammy."

She walked me back through the loft to the reception area. George was back.

"George, this is Sammy St. Clair. She's our new Online Editor. She'll be joining us in October."

"Girl, that Missoni is everything." George was obviously gay. I had several gay friends and had spent enough nights at Backstreet to have a finely tuned gaydar.

"Thank you," I responded. "I'm looking forward to working with you."

"Oh! I'm doing a show in November! Off-Off-Broadway. You must come!"

"George is a fantastic actor," Jackie added. "We go to all of his shows."

"I'd love to," I responded. "Jackie, thank you so much. You have no idea how excited I am."

"Me too," she said. The elevator door opened and I stepped inside. Had it not been for the two other people in there with me, I would have broken out into a very awkward happy dance.

I walked out of the building and back to Starbucks. The Waiter was sitting at the counter by the window reading a book. I tapped on the glass. He looked up and knew immediately by the look on my face that I had gotten the job. He came outside.

"You got it?"

I nodded.

"Oh my god, Red! Congratulations!" He picked me up and swung me around. "I told you so. Did I tell you so?"

"You told me so," I said. I was shaking.

"When do you start?"

"October 12th. I have a month to find an apartment and get moved."

"Come on," he said, taking my hand and stepping out into the street to hail a cab. "We're going to celebrate before you have to leave."

I had already checked out of the hotel and just

needed to pick up my luggage before heading to the airport. A car service was picking me up at the hotel at six.

"Where are we going?" I asked.

"To my apartment. I want one last chance to get you out of that dress."

"My lucky dress?"

"Yes," he said as we slid into the back seat of the cab. "Broadway and 74th," he instructed the driver.

It was three o'clock in the afternoon and The Waiter and I were making out like teenagers in the middle of midtown traffic. In that moment, I, just like Jackie, was completely confident. I had just landed my dream job. And, from the look of things, I may have landed my dream man too.

14. The Real Thing

Friday after work, Dana and I were sitting in Atlanta traffic on our way home to Douglasville. We were going to visit our families for the weekend while Simon played golf.

I'd already put in my two weeks' notice. Bitchy Brenda knew I was leaving. She ignored me the entire week, and for that, I was grateful. My boss was thrilled for me. He had grown up in New York and gave me a list of places I might find an affordable apartment. I called all of them and put my name on a wait list. I would take one sight-unseen if it was in a decent neighborhood.

"I still can't believe you're leaving me," Dana said. She was leaning over into the backseat, trying to retrieve something as I drove.

"We've already worked this out, Dana. You'll come to New York one weekend a month, and I'll come home one weekend. I have to or my mother will kill me."

"How is she handling this?"

"Better than expected. I think she's just happy I'm getting away from Dalton. Although she has this vision of New York in the seventies ingrained in her head, so she's really concerned about my safety. The fact that Josh is there helps."

"Ah, got em! I wanna look at these again." Dana was back in the front seat with the packet of photos from my trip. I took the disposable camera to a one-hour photo place on Tuesday during my lunch hour.

"I take it you won't be showing your mom *this* pic," she said, holding up a photo of The Waiter and me lying in bed, him shirtless and me wrapped in the sheet. He snapped the photo of us Monday morning.

"No. I don't think she'd approve of me sleeping with someone I'd only known for three weeks."

"I can't decide which is better. The chest or the cheekbones," she said, still looking at the photo.

"They're both equally impressive," I replied.

"Have you guys been having phone sex this week?"

"No," I laughed. "We haven't even had our ICQ chats. He just started his last semester of grad school, so he's been pretty busy."

"So after this, he's done with his MBA?"

"Yep. He and Nick are scouting locations for their gym. They already have investors interested."

"Flying trapeze Nick?"

I nodded.

"You have to take me to that show when I come up."

"Of course. You will love it!"

We continued the drive, listening to my new Christina Aguilera CD. I bought it Tuesday when I was getting the photos developed.

"You're gonna wear this song out fast," Dana said, referring to "Genie in a Bottle." I had it on repeat.

"This song is liquid sex. And I kinda feel bad saying that because isn't she like a Mouseketeer or something?"

"She was. I doubt she is now."

"So was Britney Spears," I said. "Must be something in the water at Disney."

I dropped Dana off at her house and went inside to say hello. Her mom and dad were like second parents to me. I had spent so many nights in this house. Every time I walked inside, I was flooded with memories of sleepovers, Rick Springfield and Duran Duran posters, and John Hughes movie marathons. It was like stepping back into my childhood.

After my brief visit, Dana walked me out to the car.

"Don't forget you're my wingman tomorrow night," I said. "I'll pick you up around six and we'll drive back to the city. Christine is going to meet us for dinner at Surin." Christine was one of our other friends from grammar school.

"I can't believe you're meeting Dalton."

"I can't believe he agreed to meet me. He's really pissed. But I have to tell him about this in person."

"I still say you don't owe him anything, Sam."

"I know. But I need to clear the air between us before I move. I mean, I've been with him since I was old enough to drink. And I'm southern. I feel like I should send him a thank-you card or something."

"Thank you for fucking up my life for the last ten years? Yeah, I don't think Hallmark makes that one."

"I'll see you tomorrow." I hugged her. "Love you."

"Love you too."

When I got to my mom's house, she had just ordered pizza. We always had pizza when I came home. And then we would watch a movie and I would fall asleep on the couch.

"So can't you just move into Josh's building so he can look after you? Surely there's an apartment available there." My mom firmly believed that a woman needed a man to take care of her. It was a Southern thing. And I was her baby. My two sisters were a lot older than me, and both of them had gotten married before leaving home. I had no intention of ever getting married and was the only one in the family that had ever lived alone. It drove my poor mom crazy. My dad, on the other hand, always knew I could take care of myself.

"It's not like that Mom. Apartments are really hard to find in Manhattan."

"Why can't you just live with Josh?"

"Um, because he only has a one-bedroom and that would be weird."

"I just don't understand what's so great about New York. But I do see how happy you are, and that's all that matters. That and your safety."

"I know Mom," I assured her. "I promise I will take all safety precautions."

The pizza arrived, and we spent the rest of the night watching *Practical Magic*. I fell asleep on the couch again. My mother covered me up and tucked me in as she always did. I slept like a rock.

Saturday morning we met my sisters at Cracker Barrel for breakfast. Another tradition. My sisters and I were trying to stick to as much of a routine as we could with Mom since Dad died. She'd been doing pretty well since the funeral, but we were all worried about her living by herself. My dad did everything for her. She had a full-time job working as a nurse, which she loved, but Dad still did everything he could to spoil her. They had been married since 1956 and Mom told us shortly after he died that she had no intention of ever getting remarried or dating again. "Your father was the only man for me. Period."

My parents' enduring relationship was one of the reasons that I always tried so hard to make it work with Dalton. It wasn't long until our breakfast conversation turned to him.

"What did Dalton say when you told him you were moving to New York?" Wendy, my oldest sister, asked.

"I haven't told him yet. I'm telling him tonight."

"I thought you weren't seeing him anymore." Leigh, my other sister, chimed in.

"It's not a date or anything. I just wanted to tell

him in person. I'm meeting him at The Dark Horse. Dana and Christine are going with me."

"Good," Wendy said. "He's not going to be happy."

"You know he called me a couple of weeks ago." My mom casually dropped that into the conversation.

"What?" All three of us turned and looked at her.

"Dalton called you?" I asked.

"Yes."

"Why? What did he say?"

"He said, 'Mrs. St. Clair, I love your daughter. How do I get her back?'"

"What did you say?" I was stunned. My mother could barely stand Dalton.

"I said, 'I know Sammy loves you Dalton. But you always seem to hurt her. And now all she wants to do is move to New York.'"

"You should have said, 'You don't get my daughter back,'" Wendy said. "I've never gotten over the fact that when you wanted to be an actor, he said he couldn't plan a future with you because you didn't have a 401K."

"You always bring that up, Wendy."

"Well, that particular nugget just sticks in my craw."

I turned back to my mom. "I can't believe he called you."

"I have to admit, I felt sorry for him," she said. I smiled at her.

"Well, it doesn't matter now. The Dalton chapter

of my life is officially over."

"Thank god!" The three of them agreed.

"When you get to New York, you should date Mike Piazza," my mom said. "He's sexy."

"Mom!" Wendy laughed.

"What? He is!" My mom was a huge Braves fan, and she rarely missed a game on television. She was quite familiar with the Mets.

"He plays for the wrong team, Mom. I'm a Yankees fan."

"You're gonna meet so many hot guys up there," Leigh said. I tried not to have a reaction, but it was pointless. "Oh my god! You've already met someone, haven't you?"

"Yes, I met someone in New York. And I really like him and we'll see what happens." That was all the information they were getting.

Later that night, Dana, Christine and I were eating dinner at Surin.

"I can't believe you picked the Dark Horse to meet him," Dana said. "Such bad mojo there." She was referring to a particular New Year's Eve that resulted in me crying at midnight while Dalton chatted up a stripper on the other side of the bar. That night, Dana had repeatedly walked over and said to him, "hey, we're over here," gesturing to me and the rest of our friends, but by the time he waltzed back over like nothing had happened, the entire night was ruined.

"Tonight is about letting bygones be bygones and moving on. It's kinda poetic, don't you think?"

"Always the writer," Dana replied.

"I honestly can't believe you didn't leave him sooner," Christine said.

"I stayed because of the sex. How fucked up is that?"

"Well you did nickname his dick 'The Real Thing,'" Dana said.

"Wait, what?" Christine looked at us.

"It's a reference to Coke," Dana replied. "Oh, sorry. I mean Coca-Cola. We are in Atlanta."

"I still don't get it," Christine said.

"The first time Sam slept with Dalton, she described his dick as being the length of a Coke bottle and the width of a Coke can."

"Yeah, that's about right," I nodded.

"Holy shit!" Christine was shocked.

"Well, you know what they say," Dana said. "The bigger the dick..."

"The bigger the dick." I finished her sentence. The three of us laughed.

After dinner, we walked across the street to the Darkhorse Tavern. Dalton was already sitting at the bar. I felt a sudden sense of panic.

"Oh god," I said as we stood there in the doorway. "Now I'm scared."

"The Real Thing," Christine semi-whispered, looking over at Dalton.

"Really, Christine?"

"Come on," Dana grabbed my arm. "Let's get this over with."

We walked over to the bar. I was totally expecting mean and brooding Dalton. I was surprised when he looked up and smiled.

"Hey babe." He stood up and hugged me.

"Hey," I replied hesitantly. "How are you?"

"Good! What do you guys want to drink?"

"Margaritas all around," Dana instantly declared. "With salt." The bartender nodded.

"Hi Christine," Dalton said. "How are you, Dana?"

"I'm fine, Dalton. Why are you so creepily happy?"

"Why wouldn't I be?"

Dana looked at me. I signaled it was okay to leave me alone with him. She pulled me away from the bar.

"He's serial killer calm, Sam," she whispered. "Dahmer calm."

"Yeah, he is. Let me figure out what's going on. Just stay close."

Dana and Christine moved down to the opposite end of the bar. Dana couldn't resist the temptation to turn around and yell loudly, "Hey! We're over here!"

"Nice one, Dana!" Dalton yelled back. Then he turned to me. "Is that why you wanted to meet me here? To replay my greatest hits?"

"Well, that was one of the shittiest things you ever did."

"Yeah it was," he responded. The bartender set my drink down in front of me and then delivered Dana and Christine's. I took a sip. Then I looked at Dalton.

"I thought you'd still be mad at me."

"I was," he replied. "But then I got some fantastic news."

"What's that?" I asked.

"I just got a long-term assignment in New York," he said. "I start October first."

Then he smiled at me. "So, what was your news?"

15. Uh-Oh!

Sunday evening I was still in shock. I must have stood there at the bar staring at him with my mouth open for five minutes before I could even respond.

"Dalton, I got a job in New York. I start October 12th."

"That's great babe! We can move up there together."

"I can't live with you in New York."

"Why not? It's corporate housing. All paid for. You won't have to pay rent."

"Because we're broken up. And because I met someone in New York."

"I don't want to talk about that."

"We have to talk about it. I know you're pissed."

"Well, I'm not happy about it, Sam." He paused a minute. "Who is this douche? Is it serious?"

"No," I replied. "Not yet anyway. But it's not toxic either. We are toxic. We can't keep doing this to each other."

"Babe. Just think about it. That's all I ask. You don't have to give me an answer now."

I agreed to think about it. But only because I needed to get out of the Dark Horse as quickly as possible so I could scream. As soon as Dana, Christine and I left, I told them what happened.

"You have got to be fucking kidding me," Dana said.

"No, he's really convinced that we can start a new life together in New York."

"What did you say to him?" Christine asked.

"I told him I'd think about it, but only because I wanted to get the heck out of dodge. This is not good." I shook my head. "This is not good."

"Okay Rain Man, calm down." Dana said. "Let's go back to your apartment and open a bottle of wine."

The conversation continued at my apartment as Dana poured each of us a glass of Cabernet.

"You do realize," she said, "that the only reason he arranged an assignment in New York is because he found out you were seeing someone."

"My mom told him all I wanted to do was move to New York. He called her a couple of weeks ago. This is the grand gesture."

"Are you serious?" Christine asked. "He called your mom?"

"I'm surprised she didn't hang up on him," Dana said.

"No, they had a long conversation. She said she felt sorry for him."

"Sam, this is not a *Titanic* moment," Dana said. "Don't romanticize it."

"Which *Titanic* moment? 'You jump, I jump' or the one where he dies at the end and she accomplishes everything she ever dreamed of?"

"You know what I mean," she said. I did know what she meant, but I was trying to inject some humor into the conversation.

"Sam, he's a Cal. Not a Jack. You can't actually be considering moving in with him."

"Of course not. Although the idea of not having to pay rent in Manhattan is quite tempting."

"Oh, you'd pay alright. Because he would constantly hold it over your head. This is the ultimate power play. He knows you want to move to New York more than anything, and he wants to be the one that makes it happen for you. He has to be in control."

I was still thinking about that statement in the laundry room of my building as I waited for my clothes to dry. I had one more week of work in Atlanta. Well, four days actually. I took a vacation day on Friday because movers were coming to take my furniture to a storage unit. My co-workers were having a going away party for me on Thursday night. Then I would have two weeks to get myself moved to New York. Of course, I still didn't have an apartment.

I retrieved my clothes from the dryer and headed back upstairs. It was almost ten o'clock. I still hadn't told The Waiter about this recent turn of events. I hadn't actually spoken to him since Wednesday night. We'd both been incredibly busy this week. Me with online apartment hunting and him with school. But it was the longest we'd gone without talking to each other since we met.

I logged onto ICQ and saw that he was online. "Hi stranger," I typed. He logged off without a reply. My heart sank immediately. I knew something was up. I wasn't sure if I should call him or not. I was afraid I might get bad news. But not knowing would have been even worse. So I called him.

"Hey," he answered. I could hear it in his voice.

"What's going on?"

"Nothing," he replied. "I've just been busy, you know."

"I know something's up so just say it." I looked down at my hands. They were shaking.

"It's just that," he hesitated.

"Just what?"

"I'm excited that you're moving up here and all, but..."

"But what?"

"I'm just not ready for a serious relationship right now," he said.

There was a ringing in my ear. My face suddenly burned with anger.

"I don't remember offering you one," I replied. And then I hung up.

He called me right back. I didn't answer. I turned my phone off and just sat there on the bed. My hands were still shaking. I couldn't believe this was happening.

There were no tears. Not yet anyway. I was hurt. But more than that, I was angry. At myself. *You stupid bitch. You should have seen this coming. What the hell were you thinking?*

"Uh Oh!" The familiar ICQ alert sound shouted from my computer as if it were mocking me. *Uh Oh! indeed.* I got up and went over to my desk. The Waiter had logged back into ICQ and sent me a message.

"I'm sorry, Red. Please talk to me."

I started to log off. Then I thought about all the things I really wanted to say to him right now. Instead, I replied with one simple sentence. *You don't get to call me Red anymore.* And then I logged off.

I was stunned. I did not see this coming. Not at all. Deep down, I actually thought he was different. But then again, how can you really know someone in just three weeks? This was on me.

I went to the kitchen and took a dose of NyQuil. I would not lose sleep over another failed relationship. Not even a relationship. Not even a month. It was nothing but a fling, I told myself. And now it was over.

16. The Comfort Zone

My co-workers were all gathered at El Azteca for my going away party. I chose this location because it was close to the office and because I was planning on getting shit-faced drunk. I wanted to be able to walk back to my apartment.

We had a large table in the back of the restaurant. Deb was sitting on one side of me and my boss on the other. At the end of the table was Bitchy Brenda. She tried her best the entire evening to pretend like I wasn't there, even though it was my party.

After a couple of hours of heartfelt toasts, funny work stories, and way too many pitchers of margaritas, people started to leave. We had basically closed down the restaurant. It was still a work night for everyone but me. I said my goodbyes as they left, promising to visit the office whenever I was in Atlanta and inviting them to visit me in New York. Deb and I stayed a while longer.

I poured myself another margarita from the

pitcher. Deb looked concerned. "So you're just never gonna talk to him again? You're just gonna keep ignoring his calls and emails?" She was referring to The Waiter.

"Yep. That ship has sailed. No, wait. It didn't sail. It sank."

"I think he just got scared. I mean, it was all fun and exciting when you were just visiting, but now you're moving there. It's riskier for him."

"He's a dick. All men are dicks. Sean excluded of course." Deb had been dating Sean since our night out at the Clermont.

"Oh, Sean's a dick too. But so far, he's manageable. He's picking me up soon."

"I like Sean. I'm glad you guys are dating."

"Sam, you know I love you, but I have to say this."

"I'm so drunk I probably won't remember it tomorrow."

"I think you should give him another chance. Just talk to him. I mean, how many second chances have you given Dalton?"

I was silent. She had a point. But I was so pissed at The Waiter that I wanted to punish him. Cutting him out of my life completely was the best way to do just that.

"Speaking of Dalton, when is he moving to New York?"

"Wednesday. He finishes up his assignment here tomorrow."

"Are you going to move in with him?"

"I might have to if I can't find an apartment," I

joked.

"Come wait outside with me," Deb said. "Sean will be here any minute."

We went outside just as Sean pulled up in front of the restaurant.

"Do you want a ride?"

"No, you guys are going in the opposite direction. And I'm like right there. I wanna enjoy the walk."

"Okay."

"I'll see you again before I move," I said, hugging her and waving to Sean.

"You better. And think about what I said. About second chances."

I nodded as she got into Sean's car. I waved goodbye and started walking back to my apartment. Then I heard something in the parking lot. I looked to my left. It was Bitchy Brenda. Her car was parked in the back of the restaurant and she was standing beside it, throwing up. I walked over to her.

"Brenda, are you okay?"

She made an inaudible sound and fell to her knees. Now she was on all fours, still throwing up. I looked around and didn't see anyone else from the office. Her car was the only one left in the parking lot. *Oh god. I can't leave her here like this.*

"Brenda, give me your keys. You can't drive," I said. She mumbled incoherently again. Then she passed out cold. Right there on the pavement. I knew there was no way I could get all five-foot-ten-inches of her in the car by myself. She was twice my size. And I certainly couldn't drive her home since I'd been drinking too. I started to call Deb and Sean, but then I looked at Brenda. I actually felt sorry for her. Deb would tell everyone in the office. I didn't want to humiliate Brenda, even though she totally deserved it after the way she treated me all these years.

I took out my phone and called Dalton. He answered.

"I need you," I said. "Brenda is passed out in the parking lot at El Azteca and I can't get her in the car. Everybody else has already left."

"I'll be there in ten minutes," he replied. He was still at his office in downtown Atlanta which wasn't very far.

I fished through Brenda's purse and retrieved her car keys and driver's licenses to get her address. I knew she lived in Buckhead but wasn't sure where.

When Dalton arrived, he parked right next to her car. He got out and walked over to us.

"Are you okay?"

"Well, I had a really good buzz going until she killed it."

He looked down at her. "Damn, she's out cold."

"Can you help me get her in the car? We need to drive her home and take a cab back."

He leaned down and scooped her up like it was nothing and put her in the back seat. I handed him the keys and got in the passenger side.

We drove Brenda's car to her apartment. When we got there, Dalton carried her in over his shoulder, the same way he carried me out of the Clermont Lounge. He laid her down on the sofa. I put her car keys and purse on the coffee table beside her. Then we left.

"Dalton," I said in the cab on the way back to his car, "thank you." He didn't say anything. He just reached over and grabbed my hand and kissed it.

I looked over at him. He was still the most beautiful man I'd ever seen. And I was still in love with him. Then I did something I knew I was going to regret. I told him.

"I love you."

"I love you too baby," he said. He put his arm around me and I leaned into him for the rest of the cab ride.

We picked up his car. Then he drove me back to the Ford Factory. He pulled into a parking spot right in front of the entrance. The car was still running.

"Well," I said. "Come on."

He looked at me. Then he turned off the engine. I got out of the car. He got out of the car. I took him by the hand and led him into the building.

We walked into my apartment. As soon as I shut the door, he pinned me against the wall. Then he kissed me. The kiss was passionate and possessive, as if he were reclaiming what was rightfully his and erasing the memory of The Waiter from my lips.

I don't know if it was because I was so grateful that he showed up when I needed him or that subconsciously, it was another way to punish The Waiter, but I'd never wanted Dalton more than I did right now.

"God, I've missed you," he said.

"I've missed you too," I replied. And then I started crying. "I'm sorry, Dalton."

"No, I'm sorry," he said. "Don't cry baby." He picked me up and carried me to the bedroom. When he put me down, he lifted my dress over my head and tossed it on the floor. He smelled incredible. There was the familiar scent of Eternity, but he just smelled like a man. Like my man.

He ran his hands down my waist to my hips, hooking his thumbs under the straps of my thong and then ripping it off with one forceful pull.

"Hey! That's Victoria's Secret. It wasn't cheap."

"I'll buy you another pair," he whispered. Then he laid me down on the bed. Feeling him on top of me again, the weight of him, the way he touched me...everything felt right. This man knew my body like the back of his hand. A hand that was now between my legs.

"You're moving to New York with me," he said, looking down at me.

His hair fell over my face. The Real Thing found its way inside. And just like that, I was right back where I said I would never be. Again.

17. Manhattan, We Have a Problem

I t was our first Saturday night in the city. Dalton and I were on our way to Mercer Kitchen to meet everyone for dinner. We moved into a fully furnished apartment on East 74th Street on Wednesday. Dalton started his new assignment yesterday. I still had a week before my start date and was excited about having plenty of time to explore my new neighborhood.

I met Katie and Lucy out for drinks at Korova Milk Bar on Thursday and told them the whole story about The Waiter and how I'd ended up back with Dalton. They were shocked at both developments, but happy that I was finally in New York. They couldn't wait to meet Dalton tonight so they could size him up. Josh wasn't surprised at all that I was back with Dalton. What he couldn't believe was that The Waiter had bailed on me.

We arrived at the restaurant around eight. I introduced Dalton to Katie, Lucy and Kyle. The six of us descended down the staircase into a cavernous dining space with exposed brick walls and candlelight everywhere. We ordered a round of drinks at the bar while we waited for our table.

"Damn, girl," Lucy said. "I can see why you keep taking him back. He's fucking beautiful. And so tall."

Katie was a little more cautious. "He's obviously on his best behavior. But after everything you told me about him, I kind of just want to smack him. And you too, for taking him back."

"I know. But so far, things have been great. I love our new apartment. It's right around the corner from Scoop's east side location."

"Well," Lucy stated, "since you're not having to pay Manhattan rent, you'll have a lot more disposable income to spend there."

"Cheers to that," I said.

"So," Katie leaned in. "Have you heard from him since you've been here?" I knew she was referring to The Waiter.

"No. And I don't want to. I'm avoiding the Upper West Side."

"Girl," Lucy said, "if you start limiting your neighborhoods because of bad dating experiences, you'll be drinking and dining in Jersey."

"I just don't want to run into him. It still stings. And I certainly don't want to run into him when I'm with Dalton."

We were seated at the end of a long communal table right next to an open-style kitchen. I sat between Dalton and Josh. Lucy sat opposite me on the other side of the table between Kyle and Katie.

Our almost two-hour dinner was filled with hilarious Josh stories, toasts to my new status as a New Yorker, and several bottles of wine. I had smiled so much throughout the evening that my face was actually sore.

When we finished, Dalton picked up the tab for everyone. I was so proud of him. He'd made a great first impression on my friends, and I was really starting to feel like we had indeed started a new chapter.

Then Josh decided it was time for karaoke. "Let's head up to The Parlour," he announced. I quickly shot him a *you know why I don't want to go to the Upper West Side look* and shook my head. "Oh, right," he nodded. "We'll go to K-town instead."

"Wait," Dalton said. "What was that about? Why don't you want to go to The Parlour?"

"Um, Sam had a really bad food experience there," Josh replied, in his best attempt to cover for me. Dalton wasn't buying it.

"No, she's afraid she'll run into her boy-toy," he said snidely.

Suddenly everyone at the table was uncomfortable. Josh looked at me apologetically. I could feel my face turning red. I needed to do something quickly to lighten the tone. I thought about Lucy's advice on not limiting my neighborhoods. Why should I let what happened with The Waiter keep me from hanging out with my friends on the Upper West Side? I had way more good memories there with Josh than I did with The Waiter. Plus, Josh had become something of a celebrity at The Parlour. Why should he have to suffer because of my bruised ego?

"Fine," I said. "Let's go to The Parlour. Dalton needs to witness your karaoke prowess in action, anyway."

We made our way upstairs and out into the street to hail a cab.

"You guys take this one and Dalton and I will grab the next one," I said as a cab stopped in front of us. I wanted a chance to be alone with Dalton and talk about what just happened.

"Okay," Josh said. "See you guys up there."

As they left, I turned around and looked at Dalton.

"Did you really have to do that?"

"Do what? Call you out on your little fling?"

"You didn't have to make everyone uncomfortable. We'd just had such a perfect time." I held my hand up to the approaching cab.

"I just wanna know why you're trying so hard to avoid this guy. Sounds to me like you might still have a little thing for him. If that's the case, we have a problem."

The cab stopped. Dalton opened the door for me.

"Dalton, you're being ridiculous."

"Get in the fucking cab, Sam."

"86th and Broadway," I informed the driver.

"I just don't want anything to ruin our new start, Dalton. That's all."

"Well, maybe you should have thought about that before you fucked somebody else."

It was a long, silent ride uptown. The joy I'd felt throughout dinner had quickly dissipated. Now all I wanted to do was get to The Parlour and get drunk. Dalton and I had been back together for a little over a week, and up until now, everything had been blissful and passionate and exciting. But I was starting to realize that he had no intention of letting my little dalliance with The Waiter go unchecked. He was going to make me pay for it.

When we got to The Parlour, Josh was already queued up to be next for karaoke. Dalton and I went to the bar, and I quickly ordered a drink.

"This is for you cuz," Josh said as he grabbed the microphone.

I had absolutely no idea what he was about to sing. When he started into Cheap Trick's "California Man," I started dancing like a maniac. In the mideighties, when Josh and I started driving, this song was constantly blaring from either his Jeep or my Pontiac Fiero. It was exactly what I needed tonight. And Josh knew it.

I looked over at Katie. "Your man is the karaoke king!"

"It's just one of the things I love about him." She saw the look on my face. "Oh god, I can't believe I just said that out loud."

"Katie, are you in love with my cousin?"

"Don't tell him, okay?"

"I promise." I was pretty sure Josh felt the same way about her, but knowing him the way I did, it would be a long time before he said it.

When he finished singing, I gave him a big hug.

"That was epic!"

"Yeah man," Dalton said. "You're like a rockstar here." Then he looked at me. "I'll be right back, babe. I have to go to the bathroom before I piss myself."

As soon as Dalton was out of sight, I apologized to everyone.

"Guys, I'm so sorry about what happened at the restaurant."

"Why are you sorry?" Katie asked. "You weren't the one being a jerk."

"Yeah, Sam," Josh said. "He's still pissed, obviously."

"I think he's just stressed with the move and the new assignment and everything."

"Girl, you are so making excuses for him," Lucy stated.

"I know guys. I just really, really, want it to work out this time."

"I'm staying out of this," Kyle said. "I just met the guy." Just then, I felt someone come up behind me.

"Hey Red." I panicked. I turned around. It was Darryl. *Thank god it was Darryl.* I'd never been particularly happy to see him, but this time was different.

"Hey Darryl!" I gave him a quick hug.

"Um, Darryl, you probably shouldn't be touching my cousin when Dalton gets back," Josh warned him.

"Who's Dalton?"

"Sam's boyfriend."

Dalton came back to the bar. I introduced him. "Dalton, this is another one of Josh's friends Darryl."

Darryl looked up at Dalton. "Dude, you're a beast!" he said. Dalton laughed and shook his hand.

"I should have known Conan the Barbarian was your boyfriend," Darryl said to me. Then he looked back at Dalton. "I hope you treat her right, dude. She wouldn't give me the time of day."

I laughed. Dalton didn't.

"Let's do a song," Lucy said. "The three of us. You, me and Katie."

Katie grabbed the song book and began looking through it.

"You guys know I can't sing. I didn't get Josh's voice."

"You're singing," Katie said.

"I'm gonna need a little more alcohol in me." I turned to Dalton. "Please don't be mad at me."

"I'm not mad at you, baby." He put his arms around me. I stood on my tip-toes and gave him a long kiss.

"Jesus, get a room," Lucy said as she handed both me and Dalton kamikaze shots. She had ordered them for all of us. "To Sam making her karaoke debut!"

"Hear, hear!" Josh said loudly. We all downed the

shots and then Lucy grabbed me by the hand and pulled me and Katie in front of the karaoke screen.

"We picked the perfect song," Katie said. And then I had no choice but to lose my karaoke virginity to The Spice Girls. We sang "If You Wanna Be My Lover." Apparently we weren't that bad. We received a rowdy reception from the crowd. Not Josh-level rowdy, but respectable.

Afterwards, Kyle was craving pizza, so we decided to go to Big Nick's. We stumbled out of The Parlour and began walking down Broadway. I couldn't believe this was my first Saturday night living in Manhattan. I'd done it. I'd made my dream come true. And while I never expected to be living here with Dalton, here we were.

Then I realized where we actually were. We were stopped on 77th and Broadway, waiting to cross the street. We were right across from On The Ave Hotel. Memories of The Waiter flooded my thoughts. Suddenly I couldn't breathe. My entire demeanor changed. Katie noticed and caught my eye.

"Are you okay?" she mouthed the words. I nodded "yes" even though I wasn't.

Standing there on the corner, I finally felt the heartache I'd been trying to avoid since he said the words. *I'm just not ready for a serious relationship right now.*

It took every ounce of control I could summon in my drunken state not to burst into tears. The truth was, I did still have feelings for The Waiter. Strong ones. And that was definitely going to be a problem.

18. Play Me

Today I was officially starting my new job. I woke up incredibly early and spent two hours getting ready. I wanted to look perfect and make a great first impression.

I spent the previous week exploring my new neighborhood and shopping at Scoop. I also signed up for a flexible membership pass at New York Sports Club so I could work out with Lucy and Katie. All week long, I had been hitting the gym hard to keep my mind occupied with anything but thoughts of The Waiter. Plus, Dalton had been working late every night, so I had plenty of time on my hands.

I rehearsed my morning commute every day, figuring out the subway and how long it would take me to get to work. I would take the 6 train downtown from East 77th Street and transfer to the N&R at 59th. Then I'd get off at Fifth Avenue and walk across Central Park South. I could make the trip in about thirty minutes, but I would always give myself at least an hour. I had already found a shortcut through Central Park right past Seventh Avenue that put me out directly in front of the Columbus Circle fountain. I'd been stopping at the Starbucks on the corner each morning and ordering a Venti Iced White Chocolate Mocha. I was trying to get over the memory of The Waiter sitting there the day I got the job. And the memory of how we celebrated afterwards with a three-hour sexcapade that made me almost miss my flight.

The weather was starting to feel more like fall, which gave me the perfect excuse to break out my Kenneth Cole camel-colored knee boots. I wore them with my latest Scoop acquisition - a black long-sleeved Helmut Lang asymmetrical dress. My hair was pulled up in my signature messy bun, and between my Coach backpack and Scoop tote, I had packed everything I'd need for my first day.

I skipped Starbucks this morning. I didn't want coffee breath while meeting my new co-workers. I also remembered there was a full cappuccino bar inside the office, which I planned on taking full advantage of.

When I walked in, George greeted me immediately.

"Sammy! You're here! I'm so excited!" He ran over and gave me a hug.

"Hi George! It's so great to see you again."

"Can I just say that I am loving this outfit?"

"George, you are so good for my ego. I love you

already."

"I love you, Ginger Spice. That's your official nickname. I nickname everyone. It's part of my job description."

"What's Jackie's nickname?"

"Oh, The Queen, of course. Come on," he said, locking his arm in mine. "I'll give you a tour of the office."

He began explaining that the loft was arranged by departments. Directly across from his receptionist desk on the left was IT. Then about midway through and stretching all the way back to Jackie's office was Creative. Behind George's desk in the middle were two small areas covering HR and Finance, and then a larger area for Sales and Marketing. On the opposite side in the back corner was a kitchen and the cappuccino bar. Next to that was a decent sized photo studio and a lounge area that led back to the elevator and bathrooms.

He showed me over to my desk in the Creative Department. It was next to an enormous window that looked out at a brick wall. I wasn't complaining. This was still the coolest office space I'd ever had. My desk was an ultra-modern curved design with a lever to adjust the height in case I wanted to stand. On top of it was an orange iMac and behind it a matching orange Aeron chair.

"Wait, I have an Aeron chair? Are you serious?"

"Everybody's got one. Herman Miller gave us a great deal in exchange for photos of all of us fashionable people sitting in their chairs. Apparently the buzz worked because now the wait for an Aeron is longer than a Birkin."

I laughed. Then I looked around and noticed that each department had different colored modular furniture, chairs and iMacs. The Creative Department was orange. IT was purple. Finance was blue. Human Resources was red. And Sales and Marketing was green. The entire office reminded me of The Time, a hotel in Times Square I'd stayed at once when visiting Josh where all the rooms were designed according to a primary color.

I sat my things down at my new desk, and then George began introducing me to everyone. I was blown away by the diversity of the company. It was about an even split men and women and it was the first place I'd ever worked where the majority of the people weren't white. Just another reason I loved New York.

Around nine-thirty, Jackie arrived at the office carrying an enormous vase of beautiful fall flowers. She walked over to my desk and set them down. I stood up to greet her.

"Welcome Sammy!" she said, giving me a hug. "I'm so glad you're here."

"Thank you. Me too! Your flowers are gorgeous."

"These are your flowers," she replied. "I got mine yesterday."

I had never met anyone like Jackie. She was the freaking CEO of the company and she was bringing me flowers. I adored her already.

"Come with me," she said. "I have another surprise for you."

I followed her back to her office.

"Your first article is fantastic! We're launching it today along with an introduction. I thought you should be the one to hit the publish button."

She turned her monitor around and showed me the layout of my article. There, on the homepage of the website, was a photo of me wearing the Missoni dress and above it, the headline, "Welcome to the team, Sammy!" Below was a brief intro about my background and experience with the ad agency in Atlanta. Then a link that said, "check out Sammy's first article, *What to Wear to a Job Interview*."

"What do you think?" Jackie asked.

"It looks great! This is so exciting."

"Well then. Just click the button here and you and your article will officially be live."

I leaned over and double-clicked the mouse. I was published. Sammy St. Clair had arrived in New York City. I was ecstatic.

I floated back to my desk and got started on all the paperwork Victoria from HR had given me. Around noon, George was back.

"We're ordering lunch from The Flame Diner. Do you want anything?"

"I would kill for a grilled cheese and fries right now." I reached for my bag.

"Oh no, girl. There is no way you're paying for lunch on your first day."

"Thanks, George."

"I'll let you know when it's here and we'll eat in

the lounge."

About an hour later, the food arrived. I joined George and Patricia, the Editorial Assistant who sat next to me, in the lounge.

"So, George, what's happening with your show?"

"I start rehearsals November 1st and it opens November 30th. It's an evening of original ten-minute plays and I'm in two of them. It's in the downstairs theatre space at The Drama Bookshop on 40th."

"I will definitely come. I'll bring my friends."

"Did George tell you he wants you to be Ginger Spice for the Halloween party?" Patricia asked.

"What Halloween party?"

"Oh, we're having a big party here in the office the Saturday before Halloween," George said. "We're dressing like the Spice Girls. You're Ginger, Patricia is Scary, Ann Marie in IT is Sporty, Emily in Sales is Baby, and, of course, I'm Posh."

"Of course you're Posh."

Patricia laughed. "I had to be Scary. George racially profiled me."

"I profiled Sammy too because of her red hair."

"Can we invite people to this party?" I asked. "My best friend Dana and her boyfriend are visiting that weekend."

"Of course. Invite as many people as you want. But they all have to wear costumes."

"Okay."

"Oh, and I hope you don't have any plans after work tonight because we're taking you out to Peter's for happy hour."

I didn't have any plans other than to go home, change clothes and hit the gym. Happy Hour on a random Tuesday sounded just fine, especially since Dalton wouldn't be home from work until after nine.

Later that afternoon, Eric from the IT Department came over to set up my iMac. He handed me a piece of paper with my login info.

"Try to login and see if that works," he said. "I'll be right back with your iBook."

"I get an iBook too?"

"Everybody's got one," Eric replied nonchalantly. I was starting to realize how incredibly different the culture of a startup was compared to any other place I'd worked before. There were certainly a lot of perks that came with the job.

Eric returned with my iBook.

"It's so cute!" I squealed. It looked like a clamshell and it had a handle, like a purse. And, of course, it was orange.

"Every girl says that," Eric laughed.

"What do the guys say?"

"They just say, 'cool.' Or they ask for a Dell."

Eric made sure I could login on both devices before he disappeared. I was reading my article on the company's website when George came back over to my desk carrying a large box with a bow on it.

"This just came for you," he said, setting it down on my desk.

"Oh, wow," I said. "Who's it from?"

"Open it and see!"

I unwrapped the bow and opened the box. Inside was a large fancy bottle of sparkling grape juice with another smaller box sitting right next to it. There was an unsigned card that simply said "Congrats on your first day. And I'm sorry." I knew exactly who it was from.

"Oh, do you not drink alcohol?" George asked, looking at the bottle. He sounded concerned.

"I definitely drink alcohol. This is a private joke."

"Good. Because it's almost time for happy hour. I'm going to go pack up and then we'll head out."

As George walked away, I picked up the smaller box. I was afraid to open it. I was afraid I would start crying right there, no matter what was in it. The sentimental gift of the grape juice had already taken me back to that day at the GreenFlea and stirred up feelings that didn't need stirring. I thought about not even opening it and just tossing it in the trash. But I couldn't. My heart pounded as I opened the box. Inside was a blank CD with a note from The Waiter.

It simply said, "Play Me."

19. Anticipation

"Where's Peter's?" I asked as we walked up Columbus Avenue. I couldn't help but notice that every block was bringing me closer to Pomodoro.

"Columbus and 68th," George said. "Not too far."

It was not too far alright. Pomodoro was on Columbus and 70th. I had no idea if The Waiter was working, but the thought of being so close to him made me nervous. The CD he'd sent was in my bag and I still didn't know what was on it. I'd have to wait until I got home to find out.

When we arrived at Peter's, we grabbed a high top table near the bar and ordered a round of drinks.

"So, how often do you guys do happy hour?"

"Every Friday," Patricia responded. "And whenever George is in the mood, like tonight."

"Yeah, but The Queen always comes on Fridays," George said. "And she picks up the tab."

"Jackie is amazing," I said. "I've never met anyone

like her. I've certainly never worked for anyone like her."

"Me either," Patricia agreed. "She takes great care of her team. And we all work our asses off for her."

"What's her story? Is she married? Single?"

"Oh, The Queen is single," George answered.

"What about you, Sammy?" Patricia asked. "Are you attached?"

"Yeah, I moved here with my boyfriend. He's an IT consultant. He got a long-term assignment with his company and free corporate housing."

"Oh, that's incredible," George said. "Where?"

"On the Upper East Side."

"Oh no, that's sad."

"Why is it sad?"

"The Upper East Side is a wasteland. Stuffy old rich people live there."

"Where do you guys live?"

"I live in Queens," George replied.

"Brooklyn," Patricia said.

"Where does Jackie live?"

"Central Park West. She walks to work every day."

"Jackie comes from old money, although you'd never know it because she's so down to earth," Patricia added. "Her parents were in commercial real estate."

"Her parents live on the Upper East Side," George said. "See, old money."

"How long have you been with your boyfriend?" Patricia asked.

"Almost ten years, on and off."

"Ten years?" George yelled. "Are you serious? Why aren't you guys married by now?"

"Neither of us is the marrying type. It's never really been something I wanted."

"Damn girl," Patricia said. "Ten years is a long time."

"He must be really hot," George chimed in. "What's his name?"

"Dalton."

"Oh wow, like Patrick Swayze in *Roadhouse* Dalton? Yeah, definitely hot. Minus the mullet."

"I can't believe you've seen that movie, George."

"I'm crazy for Swayze. You should call your man and tell him to come meet us."

I knew Dalton wouldn't come even if I called him. I also didn't want to prolong happy hour because I was dying to get back to the apartment so I could listen to the CD. The suspense was killing me. But I didn't want to diss my coworkers on my first day.

"He's been working late every night on a project. But you'll definitely meet him at the Halloween Party."

We stayed at Peter's until seven. Then I caught a cab on Central Park West instead of Columbus so I wouldn't have to pass Pomodoro on my way home.

When I walked in the apartment, I was surprised to find Dalton lying on the couch watching television.

"Hey babe!" he said. "How was your first day?"

"It was good." I walked to the bedroom and put my bags down. "I'm surprised you're home so early." "I just got home a few minutes before you. Why don't you take off all your clothes and come tell me all about it?" I laughed. "Do I need to be naked in order to tell you about my day?" "No, but I'd be a lot more interested if you were." I took my new iBook out of my Scoop bag. As I did, I shoved the CD from The Waiter down to the bottom so Dalton wouldn't see it. Then I walked back into the living room.

"Look what I got today." I modeled my laptop as if it were a new handbag.

"Typical startup. Apple-obsessed. I guarantee you the programmers aren't using Macs."

"Everybody's got iMacs and iBooks. And they're all color coordinated."

"Of course they are." He opened my iBook. "This is a piece of junk designed by a punk."

"Oh god, do I really have to listen to another lecture about how Bill Gates could kick Steve Jobs' ass?"

"He could."

"Yeah, but nobody wants to have sex with Bill Gates. I'd totally do Steve Jobs."

"Well," he said, setting my iBook aside and pulling me down on top of him. "Steve Jobs isn't here."

What I really wanted to do was grab my Walkman and headphones, lock myself in the bathroom, and listen to the CD. But I'd never turned down sex with Dalton, and if I did now, he'd know something was up. He'd automatically assume it had something to do with The Waiter, which of course, it would.

"Take off your dress," Dalton ordered. "But those boots stay on."

"You're such a perv."

"I am. And you fucking love it."

I stood up and pulled the dress over my head. He pulled me back down on top of him. The whole time I was having sex with Dalton, I was thinking about The Waiter. I felt bad, but I couldn't help it. Right there in the room next to us, in the bottom of my Scoop bag, was a message from him. A message I had yet to receive. Maybe it was an apology. Maybe it was, "hey, can't we just be friends?" Maybe it was something in between. Whatever it was, I would have to wait a little longer to find out.

An hour later, I had the perfect excuse to make my escape.

"Well, now that you've worn me out, I'm going to go take a nice, long bubble bath. I'm exhausted."

"Okay." He reached for the remote and began flipping the channels, still lying there naked on the couch. Then he turned up the volume.

"Oh, and two things," I yelled over the sound of the television. "One, you have to wear a costume to the Halloween party and two, I told my mom we're staying in New York for Thanksgiving so we can go to the parade."

"What'd she say?"

"She was fine as long I'm home for Christmas. I told her Josh wants to initiate us into the Upper West Side night-before-Thanksgiving festivities. You know, balloon inflation followed by a pub crawl followed by the inevitable karaoke marathon at The Parlour."

"And you think that after all that you'll actually get up super-early to go to the parade?"

"Maybe we'll just pull an all-nighter." I went into the bedroom and put on my bathrobe. I grabbed a towel from the laundry basket and used it to hide my Walkman and the CD.

"I'm gonna be in the tub for a while," I said to Dalton as I passed back through the living room. "Do you need to get in here before I run my bath water?"

"No babe, I'm good."

I walked into the bathroom and closed the door. Then I locked it. I figured if he tried to come in and asked why the door was locked, I could always say "oh, I don't know, habit."

I turned on the water. Then I sat down on the side of the tub and took the CD out of the plastic case. I put it in my Walkman and placed the headphones over my ears. Then I took a deep breath and pressed play.

Terrence Trent D'arby began to sing. It was his cover of "Who's Loving You" from the *Introducing the Hardline According to Terrence Trent D'Arby* album. I immediately started to cry. It was that horrible ugly cry where your face contorts and you wanna scream but nothing comes out because you're not actually breathing. I had to cry silently because I didn't want Dalton to hear me. And the more the song played, the harder I cried. It was guttural. Uncontrollable. Part of me wanted to run out of the apartment and across Central Park just to knock on The Waiter's door so I could see his face. Another part of me felt incredibly guilty because Dalton was in the next room.

I thought about logging on to ICQ after Dalton went to sleep and messaging The Waiter. But how on earth would I ever be able to explain that not only had I gotten back with Dalton, but that I was, in fact, living with him? In New York. And what would happen if Dalton caught me? I couldn't do it.

When the song was over, I just sat there, still sobbing silently. I realized that I was in love with both of them, but in two very different ways. What always has been. And what could be.

I took off the headphones, took off my bathrobe, and climbed into the tub. I had absolutely no idea what I was going to do about Dalton or The Waiter, if anything. All I knew was that my heart was absolutely aching. For both of them.

20. The Great Escape

It had been over two weeks since the CD incident and I still hadn't responded to The Waiter. I couldn't. I was living with Dalton and it wouldn't be fair to either of them.

I called Dana this morning on my way to work to let her know that she and Simon would need to bring a Halloween costume when they came to visit. Then I admitted to her that I couldn't stop thinking about The Waiter.

"Sam, what are you going to do? Do you still love Dalton?"

"Of course I love Dalton. But I've gotta tell you. Things have been weird between us."

"Weird how?"

"He's just distant. He's been working late - like really late - every night. And whenever we go out to eat, if we have a male waiter, he asks if I fucked him too."

"Dude. That's bullshit."

"Yeah. He likes to punish me on a daily basis. I don't know if he'll ever get over this."

"How much of his bullshit have you had to get over?"

"Too much. But I owe it to him to really try and make it work this time. I mean, he did move here for me and I do have a free place to live."

"Do I even have to say it?"

"Say what?"

"I told you so. Remember when we had that conversation at your apartment and I told you the only reason he got the job there was so he could manipulate and control you? It's already happening."

She was right. And Lucy and Katie agreed with her. We'd had brunch together on Sunday, and the consensus was that I should get my own place as soon as possible. It wasn't a bad idea. I had plenty of money saved. I'd sold my car before I left Atlanta, so I'd have no problem coming up with a security deposit and broker fee. Plus, I was making a lot more money at e-Styled than at the advertising firm. But I knew that if I got my own place, it would be the end of Dalton and me.

I was sitting in the conference room around four-thirty with Jackie and the creative team discussing the follow-up to my last article, "What to Wear on Halloween." We'd featured several costumes from Ricky's NYC and "tips-and-tricks (or-treats)" from a special effects makeup artist. Ricky's had even gifted us Spice Girls costumes for our Halloween party, which was coming up in two days. I received a spectacular Union Jack mini-dress and a pair of red platform boots. We hired a photographer to document the party and costumes so I could write a follow-up article.

"Don't forget happy hour tomorrow night is at the Evelyn Lounge," George said as our meeting was wrapping up.

"George, you're our very own 'Julie the Cruise Director.'"

"I think he's more 'Isaac the Bartender,'" Jackie said.

"I miss *The Love Boat*."

"The writing and acting were horrendous. But the fashions were incredible."

"Remember the episode with Halston and Bob Mackie?"

"And Geoffrey Beene and Gloria Vanderbilt? It was my favorite episode," Jackie said. "I have the Halston dress that Pat Cleveland was wearing."

"You are a goddess!"

"You'll have to come over sometime and see my entire vintage collection," she said. "You can write about it."

"I would love that!"

After work, I changed clothes in the bathroom and headed to the gym. I'd been taking a really great cardio kick-boxing class at New York Sports Club every night, but the dressing room was always crowded, so it was easier for me to change at work.

When I got home from the gym around eight-thirty, I was shocked to find that Dalton was actually home and in the shower. I went to the kitchen to grab some water and saw his open laptop on the counter. An ICQ message popped up on the screen.

I miss you so much! I can't wait until you're back in Atlanta for a visit. It was from Rhonda, his so-called "platonic" friend that had conveniently forgotten to wake him up that time they were "just watching movies." I couldn't resist the temptation to scroll up and read the chat history. About five minutes later, Dalton came out of the bathroom. I stood next to his laptop with my arms folded, glaring at him. He glanced at the screen. He looked like he'd seen a ghost.

"Really, Dalton?"

"It's not what you think," he said immediately.

"Oh, it's exactly what I think. It's exactly what I thought months ago when you lied to me about falling asleep at Rhonda's. Oh, wait. That wasn't a lie. You probably did fall asleep, because you always fall asleep after sex."

"I didn't fuck her, Sam."

"Really? She's going on in that chat about how she can't wait for you do all the things you do so well to her. Fuck her! Fuck you too!"

"Okay, do you want to be the pot or the kettle here Sam?" His face had gone from pale white to fire-engine red.

"We weren't together when I had sex with somebody else! You fucked her right after my dad died. You knew what I was going through and you did it anyway! What kind of a sick person does that?"

"You need to shut the fuck up," he said.

"And all this time you've been punishing me and making me feel guilty about having feelings for someone else when you've been cheating on me all along!"

"Oh, so now you're admitting you've got feelings for this douche?"

"Yes, Dalton. After all these years, I actually have feelings for someone that isn't you."

He came towards me, and for a split second, I thought he was going to hit me. But he didn't. He just stopped and looked at me.

"I want you out," he said, in a vile voice.

"Fine," I replied. I went into the bedroom and locked the door. I grabbed my phone and called Josh. I told him what just happened.

"Come over here. You can stay at my place as long as you need."

"Thank you so much Josh."

"Do you want me to come get you?"

"No, I have to get my stuff together and then I'll get a cab. I'm not sure what time I'll be there."

"Okay, I'll be here. Call me if you need me though."

"I will." I hung up the phone.

I started throwing all of my clothes and shoes into the large duffle bag I'd packed when we moved to New York. I was amazingly calm. I think I was relieved. I'd been agonizing the last week over whether to get my own place, and Dalton had just made the decision for me. Of course, I wasn't expecting to be thrown out on the street. But I didn't care. I just wanted out.

I finished packing my clothes and went into the bathroom. I began gathering up all of my makeup and toiletries and loading them into my Scoop bag. When I closed the medicine cabinet door, I didn't recognize the person I saw looking back at me in the mirror. I felt sorry for her. Sorry that she had wasted so many years of her life believing every lie and ignoring every act of cruelty. I had been trying so hard to hold on to something that wasn't even there because I was afraid of being alone. I decided right then and there that I would rather be alone for the rest of my life than to be Dalton's emotional punching bag for another second.

I went back to the bedroom and grabbed my duffle bag and backpack. Dalton was sitting on the couch in the living room staring at the television.

"This is the last time I'm leaving you, Dalton," I said as I headed for the door. He got up and stepped in front of me.

"You're not going anywhere," he said. "Stop being so fucking dramatic." He tore the duffle bag away from me and threw it on the floor. He put his arms around me. I stiffened.

"I'm sorry, I didn't mean what I said. You just make me so angry sometimes. You make me say things I don't mean."

"I don't make you do anything, Dalton. Let go of me." I tried to move away from him. He put his hand against the door.

"Stop," he said. "Sit." He pointed to the couch. I knew he wasn't going to let me leave, so I went and sat down.

"I'm sorry. I don't want you to leave. We'll talk about this later. I'm mad. You're mad. Let's just go to bed. I'll even sleep on the couch."

"Fine." I went to the bedroom and threw the comforter and a pillow out onto the couch. I left the door open, but I turned out the light. I sat down on the edge of the bed, still holding my backpack and Scoop tote. Then I waited.

When I heard him snoring about an hour later, it was time to go. I tiptoed into the living room and slowly turned the locks, making as little noise as possible. My heart was racing. I opened the door with the same slow and quiet intensity. I picked up the duffle bag and left, quietly closing the door behind me. I snuck down the stairs and out onto the street. The air was chilly, but the sense of relief I felt when my feet hit the sidewalk was as though I'd been cured of cancer. And, in a way, I was. I turned and looked up at the third-floor window. He wanted me out. I was out. I was done. And this time, I actually meant it.

I turned around and walked up to Third Avenue. A cab stopped immediately.

"Upper West Side please," I said as I shoved all of my bags into the back seat and closed the door. "Riverside and Tiemann Place."

The cab sped up Third Avenue. If I never laid eyes on the Upper East Side again, it would be too soon.

"I thought you might be headed to the airport with all those bags," the driver said. "Thought you might be leaving town."

I smiled at his kind reflection in the rear-view mirror. "No. Not leaving. Just switching sides."

21. Nobody Fucks With Ginger Spice

I arrived at Josh's apartment around eleven. When he opened the door, he immediately took my bags and set them down. Then he gave me a really long hug.

"I'm so sorry cuz," he said. "Are you okay?" He handed me a glass of wine.

"Yeah, I'm fine."

"What the hell happened?"

"He was cheating on me, Josh. He's probably been cheating on me for years."

"With who?"

"Rhonda! And I knew it! I knew what happened that night. I knew he was lying, and yet I still took him back. I'm so fucking stupid."

"He's the stupid one, Sam. I wanna kill him."

"Okay," I said. We both started laughing.

"So, what are you gonna do?"

"Well, first, I have to find an apartment. Any chance there's an opening here in your building?"

"Actually," he said. "There is."

"Are you kidding? Please say you're not kidding."

"No. I'm not. This apartment is available."

"What do you mean?"

"I'm moving in with Katie. You can have my apartment."

"Oh my god! Josh! Are you serious?"

"Yeah. We've been talking about it for a while. I'm crazy about her, Sam."

"I'm crazy about her too! I love her! I love you and her together!"

"I've been spending practically every night over there, anyway. Her apartment is a lot bigger than mine. Plus, we'll both save a ton of money."

"Josh, this is huge! I'm so happy for you guys!"

"Well, if it weren't for you, we might not be together. So consider the apartment payback."

"I can really just move in here? Do I need to talk to your landlord?"

"No, you can just sublease from me. It's eleven-hundred a month. Rent-stabilized."

"Josh, I will never be able to thank you enough for this. You just made my life."

"You can help me move," he said.

"Absolutely! And to think, just a few minutes ago I was homeless."

"Well, not to get all Zen on you or anything, but everything happens for a reason. The other night

Katie was saying that you needed to get your own place, and I was like, 'she can have mine!' I just didn't realize you'd be needing it so soon."

"Yeah, me either."

We finished off the bottle of wine and then he went to bed. He promised to wake me up in the morning after he got out of the shower so I could get ready for work. I plugged my phone into the charger and turned it off. I knew when Dalton woke up it would start ringing and I had no intention of answering. Then I snuggled up under a blanket on the couch and looked around the room. *This is my apartment.*

The next morning I enjoyed a completely different commute. I took the 1 train, which is only a half-block from my new apartment. It was just nine stops from 125th Street to the 59th Street station. A lot faster than my east-side commute.

I got to work really early, so I made myself a cappuccino and called Dana. She and Simon were flying up tomorrow, and I needed to tell her what happened. I sat down at my desk and took my phone out. I turned it on to find several messages from Dalton, which I promptly deleted without listening to. Then I dialed Dana.

"So, I've got good news and bad news," I said when she picked up. "Which do you want to hear first?"

"Oh god, give me the bad news."

"I broke up with Dalton last night."

"That's good news," she responded. "What happened?"

"He kicked me out of the apartment."

"What? Why?"

"I found out he was cheating on me."

"No way! With who?"

"Fucking Rhonda. Literally, he was fucking Rhonda."

"Oh, Sam. I'm so sorry. Are you okay? Where are you?"

"I'm at work. I went to Josh's last night. Here's the good news. Josh is moving in with Katie and he gave me his apartment."

"Oh my god! That's perfect! So you're done. You're really done with Dalton this time?"

"Beyond done. We'll celebrate tomorrow. Call me when you get to the hotel and I'll come meet you guys."

"Can't wait. I'm so proud of you, Sam."

I turned off my phone and put it back in my bag. Then I heard George arrive. I went over to his desk and told him what was going on. I asked if I could forward my phone to him because I knew Dalton would be calling. He seemed to relish the responsibility.

"Nobody fucks with Ginger Spice today," he said, causing me to laugh out loud. "You don't seem that upset."

"Actually, I'm not. It's something I should have done a long time ago."

He got up and hugged me. "You can tell me all about it at happy hour tonight."

I threw myself into my latest article, which was about what to wear for Thanksgiving. One of our in-house stylists was helping me to put together looks for various scenarios: *traveling home for Thanksgiving, spending Thanksgiving at the beach, spending Thanksgiving on the slopes,* and *attending the Macy's Thanksgiving Day Parade.* Macy's was sponsoring the article, so they had sent over tons of clothes and accessories they wanted featured.

I couldn't help but think about the fact that this would be the first time I wouldn't be traveling home for Thanksgiving. I'd tried to get my family to come up for the parade, but I got the same response from my mom and sisters: "too cold."

Later, as George and I were heading out for happy hour, the decorators for the Halloween party were coming in.

"I hope your costume survived being tossed out onto the street last night," George joked. "We are going to be the best Spice Girls ever."

"It survived. Just like I survived."

That prompted George to sing Gloria Gaynor as we exited the elevator. He was still singing and I was laughing hysterically when we walked out of the building. Suddenly, someone grabbed me violently by the arm. It was Dalton.

"We need to talk." His grip on my arm was tight, like a blood pressure cuff right before release.

"Let go of me, Dalton. You're hurting me."

"Yeah, let go of her Tarzan!" George yelled loudly.

His grip tightened as he pulled me into the courtyard next to the building.

"What the fuck is wrong with you?" he said as he shoved me up against the metal handrail. I'd never seen him so mad, and for the first time in my life, I was afraid of him. "You think you can just sneak out and leave me in the middle of the night? What the fuck, Sam?"

By now I was terrified. And I was crying. "Dalton, please let go of me."

"You ran straight to him, didn't you?"

"No!" I could no longer feel any circulation in my arm, and I was starting to hyperventilate. Then George came around the side of the building with Jackie, cell phone in hand.

"Hey, jackass! Take your hands off of her," she demanded.

"This is none of your business," Dalton yelled back without even looking at her.

"Sam works for me. And this is my building, so yeah, it kind of is my business. And if you don't let go of her, I'm going to call my brother, who happens to be NYPD."

Dalton let go of me. I stood there frozen. My arm was completely numb.

"This isn't over, Sam," he said. And then walked away. I was shaking. I sat down on the steps and continued crying. George kneeled in front of me and Jackie sat next to me.

"Are you okay?" George asked. I nodded.

"Who the hell was that?" Jackie asked.

I was so embarrassed. I didn't want to admit that

Dalton was my boyfriend. Ex-boyfriend. I didn't want her to think less of me. But I wasn't about to lie to my boss.

"My ex. I'm so sorry, Jackie. This is beyond humiliating."

"Oh honey," she said. "I've been there. You've got nothing to be sorry or embarrassed about."

She gave me a long hug. Then she stood up and extended her hand. "Let's go hit that happy hour, shall we? You look like you need a drink."

I laughed and nodded and took her hand. She noticed how badly I was shaking and put her arm around me. We walked over to Amsterdam where she hailed a cab uptown. The three of us got in the backseat.

"Columbus and 78th," Jackie instructed the driver.

"Okay, I don't know if I should say this or not," George said, looking over at me.

"Say what?"

"Your ex is obviously a jerk, but he's like really hot."

"Yeah, he is. And I put up with his shit for a decade because I liked the way he looked. What does that say about me? I'm the superficial jerk."

"Don't beat yourself up, Sam," Jackie said. "Live and learn. That one wasn't worthy of you. Just make sure the next one is."

22. The Halloween Party

H an Solo and Princess Leia stood on the corner of 77th and Broadway. Ginger Spice arrived to pick them up in a cab.

"You guys look incredible!" I said as they climbed into the back seat. Dana wasn't comfortable taking the subway in her gold bikini and purple sarong. I was equally self-conscious in my microminidress and platform boots. Josh, Katie, Lucy and Kyle were meeting us at the party. They wanted their costumes to be a surprise.

Dana and Simon arrived this morning and were staying at On the Ave. Josh and I took them to Mama Mexico for lunch where we promptly celebrated their arrival in Manhattan and my departure from Dalton. Muchas margaritas were consumed.

After lunch, Josh left to pick up a few things for his costume. Then he was meeting Katie back at her apartment when she got off work. Dana, Simon and

I were attempting to walk off our buzz in Central Park.

"Can we go to that flea market place you're always talking about?" Dana asked.

"It's only open on Sundays." I hadn't been there since my first date with The Waiter. I wasn't sure I was ready to go back.

"Can we go tomorrow then?"

"Sure." I guess I was ready. "I can pick up some things for my new apartment."

"When is Josh moving out?" Simon asked.

"Next weekend. The only thing I've ordered so far is a convertible futon sofa. I can't really decorate until I see the place without all of Josh's stuff in it."

"Where is he putting all of his stuff?"

"Katie has a two-bedroom. Her roommate moved out, so she's got plenty of space."

"I have never seen Josh this happy," Dana said.

"You are going to love, love, love Katie! I can't wait for you guys to meet her tonight."

Dana and Simon went back to the hotel to get ready. I took the subway home. I had a nasty bruise on my arm from Dalton's death grip and I knew it would take a while to cover up. It was black and purple and wrapped all the way around my arm in the perfect shape of Dalton's gigantic hand. It would have been completely visible in my sleeveless Ginger Spice dress had I not meticulously applied several layers of Dermablend.

When we arrived at the party, George - aka Posh Spice - was the first to greet us.

"Ginger! You look fabulous! And who are your fabulous friends?"

"George, this is Dana, my best friend since sixth grade. And this is her boyfriend, Simon."

George hugged Dana. "I feel like I know you already." Then he looked at Simon. "I have to say this because you're Han Solo. I love you."

"I know," Simon replied without missing a beat. Dana and I laughed.

"Come on! Let's get drinks!" George led us over to his desk, which had been transformed into a huge rectangular-shaped bar with glow-in-the-dark barstools. "Look! There's dry ice and everything!"

There was indeed dry ice emanating from a large cauldron behind the makeshift bar.

"What's in the cauldron?" Simon asked one of the bartenders.

"Witches' brew. Vodka, triple sec, pineapple juice, orange sherbet."

"I'll just take a beer."

"I'll try the witches' brew," Dana said.

"Apple martini for me."

"You want a caramel appletini?" the bartender asked.

"What's the difference?"

"Butterscotch schnapps."

"That sounds great."

"When you get your drinks, come over to the photo studio," George said. "We have to take good costume photos before we all get wasted. I'll round up the rest of the Spice Girls."

"Okay."

"He's a doll," Dana said. "He must be a lot of fun to work with."

"He is Julie the Cruise Director." We walked over to the photo studio where I was reunited with Posh, Scary, Baby, and Sporty. The photographer snapped several pictures.

"Where's Jackie?" I asked George as we struck another pose.

"Oh, she'll be here around nine. Her costume is always a surprise, so there's a grand entrance. Trust me, you'll know when it happens."

"How long have you guys been doing this Halloween party?" Dana asked.

"Since I started working here, so three years now," George said.

I was incredibly impressed with all the work that had gone into the party. The entire loft had been decorated by professional set designers. Orange and black balloons covered the ceiling. Giant black spiders were everywhere. There was a buffet set up in the middle where the sales team usually sits, but all of their furniture had been moved out to make room for the spread. In the kitchen area was every type of Halloween candy you could imagine lined up in glass cylinders. The conference room had been transformed into a mini-theatre with tiered seating and *Halloween* showing on the drop-down screen. The lounge area where we usually eat lunch was now a disco, complete with electronic dance floor tiles that changed colors and a huge disco ball hanging from the ceiling. The DJ was spinning some of my favorite classic disco songs and I was ready to dance.

As we approached the dance floor, I spotted Lucy and Kyle getting off the elevator. They were dressed as Trinity and Neo from *The Matrix*. I screamed and ran over to them.

"You guys look amazing! Okay, the bar is right over there. Grab a drink and join us on the dance floor. I want you to meet my friend Dana!"

George, Dana and Simon were dancing to Donna Summer's "I'm Coming Out." I joined them.

"This should be your new theme song," Dana yelled over the music.

"Why? Am I coming out as gay?"

"No. Just as a new you. Sans Dalton."

I smiled. I did kind of feel like I had a new start, but that was much more the result of having a new apartment than finally being done with Dalton. In any case, at this very moment, I was just happy. And a little drunk.

"Yeah baby!" I heard someone yell loudly behind me. I turned around to find Josh dressed like Austin Powers and Katie as Vanessa Kensington, complete with a silver minidress and matching knee boots. She was even wearing a brown bouffant wig.

"Oh my god!" I screamed at the top of my lungs, jumping up and down and hugging them both. "Perfect! You guys are absolutely perfect!"

I immediately introduced Katie to Dana and Simon. Then Lucy and Kyle joined us, and I introduced them as well. Josh and Katie headed to the bar. Michael Jackson's "Thriller" began to play.

"The Queen has arrived!" George informed the crowd.

We turned around to see Jackie emerging from the elevator dressed as Cleopatra. More specifically, Elizabeth Taylor as Cleopatra. Everyone began to clap. I thought George was going to faint.

"In my next life, I want to come back as her," he said.

"Who? Cleopatra? Elizabeth Taylor, or Jackie?"

"All of them."

"That's your boss?" Dana asked.

I nodded. Jackie made her way through the loft greeting everyone and posing for photos. I introduced her to all of my friends. She commented on how much she loved their costumes, graciously thanked them for coming to the party, and even asked if she could get anyone a drink.

Now the DJ was playing "You Should Be Dancing" and Josh was in full-on John Travolta mode.

"That's who he should be for Halloween next year," I said to Katie. "Tony Manero."

"What was Dalton gonna be tonight?" Dana asked.

"He refused to wear a costume."

"So he was just coming as an asshole," Lucy said.

"Exactly."

"You know who you should have invited," Katie said, giving me a look. I knew she was talking about The Waiter.

"Too soon."

"Not too soon!" Katie, Lucy and Dana all said in unison.

"Next week guys. I promise I'm going to get in touch with him next week."

"I hope it's not too late," Katie replied.

Her comment startled me. *What if it was too late?* What if he was already seeing somebody else? I certainly couldn't blame him. I decided I would call him on Monday after Dana and Simon left and hope for the best.

My platform boots were starting to hurt my feet. I had a pair of sneakers in my desk drawer, so I decided to go change. I passed Jackie sitting at the bar.

"Sammy," she said, motioning me over. "Come, sit."

I took a seat next to her.

"How have you been? Everything okay?"

"Yeah. Thank you so much for yesterday. Thank you for this party, for everything. I really love it here."

"We love having you here. You're doing great work."

"That's because you inspire me. You inspire all of us."

"That's sweet," she said. "I truly hope I do. I just want work to be productive and fun. Otherwise, what's the point of getting out of bed every morning, right?"

I smiled. "Have you always been this confident?"

"God no. It's taken me a really long time and a

shit ton of mistakes. Don't let it take you that long."

"I'm definitely done making the bad relationship mistake," I stated emphatically.

"Oh, you'll make more, trust me," she said. "Don't close yourself off. This city has so many experiences to offer you. Just be open. Don't let fear stop you from living your life out loud."

I nodded.

"And with that," she said, "I'm going to go shake my groove thing." She got up and sauntered over to the dance floor.

I went to my desk and sat down to take my boots off. When I opened the drawer to get my sneakers, there sat the fancy bottle of sparkling grape juice. I smiled. Then I made a mental note to make sure that Dana and Simon tried the grape juice at the GreenFlea tomorrow. I made another mental note to call The Waiter on Monday.

God, I hope it's not too late.

23. The Street Where You Live

The next morning, I took Dana and Simon to Cafe Lalo for a late brunch. Late because we didn't leave the Halloween party until two and we all wanted to sleep in. Dana had been dying to go to Cafe Lalo ever since she saw it in You've Got Mail.

"Wow, this place is tiny," she said as we sat down. "It looked a lot bigger on-screen."

"I need coffee," I whined.

"That was the best Halloween party I've ever been to. Your coworkers are so much fun."

"It was fun. But my entire body is paying for it right now."

"Mine too," Simon agreed. "I'm gonna need a nap before we go to the parade."

The waitress came over to take our order. After she left, Dana looked at me. "So, how are you, really?"

"I am really hungover."

"No, I meant with the whole Dalton situation."

"There is no Dalton situation anymore."

"Sam, I know you're hurting. Do you want to talk about it?"

Was I hurting? It had only been two days since I'd left him, and I'd been so busy that I hadn't really had time to think about it. My arm still hurt. Today I hid the bruise underneath a long-sleeved cashmere sweater.

"Well, I'm pissed that he cheated on me. My ego is bruised. I mean, Rhonda? Seriously?"

"You are way more attractive than she is Sammy. It's not even close."

"You have to say that. You're my best friend."

"Nah, she's right," Simon said. "Rhonda's not even pretty. She's just average."

"And you have to say that because you're my best friend's boyfriend. But I love you both for trying to cheer me up."

"See!" Dana said. "I knew you were upset."

"The strange thing is that I'm not even that mad at him. I'm mad at myself for being so stupid."

"You weren't stupid, Sam. You were in love."

"No, I was insane. The poster child for insanity. Repeating the same mistake over and over again and expecting a different result."

"So you spent the last ten years in the looney bin," Simon said. "Now you're out. I mean, I don't know how sane you are now, but at least you're out."

Dana and I both laughed. "Well, in any case, Dalton has a new punching bag now," she said.

"I wouldn't wish that on anybody, Dana. Not even Rhonda."

"And yet, you had no trouble putting yourself through it for how many years?"

Our coffee arrived and the three of us proceeded to plan out the rest of our day. We'd finish breakfast and head down to the GreenFlea. Afterwards, much-needed naptime followed by Mexican food at Cowgirl Hall of Fame. Then the parade.

"I wish you guys didn't have to leave tomorrow."

"I know. Our December trip will be a lot longer."

"I wish you were coming up for Thanksgiving."

"You know my mom would kill me. She'd kill you too. She's sad you won't be there this year."

"My mom, too. And Josh's mom. But they'd rather have us home for Christmas."

We finished breakfast and took a few photos in front of the restaurant before leaving. Then we walked down to the GreenFlea. I hadn't gone anywhere near it since I moved here because I thought it would be too painful. I did feel a tinge of sadness as we approached the entrance. But it didn't last when I saw all the children running around in their Halloween costumes. They were having a trick-or-treat event at the market today.

As soon as we walked in, I spotted the farmer's stand with the fresh grape juice. "Come with me immediately," I said to Dana and Simon. "You guys have to try this."

We walked over to the stand and I ordered three

cups.

"When Jesus turned the water into wine, this is what it tasted like." I paid the vendor and handed a cup to Dana and then one to Simon.

"Wow!" Dana said after taking a sip. "I think I need to sit down."

"Right?"

"That's really good," Simon agreed.

We took our cups and started exploring the market. Dana quickly found an antique silver necklace that she loved and promptly purchased. Simon was shopping for baseball cards. I was just standing there, watching them discover every hidden gem the same way I did the first time I was here.

We turned the corner and there was the vintage record booth with the same older couple I'd seen before. This time, they were dancing to Dean Martin's version of "On the Street Where You Live." I couldn't help but smile. And the closer we got to them, the wider my smile became. "This is one of my favorite booths. Aren't they lovely?"

We walked into the booth and began browsing the record collection. Then Simon started dancing with Dana. The older gentleman held out his hand, inviting me to dance with him. His wife smiled and insisted. I couldn't say no.

"I really love your shop," I said as he twirled me around. "How long have you and your wife been together?"

"Fifty-five years," he replied proudly.

"Wow. What's the secret?"

"Dancing," he said, smiling. We continued to dance as he told me the history of the song. It was originally from *My Fair Lady*. Then it was recorded by Vic Damone in 1956. But his favorite version was Dean Martin's, and that's why he always played it.

"Do you mind if I cut in?"

I heard a familiar voice behind me. My stomach dropped like a roller-coaster. I turned around. It was The Waiter.

He had a look on his face like he wasn't sure if I was going to hit him or hug him. I could hear Jackie's voice in my head. *Just be open, Sammy.* I threw my arms around him.

"I'm so sorry," he said, holding me tighter than I'd ever been held before. "I got scared. I'm an idiot."

"I can't believe you're here."

"I'm here every Sunday."

I looked up at him and started to cry. He leaned down and kissed me as Dean Martin continued singing.

"You taste like grape juice," he said smiling. I started laughing as the tears rolled down my face.

"Young man," the elderly gentleman tapped him on the shoulder. "She wasn't crying when she was dancing with me. I'm just saying."

Then we were both laughing. I looked over to see Dana and Simon just standing there staring at us. I took The Waiter by the hand and walked over to introduce him.

"I know exactly who you are," Dana said. "And I am so happy to finally meet you."

"Sammy's told me so much about you," The Waiter said.

"Dana and Simon came in yesterday. We're going to the Village Halloween Parade tonight."

"Do you want to come with us?" Dana asked immediately.

"I'd love to," he replied, looking down at me. "If that's okay with you."

"Of course. You're not working today?"

"No."

"Great," Dana said. "And now, Simon and I are gonna check out the rest of the market and let you guys catch up. Call me later Sam and let me know what time we're going out." She hugged me and dragged Simon away.

"I guess we have some catching up to do," The Waiter said.

"Definitely. But first I have to do something." I walked over to the older gentleman. "Can I buy that album? Or one with that song on it? And one of your vintage record players, too."

"You certainly can my dear," he said with a wink. "That's why we're here."

I turned to The Waiter. "Come help me pick out a record player." I introduced myself and The Waiter to the couple. Their names were John and Adriana.

"This is the first official purchase for my new apartment," I said to them. "Well, I ordered a futon, but that hasn't arrived yet so it doesn't count."

"New apartment?" The Waiter asked. "Where?"

"Tiemann Place and Riverside."

"Isn't that where Josh lives?"

"It's exactly where Josh lives. I got his apartment. He's moving in with Katie next weekend."

"Wow. That's great. So where were you living before?"

I was going to have to tell him. Everything. "That is a very long story."

"I've got time. Wanna get some coffee?"

"I'd love to. Right after I pay for this." I pointed to the cutest light blue record player I'd ever seen. It was similar to one my sisters had in the seventies. One that I wasn't allowed to touch.

"Let me buy it for you," The Waiter said. I shook my head.

"Thank you, but no. You can buy me a Sinatra record if you want."

"Deal."

The record player wasn't cheap. Luckily, I had brought plenty of cash, as I was hoping to purchase one of those big mirrors I'd seen the first time I was here. Instead, I'd be walking away with a vintage 1960s Sears & Roebuck light blue suitcase-style record player, Dean Martin's *This Time I'm Swingin'* album, Frank Sinatra and Count Basie's *The Complete Reprise Studio Recordings*, and The Waiter.

We walked across the street to Isabella's and ordered cappuccinos. I sat across the table from him and told him everything. How I'd gotten back together with Dalton. How he'd taken a long-term assignment here in New York. And how he'd kicked me out onto the street when I confronted him about cheating on me. I was totally expecting him to say, "I knew it," or "I told you so." Instead, he just reached across the table and held my hand.

"I am so sorry you had to go through that. And I'm really sorry if my freaking out played any role in you taking him back."

I smiled at him. "No, that was all on me."

He got up and moved his chair over next to me. We were face to face.

"I just have one very important question for you," he said.

"Okay." I braced myself, knowing he was going to ask how he could trust me not to take Dalton back just one more time.

He leaned in and kissed me softly on the cheek.

"Is it okay for me to call you 'Red' again?"

24. Falling

The look on Katie's face when she saw me walk in with The Waiter was somewhere between shock and glee. She and Josh were standing at the bar, but Josh had his back to us. As we got closer, Katie nudged him. He turned around.

"Hey man!" he said to The Waiter, shaking his hand excitedly. "Great to see you!" He seemed happier to see him than he was me. For a second, I thought he was actually going to hug him.

"Great to see you guys too."

Katie hugged me as Josh greeted Dana and Simon. "Not too late," she said under her breath.

"Not too soon," I replied.

"So," Josh said, smirking. "How did this happen?" Then he stopped himself. "You know what? I don't even care how it happened. I'm just glad it did."

"Me too," The Waiter said, wrapping his arms around me. I leaned back into his chest. It felt incredible and familiar. And safe.

We headed to our table just as Lucy and Kyle walked in. Lucy immediately put her hand up in front of The Waiter and me.

"Wait! What's happening here?"

I didn't quite know how to answer her. After our cappuccinos at Isabella's, the only thing The Waiter and I had agreed on was that he could call me 'Red' again. Then he headed to the gym while I went home to take a nap. We met Dana and Simon back at the hotel and then we all came here.

The Waiter responded to Lucy's question. "Sam's giving me a second chance and I'm not gonna fuck it up this time."

She smiled at both of us approvingly. I smiled too.

"Good," she said. "Don't." Then she locked her arm in mine as we walked back to the table. "I'll need details later, of course."

"Of course."

All through dinner, all I could think about was how I just wanted to be alone with The Waiter. But Dana and Simon were flying out tomorrow morning, and I wasn't going to bail on them, even though Dana would have totally understood. Plus, the anticipation was delicious. The way he would lean in close every time he said something to me. The sensation of his breath on my neck. His hand on my knee. Every touch. Every look. Everything felt as if it were happening for the first time all over again.

After dinner, we found the perfect spot to watch the parade on the corner of West 9th Street and

Sixth Avenue, right across from the Jefferson Market Library and in the shadow of a huge black spooky spider that was hanging down from the building's clock tower. The eight of us, all quite jovial from too many margaritas, packed in with the rest of the crowd and cheered on the giant puppets and costumed paraders. But the best thing about the parade wasn't the costumes or the floats or the music. It was experiencing it with all of my friends, and with The Waiter.

"God, I've missed you," he said as he buried his face in my hair. I wanted him more at this very moment than I did the first night we were together after *De La Guarda*.

We stayed at the parade for a couple of hours. Then Dana said she wanted to see Josh's karaoke skills in action.

"Let's go to Winnie's," Josh suggested.

"In Chinatown?" Kyle asked.

"Yeah. Bayard and Baxter."

My libido would have to remain in check for at least another hour or two. We maneuvered through the crowd and over to the 6 train at Broadway and 8th.

The MTA on my daily commute to work is interesting enough. On the weekends, it's what I would call entertaining. On Halloween night, it's a freak show. Half the people were dressed in costumes, although I wouldn't really describe them as "dressed" at all. If this year's Halloween had a theme, apparently it was ass chaps.

We got to Winnie's and headed straight for the bar. "Don't order the Hawaiian Punch," The Waiter said, "unless you wanna wake up on the floor."

"I wanna wake up next to you," I replied.

"That can be arranged."

Josh began handing out drinks to everyone.

"What is this?"

"Hawaiian Punch," he replied. The Waiter and I both laughed. Josh took his drink and went up to start his first karaoke song - Elton John's "I Guess That's Why They Call it The Blues." It was a special request from Dana.

"Man, this song reminds me of Friday night football games," I said to her. "And freezing our asses off in our skimpy majorette uniforms."

"You guys were majorettes in high school?" Kyle asked.

"We were."

Katie was intrigued. "Do you remember any of your routines?"

Dana and I looked at each other. "Proud Mary."

"Proud Mary?" Lucy said. "You twirled a baton to Tina Turner?"

"Well, it was in Georgia, so it was more like the Credence Clearwater Revival version."

"And it was just a dance," Dana added. "The band played it during games and pep rallies, and the majorettes and cheerleaders would do this silly little routine."

Lucy grabbed the karaoke song book. She started flipping through. "If that song is in here, you bitches are dancing."

"No!" I screamed. "I am not anywhere near drunk enough to do that!"

"Oh, you're doing it," The Waiter said. "Drink your punch baby."

Lucy looked up from the book. "It's here."

"Let's do it!" Dana was game.

"Katie and I will sing," Lucy said. "You two will be our backup dancers."

Josh finished his song and Lucy and Katie dragged Dana and me to the front. Then she grabbed the mic and spoke to the crowd.

"So, our friend Dana is visiting from Georgia and she and Sammy here made the mistake of telling me they remember their high school dance routine. Now they gotta prove it."

The bar patrons clapped and yelled and started a rhythmic clapping to the song as Lucy and Katie sang and Dana and I danced. We remembered every move. When the song was over, we received a big round of applause and even an "Encore! Encore!"

As I was walking back to the bar, I tripped and fell right into The Waiter.

"Okay, you're cut off," he said as he steadied me on my feet.

"And I was worried about embarrassing myself dancing. Dancing I can do. Walking, not so much."

"I love you," he said laughing. And because he was laughing when he said it, I thought nothing of it.

"You love that I made a complete fool of myself for your entertainment."

He pulled me close. "I love how you are with your friends. I love that you smile at random people on the subway for no reason. I love the way you blushed that first day when Josh told me you were single. I love all of it, Red. I love you."

People in the bar were still clapping and cheering, but the noise faded into the background. I looked up at The Waiter. He was serious. I felt like everything was happening in slow motion. Everything except my heart rate. I don't even think I was breathing. But I managed to say it.

"I love you too."

He leaned down and kissed me. "Let's get out of here," he said. "My place."

I turned to Dana and Simon. "We're gonna call it a night if that's okay with you guys."

"Us too," Dana replied. "We have an early flight tomorrow morning."

"We'll share a cab," The Waiter said.

Josh, Katie, Lucy and Kyle decided to stay for one more drink. We all hugged goodbye and then the four of us left and flagged down a cab. The Waiter sat up front with the driver and Dana, Simon and I climbed into the back seat. Dana and I rehashed the evening and she promised to send me copies of all the photos she'd taken this weekend. Occasionally, The Waiter would look over his shoulder at me in the back seat and smile. A knowing smile, as if the two of us had a secret that nobody else knew. And we did.

He'd said those three little words. *He loved me.*

And I loved him, too.

25. Happy Endings

"You got laid last night."

It was the first thing George said to me when I walked into the office.

"What are you talking about?" How the hell did he know that I did, indeed, get laid last night? And twice this morning.

"You got laid. I can tell. You look different."

"That's because I'm still recovering from the Halloween party, George."

"No, it's not. Oh god. You got back with that beast, didn't you?"

I smiled at him. "No, George, I did not get back with Dalton. I'm gonna go make myself a much-needed cappuccino. Can I make one for you as well?"

"Much-needed because you were up all night getting laid. I'll go with you and you can tell me everything."

George followed me to my desk as I put my

things down and then we headed to the kitchen. You would never know there was a party here in the office on Saturday night, aside from all the leftover Halloween candy.

"So, what's with the glow? Did you sleep with a celebrity or something?"

I laughed. And then I told him the whole story about The Waiter.

"I need to meet him. Let's get together one night this week after rehearsal."

"Oh, that's right! You start rehearsals today. Are you excited?"

"Yes. There are two incredibly hot guys in the cast and I plan on hooking up with both of them."

"At the same time?"

"If the opportunity should present itself."

We took our cappuccinos with freshly frothed foam back to our desks just as Jackie was walking in with a fresh bouquet of flowers.

"Sammy got laid last night," George informed her.

"Good for you, Sammy," she said with a hi-five and a smile. "So did I." She sashayed right into her office and began arranging the flowers in a vase. George and I looked at each other.

"Legend," George said.

"Total legend."

I sat down at my desk and logged on to my iMac. I started to check my email, but my mind was elsewhere. And by elsewhere, I mean still in bed with The Waiter. I could feel my face morphing into a ridiculous grin as I remembered every detail.

After we said goodbye to Dana and Simon at the hotel, we walked hand-in-hand down Broadway the three blocks to his apartment. The last time I'd been here was in the daytime, and I remember thinking that the Ansonia looked like a castle. Now, at midnight, all lit up, it was even more romantic.

"I love your building," I said as we walked through the marbled floor lobby to the open elevator.

"It used to be a sex club."

"What?"

"Yeah. The basement used to be Plato's Retreat."

"Wow. If these walls could talk."

The elevator doors opened on the sixteenth floor and The Waiter took my hand.

"Let's give 'em something new to talk about," he said. When he opened the door to his apartment, I was shocked at how different it looked at night. I was greeted by the most beautiful view of the Upper West Side through the two large windows that faced his bed, which was directly to the left of the entrance. He didn't even bother turning on the light. He just kissed me. It was passionate and deep and all-consuming. It was also long overdue. I'd missed him so much. I took off my leather jacket as he was kissing me and threw it on the floor. He lifted my sweater over my head. Then he took off his shirt and sat down on the side of the bed. He pulled me over until I was standing right in front of him. He put his hands on my waist and kissed my stomach.

"Still tickles," I said as I ran my fingers through his hair. He unbuttoned my jeans and pulled them down. I stepped out of them. He pulled me onto the bed and positioned himself on top of me. Then he started kissing my neck.

"Oh my god I've missed that smell," he said.

"My perfume or my sweat?"

"Both." He sat up with his knees on either side of my hips, exposing his insanely sculpted six-pack. "In fact, I missed the smell of you so much that I went to Macy's and sniffed every Gucci perfume until I found the one you wear."

"You did not."

"I can prove it," he said. He reached over to the side table and opened the drawer. I ran my hand down his left side just so I could feel his muscles. I couldn't decide which was sexier. The view of The Waiter sitting on top of me without his shirt on or the view of the San Remo through the window behind him. From the drawer, he pulled out two boxes. One was a box of condoms. "We'll definitely be needing these," he said. The other was a box of Gucci Rush.

"Wow, the big one. That's not cheap. The salesperson must have seen you coming from a mile away."

"Yeah. I just told her I wanted to buy perfume for my girlfriend and that I knew it was Gucci but wasn't sure which one." He sat the box over on the table. "I guess you can have this now."

I smiled up at him. "So, I'm your girlfriend?"

"You want me to prove that too?"

"I think you better."

And prove it he did. The sex was on a different level than last time. Slower. More intimate. More intense. Honestly, I could have orgasmed just on the smell of his hair alone if I'd had to. But I didn't. I fell asleep with my head on his chest, looking out the window at the city that had been watching us voyeuristically the whole time.

When the alarm went off at six, I leaned over him and hit the snooze. He pulled me over on top of him.

"You can't go," he said. "It's still dark outside."

"I have to go home and shower and get ready for work."

"One more hour," he pleaded. I couldn't say no. His groggy morning voice was just too sexy. So I stayed for one more hour and two happy endings. For both of us. When I got up to put my clothes on, The Waiter grabbed my wrist.

"Oh my god! Did I do that to you last night?" He was referring to the bruise on my arm.

"No, you didn't." I wasn't going to lie to him about its origins.

"Do I even have to ask?" He sat up in the bed and took a closer look at my arm.

"No, you don't."

"I will fucking kill him."

"He's not worth it, and that's beyond over. And not to make excuses or anything, but that was the first - and the last - time he ever left a mark on me."

"It was definitely the last," The Waiter said. Then

he kissed my arm and just held me for a minute. Afterwards, I left and took a cab back to my apartment and got ready for work.

And now I sit here, trying to do just that. Work. The phone on my desk started ringing. I answered.

"We need to talk." It was Dalton. Suddenly, I was jolted out of my decadent daydream and back in my never-ending nightmare.

"I can't talk. I'm at work."

"Meet me downstairs right now or I'm coming up."

Mother-fucker.

"You can't be near my building, Dalton. Meet me at the Starbucks on the corner." I figured at least I'd be surrounded by other people there.

"Fine," he said and hung up. I grabbed my bag and pretended to be talking on my cell phone as I headed towards the elevator. I didn't want George to ask where I was going or offer to go with me. When I walked into Starbucks, Dalton was sitting at the counter by the window, almost in the exact same spot The Waiter had sat when I'd had my job interview. That made me even angrier.

"What the actual fuck, Dalton?"

"Sit down, Sam," he said. I didn't.

"Say what you've gotta say and then I'm going back to work."

"Where are you living?"

"Why do you care?"

"Are you living with him?"

"That's none of your business."

"If my girlfriend is shacking up with another guy, then yeah, it's my business."

"I'm not your girlfriend anymore. You wanted me out, remember?'

"You know I didn't mean that." He reached for my hand.

"Don't even think about touching me."

"I know you're pissed, Sam. But I fucking moved here for you. I did all of this for you. Can't we just work it out?"

"No, we can't. Now leave me alone. I mean it, Dalton." I turned around and left him sitting there.

"You know you'll come back," he said as I walked away. "You always do."

I didn't even bother to look back at him. *Not this time, asshole. Not this time.*

26. Surprise! Surprise!

On Saturday, The Waiter and I were assembling the entire IKEA catalogue in my living room. Well, maybe not the entire catalogue, but judging from the number of boxes strewn across the floor, it certainly looked that way.

Josh had taken yesterday off so he and The Waiter could move the rest of his things over to Katie's. The Door Store delivered my convertible futon and platform bed this morning, and luckily, they both came with full assembly. That left The Waiter and me to set up the entertainment center, office area, and the additional closet storage I desperately needed in the bedroom.

We'd just finished putting together a pair of Billy bookcases and a Fakturist desk. They fit perfectly into the alcove space in my living room. My office was done. Now it was time to move on to the closet.

"I'm guessing this closet unit is the first thing you ordered," The Waiter said as he sat on the floor unpacking all the boxes labeled "PAX."

"No, the futon was first." I sat down on my new platform bed. "Followed by this."

He looked over at me. "How's that mattress feel?"

"Good. Firm."

"Maybe we should give it a test drive," he said.

"I don't even have sheets on it yet."

He crawled over to me. "Then I guess we don't have to worry about messing them up."

"You know, we just had sex like five hours ago at your apartment."

"What's your point?"

"My point is that this will have to be a quickie. We're meeting everyone for dinner at eight and we still have a shitload of IKEA to put together."

"I love a good quickie," he said, crawling on top of me and sliding me back onto the naked mattress. "Plus, we owe it to the bed, you know. It deserves a proper breaking in."

The quickie turned into a longie. Afterwards we were starving. We got dressed and walked across the street to Tom's Pizza and ordered slices. Then we came back to the apartment and finished my closet.

"What's left?" The Waiter asked.

"Just the curtains and the wine rack." I'd purchased long red Merete curtains to hang behind the futon in the living room to separate it from the kitchen. And I'd found a wooden wine rack at the cutest store down in the East Village called *Surprise! Surprise!*

"Both can wait until tomorrow," I said.

"Nah, let's do it now. I'm going to Nick's gym in the Bronx tomorrow before work."

"How is Nick?"

"He's good. Why don't you come with me and say hello? We'll put you in the ring."

"Yeah, right."

"No, seriously. Come with me. I'd love it. Don't you take boxing classes at your gym?"

"Yeah, kickboxing. Not real boxing."

"Come. I promise you'll have fun."

"What time? I'm having brunch with the girls at one."

"Around nine. You'll have plenty of time."

"Okay. I guess I'm going to the Bronx."

By six-thirty, The Waiter had hung the curtains and installed the wine rack above the refrigerator. My apartment was officially furnished. I took a bottle of champagne out of the fridge and grabbed two glasses from the cabinet.

"Here," I said, handing the bottle to The Waiter. "Open this. Now I have to make it official."

"Didn't we do that earlier?" He opened the champagne as I placed a final framed photo on my new entertainment center. It was the one of all of us at Luna Park the night we went to see *De La Guarda*.

"Now it's official," I said.

He handed me a glass of champagne. "Cheers, Red." I took a sip.

"We have a million boxes to break down," I said.

"You know, your apartment is much nicer than

mine now. Maybe I should move in here."

"Yeah, but your apartment has that amazing view."

"Yeah, but your apartment has you," he said.

I looked up at him, stunned. "You wanna live together? Here?"

"Sure. Why not?"

"You would give up your apartment?"

"Nah, I'd sublease it to Nick. He's been wanting to move into Manhattan, anyway."

"I've never lived with anybody before. Well, aside from my recent blip with Dalton, which resulted in my homelessness."

"I'm not Dalton."

I smiled up at him. "Thank god."

"So think about it. I know it's too soon but fuck it. I want to spend every minute with you."

"Okay, I'll think about it."

The thought actually terrified me. Yes, I was crazy in love with him. And it was that new kind of love where every minute is magic and you want to spend every waking hour together. But I had only known The Waiter for two months, and we had only been an actual couple for a week.

Later that night we met Josh, Katie, Lucy and Kyle at Calle Ocho for dinner. I also invited George since he was dying to meet The Waiter. When we walked in, George was already at the bar with Jeffrey, one of the actors from his show.

"Oh my god!" George said to The Waiter. "You look just like Harry Connick Jr.! Harry Connick Jr. in

Hope Floats. Not Harry Connick Jr. in *Copycat*."

The Waiter laughed as he ordered us a round of mojitos. "Is there a difference?"

"Big difference," George and Jeffrey both said. The Waiter looked confused.

"Well," I clarified, "in *Hope Floats* he was a total dreamboat. In *Copycat*, he was a serial killer."

"Yeah," George added. "But more like a Ted Bundy serial killer than a Charles Manson. I mean, he was still Harry Connick, Jr. for chrissake."

When everyone else arrived, the host escorted us back to our table.

"You guys must be exhausted," Lucy said to The Waiter and Josh.

"Let's just say I am now fully qualified to work at IKEA," The Waiter responded. "Sam ordered everything in the store and I got to put it all together."

"What were you wearing?" George asked The Waiter. "You know, when you were putting everything together." The entire table erupted in laughter.

After dinner, we walked down the street to Potion, a tiny club on Columbus and 78th Street known for its creative cocktails and incredible DJs. George and Jeffrey immediately hit the dance floor while Katie, Lucy and I secured a table. When the boys headed to the bar to get drinks, I told Katie and Lucy about my day.

"He wants to move in with me and I'm freaking out."

"He said that?" Lucy asked.

"Yep. Told me to think about it."

"And what do you think about it?" Katie said.

"I don't know what I think. It's so soon. I mean literally, it's like one week."

"Yeah, that's soon," Lucy agreed. "But aren't you guys spending every night together anyway?"

"Yeah."

"Do you feel like you need a break or something?"

"No, I love being with him."

"That's what happened with Josh and me," Katie said. "We were spending every night together, and it just made sense."

"Lucy, how long did you and Kyle date before you moved in together?"

"About six months, I think."

"That's not that long," I said.

"Here's the thing, Sam," Lucy began to school me. "The real estate market in New York speeds up the relationship process because apartments are incredibly rare and even more incredibly expensive."

"Yeah but look what happened when I moved in with Dalton."

"I know what happened," she replied. "He showed his true colors. You saved a shit ton of money, and now you have a new apartment and a new man. I've never seen you this happy."

"She's right," Katie agreed. "Besides, we never know how long the people we love are gonna be around. Don't you wanna spend as much time with him as you can?"

"The Lama has spoken," Lucy said. We'd nicknamed Katie "The Lama" because she always came up with profound words of wisdom precisely at the moment we needed it most. "Anyway," she added, "I think you should go for it. He's crazy about you."

"I agree," Katie said as the guys began walking back to the table with our drinks. "And I like him so much better than Dalton."

"Me too." I looked up at The Waiter as he sat my martini down on the table. He smiled at me, and in that moment, he replaced Dalton as the most beautiful man I'd ever seen. Katie was right. I had no guarantee that he - or anyone - would be around forever. And I definitely wanted to spend as much time with him as possible. The DJ started playing Prince's "Pussy Control" and George came running over to the table screaming.

"Oh my god! This is my song! I just requested it. You have to dance with me."

"I guess you're dancing," The Waiter said.

"Yes," I replied, as George pulled me, Katie and Lucy onto the dance floor. Then I turned around and yelled at The Waiter. "Hey, you know that thing we talked about earlier?"

He nodded.

"Yes to that too," I said.

"Seriously?"

"Yeah," I smiled. "Seriously."

27. Gut Punch

"You look like a tick," Josh said.

He, The Waiter and I were walking down 125th Street to catch the B train to Nick's gym. Last night, The Waiter invited everyone to come with us, but Josh was the only one that had taken him up on the offer.

I was freezing. The temperature was in the mid-forties, but being from the deep south, I considered anything below sixty degrees flat-out-frigid. As much as I loved New York, I wasn't sure I would ever get used to the cold. I was wearing a black unitard and one of The Waiter's Columbia sweatshirts. On top of that was a big blue puffer jacket.

"I don't know how you guys deal with this cold."

"This isn't cold," Josh said.

"Yeah, wait until January," The Waiter added.

We took the B train four stops to 161st Street in the Bronx. It was the first time I'd ever seen Yankee

Stadium in person. It looked like a cathedral, and I guess in a way, it was. The Yankees had just swept the Braves in the World Series a little over a week ago. I'd watched the final game at The Gin Mill with Josh, Katie, Lucy and Kyle. That was the night before I'd packed up all of my shit and left Dalton for good.

The gym was located a couple of blocks from the stadium on the top floor of a brick building. It had floor-to-ceiling windows and an incredible view of the stadium. As soon as we walked in, Nick immediately came over and greeted us.

"You don't know how happy I am to see your beautiful face." He gave me a bear hug and lifted me off the ground. "This guy's been moping around the city for weeks."

"Really?"

"You can't believe anything he says," The Waiter responded. "He's been punched in the head too many times."

"So, this is your gym," Josh said looking around. "Cool place."

It was a cool place. There were two boxing rings and several heavy bags hanging from the ceiling. There were two guys sparring in one of the rings and about a half-dozen others scattered throughout the gym.

"It's my Dad's gym actually. I just work here." Apparently Nick's dad had been a pretty successful boxer in Argentina in the sixties. When he retired, he moved the family to New York and opened this gym.

"How did you end up performing in *De La Guarda*?" I asked.

"My cousin. He was involved in the original production in Argentina. When it came to New York, he asked me if I wanted to be part of it and I said, 'hell yeah!'"

"So, boxing coach by day, Peter Pan by night?"

"Exactly. Now, are you guys ready to get in the ring?"

"Yes!" Josh said.

"No," I said. The Waiter laughed at me.

We began our workout by jumping rope. In just a few minutes, I was already sweating and it was time to lose The Waiter's sweatshirt. I was a little uncomfortable, being the only girl in the gym at the time. And I wasn't the only one feeling self-conscious.

"There's no way in hell I'm going shirtless in here," Josh said. The Waiter and Nick had already shed their shirts. "These guys look like they were created in a lab."

Josh and I started competing to see who could jump rope the longest without missing a skip. I was crushing him. After a half-hour or so, we moved on to the heavy bags.

"I have to wrap your hands babe," The Waiter said. He pulled up a stool in front of me and began unraveling a set of wraps. I looked down at him as he sat there, shirtless and sweaty. He took my right hand and began slowly wrapping the material around it. It was incredibly erotic.

"You ready to hit it?" He asked when he was done wrapping my hands.

"Oh, I'm ready to hit it alright," I replied. He shook his head.

"You need to focus," he said as he stood up. Then he leaned in and whispered in my ear. "And stop looking at me like that. I can't be walking around here with a hard-on."

I laughed. We went over to the heavy bags. Nick was working with Josh, demonstrating how to throw a right hook in precise detail. The Waiter was putting boxing gloves on me.

"You look sexy when you're all sweaty," he said.

"I feel gross."

I started punching the bag, trying to listen to everything The Waiter was telling me to do.

"Harder! Think of somebody you'd really like to punch and knock the hell out of him!"

Well, that was easy. I immediately thought about Dalton and my punching intensified. Of course, I did this all the time in my kickboxing classes. Dalton was my go-to nemesis, and he always delivered a productive workout.

"Damn," The Waiter said. "I'm pretty sure I know exactly who you're thinking about."

"Well, who do you think about when you're hitting the bag?"

"My ex-wife," he said. Suddenly I wanted to hit him instead of the bag. This was the first time I'd ever heard about an ex-anything, much less an ex-wife. The Waiter continued. "Actually, I think about the guy my ex-wife cheated on me with."

"You were married?"

"Yeah. For about two years."

"How come you never told me about this before?"

"I didn't wanna scare you away, and it's a part of my life that's over. She cheated on me. I divorced her. And that's it."

"When did you get divorced?"

"Three years ago. When I was twenty-seven."

"Does she still live in New York?"

"No. She married the guy she cheated on me with and they moved to Miami."

I was stunned. It's not like I didn't expect him to have a past, but for some reason, I was angry at him. We had moved on from the heavy bags and climbed up into the ring. The Waiter was now holding two big pads in either hand, and I was alternating punches into both of them.

"Okay, now I'm not sure if you're throwing punches at your ex or at me," he said. "Are you mad at me?"

"I'm not mad."

"You look like you really wanna hit me."

"No, I don't wanna hit you." *I wanted to hit her.*

"I know there was at least one time you definitely wanted to hit me."

"Yes, there was."

"And now?"

I had no intention of hitting him. Instead, I just threw my arms around him. And, of course, I started to cry.

"I'm sorry baby," he said. "I should have told you before."

I playfully punched him. "No, you shouldn't have. I don't wanna hear about any other girls before me."

He laughed and gave me a long kiss.

"Are you guys seriously making out in my boxing ring?" Nick asked. He and The Waiter were about to do a sparring session. Both of them put on their padded face protectors and then I helped The Waiter into his boxing gloves.

"Nick, please don't hit him in the face."

"That's why he's wearing that padding, love. To protect that beautiful face of his."

For the next forty-five minutes, Josh and I stood ringside and watched The Waiter and Nick repeatedly hit each other. Josh loved it. I didn't. I was still feeling the pain of my own gut punch.

The Waiter was married before. And not to me.

28. Home

"**B**reathe. Drink. Repeat."

Lucy had become my liquid Lamaze coach. I'd just joined her and Katie at The Heights for brunch and was half-way done with my first mimosa.

"So he was married before," Katie said. "What's the big deal? You were practically married to Dalton."

"Dana said the same thing. I called her in the cab on the way down here."

"Yeah, Sam," Lucy said. "I really don't understand why you're so freaked out about this."

"I think I'm just in shock." I ordered another mimosa.

"I'm shocked anybody would cheat on him," Katie said.

"Yeah," Lucy agreed. "I'd like to get a look at the guy she cheated on him with."

"I'd like to get a look at her."

"Why?" Katie asked. "She's his past, you're his present. And she's living in Miami."

"No, she's living rent-free in my head. And I don't even know what she looks like."

"I'm sure you're way prettier," Lucy said.

"I'm sure she's Cindy Crawford. And I'm Cindy Brady."

"Stop!" Katie said. "You're obsessing over nothing."

"Yeah, you are," Lucy agreed. "Let's talk about something else."

"How was the workout?" Katie asked. "Did Josh get hit in the face?"

"No. Josh is a much better boxer than me, but I did kick his ass jumping rope."

"How's Nick?" Lucy asked. "Is he still as hot as he was in *De La Guarda*?"

"He's good. Still hot. You guys should have come. Even though I winced every time a punch landed, I have to admit I was totally turned on watching the two of them in the ring. Shirtless."

"Okay, next time I am going with you," Lucy said.

"Me too," Katie added.

"Their startup idea is pretty amazing. Boxing, martial arts, aerial training, and now they've added climbing."

"Oh, like he did in the show?" Katie asked.

"Exactly. They've got a lot of investors interested. Nick's dad has all these contacts in the boxing world."

"They're gonna be so rich," Lucy said. "And you're gonna be Mrs. Rich."

"He already had a missus, remember?"

"And we're back to being obsessed," she said.

Katie looked at me. "I thought you said you never wanted to get married. What would you say if he asked you to marry him one day?"

"I don't know."

That was the honest truth. Marriage was not something I'd ever aspired to. Growing up, when my older sisters would pore through stacks of bridal magazines dog-earing their favorite dresses, I would flip to the back and dream about having my own heart-shaped tub like the ones in the Poconos. I had devoured enough *Cosmopolitan* magazines in my youth to view marriage as limiting. As a teenager, I had photos of Helen Gurley-Brown and Gloria Steinem on my bulletin-board. I wanted to grow up, move to the big city, and live the city girl life. And to me, that didn't include marriage. As crazy as I was about The Waiter, and as excited as I was about him moving in with me, deep down I knew I didn't want to marry him. I didn't want to marry anybody.

"Well, speaking of marriage," Lucy said, "I know my wedding is only two months away, but I want you guys to be bridesmaids."

"Of course!" Katie and I said at the same time.

"I only have two bridesmaids right now, and they're my cousins. You guys have become my best friends. I want you up there with me."

"I think I'm gonna cry," I said.

"I think you're drunk," Lucy replied.

"What do the dresses look like?"

"Anything you want. As long as it's black."

"We get to pick our own dresses?" Katie asked.

"Dresses, pantsuits, jumpsuits. You can wear overalls for all I care. As long as they're black and stylish. And as long as you're comfortable in it."

"This is so exciting!"

"So you're excited about being in a wedding," Katie said, "as long as you're not the bride."

"Correct."

"Well, at least I know who not to throw the bouquet to," Lucy said.

"Throw it to Katie."

"No! I don't want to scare Josh off."

"You couldn't scare that boy off if you tried," I replied. "He's crazy about you."

"So, Katie," Lucy teased, "if Josh asked you to marry him, what would you say?"

"Yes. In a heartbeat."

"Oh my god! We'd be family."

"We're already family," Katie said. Lucy held up her mimosa and proposed a toast. "To family."

"To family!" We clinked our glasses together. Then the conversation turned to the upcoming holidays.

"Oh, by the way, Jackie invited all of us to her place on Thanksgiving to watch the parade. George says she has the perfect view."

"She does," Lucy said. "Her apartment is right on Central Park West."

"That's so nice of her," Katie stated.

"We have to start planning Thanksgiving Eve," Lucy said.

"It's all about the pub crawl," Katie said. "But it starts with an early dinner. And then we go to the balloon inflation."

"And then we drink," Lucy added. "I was thinking we could have dinner at Carmine's first."

"Oh god, I love the frozen cosmos at Carmine's," Katie said. "I'll be drunk before the Snoopy balloon gets its first pump."

I immediately spit orange juice and champagne all over my omelet.

Lucy laughed. "Katie, that's the funniest thing I've ever heard you say."

"I agree." I blotted my eggs with a napkin.

After brunch, I decided to walk the thirteen blocks back up to my apartment. It had warmed up a bit, and I needed to walk off the mimosas. As I approached the Columbia campus, I suddenly missed The Waiter like crazy. I walked past the main gates at 116th Street. Tomorrow, he'd be right here, headed to one of his classes. I thought about how his female classmates must be crazy about him. But he was mine. Even though he was someone else's before. I knew I was going to have to get over the fact that he'd been married. Part of me wanted to hail a cab and head straight down to the restaurant just so I could see him and tell him I loved him. Then my phone rang.

"Hey Red," The Waiter said. "How was brunch?"

"I had two mimosas and I miss you like crazy."

He laughed. "Are you sure you only had two?"

"I'm sure."

"Well, the fact that you miss me makes me very happy. You make me very happy."

"You make me very happy, too."

"I get off at nine babe. Want me to bring you something from the restaurant?"

"Yes! The fettuccini with basil, please."

"You got it."

"I love you."

"Love you too. I'll see you at home."

I hung up the phone. My stomach fluttered. *Home.* He hadn't even moved in yet, but he considered my apartment home because that's where I was. And that's where he wanted to be.

The fact that he was married before suddenly didn't matter. In six hours and counting, he was coming home. To me.

29. Who's the Bitch Now?

T he day before Thanksgiving should have been an official holiday. Nobody was getting any work done. George and Jackie were huddled in her office going over the breakfast menu for tomorrow's parade watch party while the entire IT department was watching *Planes, Trains, and Automobiles* in the conference room. Their sporadic roars of laughter distracted me from finishing up an article, inspired by Josh, about what to wear with a puffer coat so you won't look like a tick. But that wasn't the only thing distracting me.

This Thanksgiving would be the first one I wasn't spending with my family in Georgia. The first one without my father. And the first one I hadn't spent with Dalton in years. It made me a little homesick and a lot of sad. Of course I was looking forward to celebrating tonight with all of my friends, and especially with The Waiter, but I still missed home. I missed my Mom. I missed Dana. She and I always got together with friends from high school the night before Thanksgiving. I'd talked to her this morning, and she told me it wouldn't be the same without me. I'd also called my Mom. She seemed to be okay with me not being there because she was so excited about meeting The Waiter. He was coming home with me for Christmas.

Around three o'clock, Jackie told everyone they could leave for the day. I was looking forward to the long weekend. The Waiter was on Thanksgiving recess from Columbia and didn't have to work until Saturday. We had officially been living together for about two weeks and I would meet his family tomorrow. I was extremely nervous, but he was quick to reassure me. "Trust me. I love you. They'll love you."

I called to tell him I was on my way home. He was studying.

"We're meeting everyone at five at Carmine's."

"Okay," he said. "Hey, if you leave right this second, we'll have time for me to give you something to really be thankful for."

"I'm heading to the subway right now."

When I got to the apartment, it was spotless. He had cleaned everything from top-to-bottom and done all the laundry.

"Okay, this is amazing and you are perfect, but when you said you'd give me something to be thankful for, I assumed it involved you being naked."

"Oh, it does. I just figured you'd be even more thankful if the sheets were clean."

"I adore you."

"I adore you too, Red." He walked me the short distance from the living room into our pristinely clean bedroom. "Let's do this Thanksgiving thing."

An hour and a half later, we joined the rest of our group at Carmine's for family-sized portions of Penne Alla Vodka, Chicken Marsala, Manicotti and pitcher after pitcher of frozen cosmos. Afterwards, we were all so stuffed that we welcomed the ten-block walk down to the Museum of Natural History for the balloon inflation. I had watched the Macy's Thanksgiving Day Parade every year for as long as I can remember. But being this up close and personal with the giant balloons made it special. I took tons of photos and we all laughed hysterically as Josh narrated the inner monologue of each balloon character in his best "Cartman" from *Southpark* voice.

The weather was ridiculously warm for late November. It had been in the mid-60s all day and thankfully I didn't need a coat to go with my black floral cheongsam dress I'd purchased in Chinatown. I wore it with my black Nine West knee boots. When I got dressed, The Waiter told me I looked like a sexy militant geisha.

First stop on our post-balloon-inflation-pub-crawl was Vermouth Lounge at 77th & Amsterdam. This was also the site of mine and The Waiter's first kiss. Katie and Lucy insisted on a re-enactment with Josh playing the role of the M7 bus interrupting us. After martinis at Vermouth, we headed to McAleer's Pub. By ten-thirty, we had reached our final destination - The Parlour. Jimmy was working the door. I introduced him to The Waiter.

"Darryl's inside doing karaoke," Jimmy said. "My ears are bleeding. Please make him stop."

We laughed as we all made our way over to the bar to find Darryl belting out "Sweet Child of Mine" and dancing like Axl Rose.

"Oh, this is a train wreck," Josh stated.

"I like Darryl," Kyle said. "He's always drunk, but he's funny as hell."

"Yeah," Lucy agreed. "He kinda grows on you, doesn't he?"

"Like mold," Katie said. We ordered a round of drinks and cheered for Darryl. This was a mistake, because he insisted on singing "Paradise City" next. Darryl was a terrible singer, but he had the entire bar whipped into a frenzy and singing at the top of their lungs.

When the song was over, we all greeted Darryl with hi-fives and hugs.

"I have to pee like a Russian racehorse," The Waiter said. "I'll be right back."

I sat on a barstool next to Lucy. "I just love watching him walk away."

"Yeah, he's got a great ass." Then she grabbed my arm. "Oh my fuck! Speaking of asses."

She motioned towards the door. I looked over. My heart stopped. It was Dalton. He was handing Jimmy his I.D. Then I saw who was with him. It was Rhonda. All the blood in my body suddenly rushed to my face.

"What the fuck is he doing here?" I said loudly enough for Josh and Katie to take notice.

"Holy shit," Josh responded when he saw Dalton. "This is so not good."

"Why is he here?" Katie asked. "And who is that?"

"That's Rhonda. He fucking brought her up here this weekend because he knew I would be here tonight. I hate him."

As Jimmy checked Rhonda's I.D., Josh and Kyle started taking bets on who was going to win the fight between Dalton and The Waiter.

"Man, I don't know," Josh said. "Dalton's a black belt, but I've seen this guy in the boxing ring."

I was starting to panic. "Nobody is fighting because we're leaving."

"Wait, why do we have to leave?" Josh said. "This is our place."

He was right. This was our place. Dalton had come here specifically just to parade Rhonda around in front of me. And to get a look at The Waiter, I'm sure. I didn't want to leave, but I knew if we stayed, things were going to get ugly. Fast.

"If you wanna leave Sam, I'll go with you," Lucy said.

"Me too," Katie agreed. It was too late, though. Dalton and Rhonda were already right in front of us.

"Well, this is awkward," Dalton said. Rhonda couldn't even make eye contact with me.

"Dalton, what are you doing here?"

"It's a public place, Sam. Happy Thanksgiving. You remember Rhonda, don't you?"

I felt like I'd been hit in the face with a sledge-hammer. I knew he'd been waiting for this moment. The moment he could slowly twist the knife that was permanently imbedded in my gut. I knew what he was trying to do, yet I couldn't help myself from responding exactly the way he wanted me to. Like I cared.

"Yeah Dalton, how could I forget Rhonda? I believe you fucked her right after my dad died and then lied to me about it. Is that right? Or was it one of your other groupies? I really can't keep up."

"Why are you being such a bitch, Sam?" he said.

Before I could even respond, Darryl stepped in front of me and punched Dalton hard in the face. So hard, in fact, that he fell backwards and hit the ground.

"Who's the bitch now?" Darryl said as he stood over him. Dalton immediately jumped up and went after Darryl just as Jimmy and one of the other bouncers stepped in between them.

"What the fuck, Darryl?" Jimmy said.

"He just called Sammy a bitch."

"Let's go buddy," Jimmy said to Dalton, grabbing him by the arm and motioning him towards the door.

"You really are a bitch," Rhonda said as she followed Dalton out.

"Good luck, Rhonda. You're gonna need it."

The Waiter came back just as Jimmy was escorting Dalton out of the bar.

"What just happened?"

"Darryl knocked Dalton on his ass!" Josh said.

"That's Dalton?" The Waiter looked over at him.

"In the fucking flesh," I said. He immediately started towards him. I pulled him back. "Please don't. He's not worth it." He turned around and looked at me.

"Baby, are you okay?"

"I'm fine." He wrapped his arms around me protectively. I looked up to see Dalton staring at me, and then at The Waiter. It was the first time they'd ever seen each other in person. You could feel the level of contempt between them from across the bar. And then Dalton and Rhonda were ushered out the door.

"My man," The Waiter turned to Darryl, extending his hand. "Whatever you're drinking, I'm buying for the rest of the night."

"You would have done the same thing." Darryl shook his hand.

"I would have killed to be the one to deck that guy."

"I never liked him," Darryl stated.

"Me neither," Kyle said.

I looked at Katie and Lucy. "You know how we feel about that jerk," Lucy said.

"And on that consensus," Josh stated, "I think we could all use a round of shots!"

"Yes!" The Waiter said. "And I'm buying."

"Well, Happy Fucking Thanksgiving then!" Josh shouted.

"Happy Fucking Thanksgiving back!" Katie, Lucy

and I all said together laughing. The guys just looked at us.

"It's from *You've Got Mail*."

"Haven't seen it," Josh stated.

"Me either," The Waiter said.

"Sounds like a chick flick," Kyle added.

"You guys suck," Lucy said.

My hands were still shaking from the sheer shock of seeing Dalton and Rhonda. The Waiter noticed.

"You wanna get out of here, Red?"

"Absolutely not. I'm not gonna let him ruin my first Thanksgiving in New York."

"That's my girl."

"Okay, is anyone gonna mention the fact that Rhonda looks exactly like the sister on *Roseanne*?" Lucy asked.

"Oh my god. She totally does," Katie said.

I couldn't help but laugh. Our shots arrived and Josh started to propose a toast.

"Wait, let me do it this time," I said.

"Go for it cuz."

I held up my shot glass. "To the greatest cousin, the greatest group of friends, the greatest boyfriend, and the greatest city in the world. I love all of you so much."

"Hear hear!" Josh replied. We all downed our shots.

"You just made me cry," Katie said, hugging me.

"You're such a wuss," Lucy said to Katie, joining in the group hug. "I love you too, girl."

The Waiter slipped his arm around my waist and

pulled me back to him.

"If you think Thanksgiving is good," he whispered in my ear, "just wait until Christmas."

"Why? What's happening at Christmas?"

"I already have your present."

"Really?" I said. "Give me a hint."

"Okay. It was ridiculously expensive and you're going to keep it for the rest of your life."

For the second time tonight, my heart stopped.

30. Christmas in Dixie

I couldn't stop staring at it. Christmas morning, The Waiter and I had just taken our seats on a flight home to Atlanta. Josh and Katie were sitting across the aisle from us. I was looking down at my gift from The Waiter and smiling so hard it hurt. I couldn't wait to show it off to everyone at home. He wasn't lying when he said it was ridiculously expensive. Or that I would keep it forever.

Last night, we went out to celebrate Christmas Eve and the fact that he finished his graduate program at Columbia on Tuesday. After viewing the windows at Bergdorf's and ice-skating at Rockefeller Center, The Waiter and I exchanged gifts, sitting underneath the live Christmas tree we'd lugged home from 96th Street weeks ago. I gave him a pair of autographed Muhammad Ali boxing gloves. He gave me a black quilted Chanel Jumbo Flap Bag. It was the most beautiful thing I'd ever laid eyes on, aside from The Waiter, of course.

Apparently, he'd asked George to help him find the perfect gift for me. George suggested the Chanel bag. Then Jackie was able to use her contacts to get him an excellent deal. She probably heard me screaming all the way down at Central Park West when I opened it. I was so happy I cried.

"I don't get you women and these bags," The Waiter said laughing. "But I love seeing you this happy."

"I love this bag. And I love you even more for giving me this bag." I spent the rest of our first Christmas Eve together showing him exactly how much I loved him. We barely got any sleep since we had to get up at six in order to make our nine o'clock flight.

Josh's dad picked us up at the airport in his Chevy Suburban, which Josh jokingly referred to as the "redneck limousine." When he introduced him to Katie, my uncle greeted her with a big hug and lifted her off the ground.

"Well, aren't you tiny?" he said with a southern drawl. Katie giggled.

"Though she be but little," Josh stated, "she is fierce."

"Quoting the bard on Christmas," I said. "Impressive."

I was next for the off-the-ground-bear-hug. "Hey Uncle Lewis. How are you?"

"Don't they feed you up north, Sammy?"

I laughed and introduced him to The Waiter, who was welcomed with a handshake and a typical southern greeting. "Nice to meet you, son. Glad you could join us."

Katie and I climbed into the back seat of the Suburban as the guys loaded the luggage.

"Josh's dad is so sweet," she said. "And Josh looks exactly like him."

"Wait until you meet my Aunt Cheryl. She's going to love you. And she's gonna tell Josh to marry you immediately." Josh was an only child and my Aunt Cheryl couldn't wait to be a grandmother.

"Well, Josh already won over my family. Last night my dad and my Uncle Mark opened up a bottle of scotch they'd been saving for decades and shared it with him."

Josh got in the front with his dad and The Waiter sat in the back next to me. We left the airport and soon we were headed west on I20. I was admiring Katie's new Coach watch that Josh gave her for Christmas.

"He says I still have one more present coming that was on back order," Katie said. "But I told him he'd already given me enough."

"Oh yeah, I know what that is. I'm the one that told him it would be the perfect Christmas gift for you."

"Any hints?"

"No. Well, only that it's very you. Very Katie."

The guys quickly became immersed in conversation about football.

"Did you play college ball son?" Uncle Lewis asked, looking at The Waiter in the rear-view mirror. "You're built like a quarterback."

"No sir," The Waiter replied. "I played hockey at Boston College."

"Hockey? Ain't that just gladiators on ice?"

The Waiter laughed. "Something like that."

"You should have seen him trying to teach me to ice skate last night."

"Yeah, I took her out for a little drag around the Rockefeller rink."

"Sammy's about as graceful as her mother. And her mother's about as graceful as a turkey."

"Uncle Lewis, I can't even imagine what my mom had to deal with growing up with you. Bless her heart."

"Bless her heart? I made her tough. I certainly wouldn't make fun of your mother today. She'd kick my ass."

When we got to my house, the rest of our extended family was already there. Aunt Cheryl came running out of the house like Paul Revere screaming, "The New Yorkers are here! The New Yorkers are here!" Both Katie and The Waiter seemed amused.

Once inside, introductions were made all around and my mom greeted The Waiter with a big smile and an even bigger hug.

"It was so nice of your family to let us steal you away on Christmas Day."

"Oh, they're in Italy for Christmas this year," he replied.

"And you came to Douglasville, Georgia instead? Bless your little heart."

"Oh, I have to work next week and I wanted to

spend the holidays with Sam, anyway."

My mom smiled. "Well, aren't you just the sweetest? Y'all must be starving. Come on and get something to eat."

The traditional Christmas Day spread was lined up along the dining room table. Ham, turkey, stuffing, baked beans, macaroni and cheese, cornbread, and every type of pie and cake you could possibly imagine.

The Waiter, Josh, Katie and I piled some food on our plates and sat down at the kitchen table.

"You want some iced tea, hon?" My Aunt Gladys - ever the flirt - asked The Waiter, handing him a glass.

"Thank you," he replied. She winked at me approvingly.

"There's like four cups of sugar in that," I said to The Waiter. He took a sip.

"Wow! That's like drinking maple syrup."

"I'll get you some water. Katie, do you want some water?"

"No, I'll take the tea," she said laughing.

My sister Leigh grabbed me by the arm as I was getting The Waiter some water and pulled me into the dining room.

"He is so hot. Oh my god, he's so hot."

"Isn't he?"

"And that New York accent," she said. "I would listen to him to read the phone book. Or the Bible."

I laughed. "Hey, how is Mom doing? I was worried about how she would handle the holidays this year without Dad."

"She's been pretty good, actually. I mean, I'm sure she's a little sad. We all are. But having the family here helps. And she's been so excited about meeting your new beau."

A couple of hours later, we were all packed tightly in the living room opening gifts. Josh was playing Santa Claus and handing out the packages. The Waiter, Katie and I were sitting on the floor, which was covered with wrapping paper, boxes, bows and presents. My mom and Aunt Cheryl made sure that there were plenty of gifts for both The Waiter and Katie.

"Your family is amazing," Katie said. "They're so funny and welcoming."

"Welcoming, yes. Welcoming you to the insanity."

Katie laughed. Then the phone rang.

"I'll get it!" My eight-year-old niece Alexis ran into the kitchen. My mom was in the process of opening a huge box from my sister that contained a new comforter.

"It's for you, Aunt Sam," Alexis said as she came back into the living room.

"It's probably Dana." I started to get up. "She and Simon are coming over later."

"No, it's Uncle Dalton," Alexis replied loudly. Suddenly all the joy was sucked out of the room. Everyone was just sitting there, staring at me, including The Waiter. Dalton had thrown a virtual hand grenade right into the middle of my family's

Christmas celebration. Katie grabbed my hand and squeezed it tight.

"Lexie, go tell him I'm not here."

"But that would be lying, Aunt Sam."

I felt like a toad. There I was, asking my sweet little niece to lie for me in front of my entire family because my dysfunctional relationship was fucking up our holiday.

"You're right, Lexie. I'm sorry." I started to get up to go answer the phone.

"Sit down, Sammy." My mom stood up and walked towards the kitchen. "I'll handle this."

I breathed a sigh of relief as Josh quickly got the festivities back on track. "This present is to Braydon from Grandma!" he said excitedly, handing a large package over to my nephew.

I leaned into The Waiter. "I'm so sorry."

"Don't be," he said, planting a kiss on my forehead. "Your mom is so badass. I love her."

"She loves you too. Obviously."

After all the packages were open, it was time for dessert. And time for the inquisition.

"So," Aunt Gladys said. "How long have y'all been dating?"

"Four months."

"Josh, how bout you and Katie?"

"Same."

"We met the same weekend, Aunt Gladys," I said.

"Well, you all just make such lovely couples. Is there gonna be a wedding anytime soon?"

"Actually, yes," Josh replied. "On Friday."

"What?" She was shocked. "Where?"

"Our friends are getting married in New York on New Year's Eve," I said. "We're all going to the wedding."

"Well then, I'm guessing you two are gonna be fightin' over that bouquet," she said, pointing at Katie and me.

"The only person I'm fighting is Wendy, for the last piece of fudge." Wendy immediately chased me into the kitchen. My mom's fudge was legendary, and every year Wendy and I fought over who would get the last piece. This year, I prevailed.

"Mom!" Wendy yelled. "You're gonna have to start making more fudge."

"And miss the two of you fighting over it?"

"So," I said, sitting down next to my mom. "What did you say to him?"

"I said you couldn't come to the phone. And then I said, 'Merry Christmas.' And then I hung up."

"And then she unplugged the phone," Wendy said.

"Thanks, Mom."

"I haven't seen you this happy in a long time. I wasn't about to let him ruin it."

"I'd be that happy too if I had this bag," Wendy said, picking up the Chanel.

"It's not the bag," Mom said. "It's the boy."

The next day, Josh, Katie, The Waiter and I met Dana, Simon, Deb and Sean at El Azteca for dinner.

"I can't get over this weather," Katie said. "I can't believe we're sitting outside in December."

"Welcome to the south," Simon said.

"It's not gonna be this warm in New York," I said.

Lucy invited Dana and Simon to the wedding. They were flying up on Thursday.

"I know," Dana said. "I'm packing appropriately."

"Where's the wedding gonna be?" Deb asked.

"It's at the Marriott Marquis. The reception will overlook Times Square and all the New Year's Eve festivities."

"Are her parents rich?" Sean asked.

"Very. Her dad's an executive at the Bank of China and her mom's a prominent artist."

"Wow," Deb said. "That's gonna be some wedding. Aren't you guys concerned about the whole Y2K thing though? I mean, being right there in the middle of Times Square?"

"Not really," Josh replied. "I figure if the world's gonna end when the clock strikes midnight, that's pretty much how I wanna go out."

"Well, speaking of signs of the apocalypse," Deb said, "Bitchy Brenda told me to tell you 'hello' and that she hopes you're doing well."

"Really?"

"Yeah. She must've found Jesus or something. She's been ridiculously nice to me ever since you left."

I thought about the last time I was here at El Azteca and how Dalton and I had taken Brenda home. That was also the night I took Dalton back. It seemed like a lifetime ago. From where we sat on the patio, I could see the Clermont Hotel sign and the water tower on top of my old apartment building. I stared off in the distance.

"You okay, Red?" The Waiter asked.

"Yeah. I just miss home."

"I can see why. It's beautiful here."

"No, our home," I said. "I miss New York."

31. y2k

"You have to stop crying!" Lucy said. "You're going to ruin that perfect makeup I paid for."

"I can't help it! I'm just so happy for you guys!"

At 6:30 p.m. on New Year's Eve, Lucy and Kyle said "I do" in front of two-hundred guests in the Marriott Marquis Manhattan Ballroom. The reception was now happening in the adjacent lounge, with floor-to-ceiling windows overlooking the absolute insanity of Times Square on New Year's Eve. I couldn't stop crying happy tears.

"She's already gotten some of that makeup on my tux," The Waiter said. "She's been like this all night."

"Just don't get it on that Gucci." Lucy managed to obtain a long backless Tom Ford number on loan from the Vogue closet for me to wear as my bridesmaid's dress.

"Don't worry. I've been treating it like a newborn."

"That's why I couldn't borrow anything from you," Katie said to Lucy. "I knew I'd be too worried about it all night. I've already spilled champagne on this dress."

"Twice," Josh added. Katie was wearing a black tea-length strapless dress with a beautiful tulle skirt that made her look like a prima ballerina. I'd helped her pick it out at Macy's.

"Lucy, this is the most amazing wedding I've ever been to in my life," Dana said. "Thank you so much for inviting us."

"I'm so glad you guys came! Now, everybody drink lots of champagne while Kyle and I make the rounds. Then we're all dancing." I watched them make their way from table-to-table, greeting their guests and graciously receiving envelopes filled with cash, checks, and general well wishes for a lifetime of happiness. Lucy, the ultimate belle of the ball, floated across the room in her custom Vera Wang gown with her handsome forever prince by her side. Once again, I was crying.

I cried when she walked down the aisle. I cried when they exchanged vows. I cried during their first dance to Billy Joel's "New York State of Mind." And now I was crying again. It was New Year's Eve in New York, and I was surrounded by people I loved. And we were surrounded by thousands of people outside in Times Square, anxiously awaiting a new millennium.

Inside the reception, a big band was playing and a Sinatraesque singer was cooing, "It Had to Be You."

The six of us - Josh, Katie, Dana, Simon, The Waiter and I - sat down at our table just as dinner was being served.

"You think I could spot Dick Clark from here?" Simon asked as he leaned over in his chair and looked out the window.

"I don't know how you could spot anyone in that sea of people," Dana replied. "It's incredible."

"They're all tourists," Josh said. "Nobody that actually lives in New York crowds into the streets of Times Square on New Year's. And you know why?"

"Why?" Simon asked.

"No alcohol," The Waiter answered.

"Exactly," Josh said. "They stand there for hours in the cold with no alcohol just for the slight chance they might end up on TV. You couldn't pay me to do that."

After dinner, the band took a break and a DJ took over. That's when we took over the dance floor. The eight of us danced nonstop for at least an hour until the wedding planner notified Lucy it was time for the bouquet toss. All the single girls were asked to gather on the dance floor, eliciting predictable groans from Katie and me.

"We'll be at the bar," Josh said. The Waiter winked at me as he and the other guys disappeared.

The wedding planner gathered the group of about fifty women and moved us all into position on the dance floor. Of course, she felt the need to put Katie, Dana and me right on the front row.

"Dana," Katie said, "This is all you. I can just imagine the look of terror on Josh's face if I ended up with it."

"Yeah," I replied. "Katie and I are just going to lean to the side and you reach out and grab it."

Dana laughed. "Oh, I'm sure there are plenty of ladies here that want it."

Nobody wanted it. In fact, nobody even attempted to grab it when Lucy threw it over her shoulder. Nobody moved. Rather than let it land on the floor, I reached out and grabbed it at the last minute. Then I immediately tossed it like a hot potato to Katie, who had no choice but to catch it. At that moment, the lights in the reception hall dimmed down to one single spotlight. On Josh. Down on one knee. Directly behind Katie.

"Turn around, Katie," I said. She did.

"Katie," Josh said, as her eyes welled up with tears. "You are the best thing that has ever happened to me in my entire life. I love you more than anything in the world." Then he popped open the box containing her final Christmas present. "Will you marry me?"

"Oh my god yes!" she answered. The entire reception crowd cheered. Josh slid the two-carat emerald-cut diamond ring on her finger. Then he stood up and kissed her. By this time, Lucy was standing right next to me and Dana. All three of us were crying.

"You guys knew about this?" Katie asked, looking over at us.

"Knew about it?" Lucy replied, wiping tears

away. "Hell, we planned it."

"I told you I helped pick out your Christmas present," I said.

Katie ran over and hugged us.

The Waiter, Kyle and Simon all swarmed Josh with masculine hi-fives and bro-hugs.

"Does this mean there will be a karaoke-themed wedding?" Kyle asked.

"Yes!" Josh said.

"No!" Katie yelled.

"Congratulations Josh and Katie," the DJ announced over the loudspeaker. "Now I'm gonna take a break and we're gonna get the band back up here. Oh, and they told me to tell you they're taking requests!"

The Waiter immediately made a beeline for the stage.

"How in the world did you guys pull this off?" Katie asked. We sat back down at our table and I took a sip of champagne.

"Remember that time we had brunch at The Heights," Lucy said, "and I asked what you would say if Josh asked you to marry him?"

"Yes. Oh my god! You guys were planning this way back then?"

"Well, I was pretty sure you'd say yes," I replied. "But we needed confirmation."

"If you'd said no, you would have totally fucked up my wedding," Lucy said.

Katie took Lucy by the hand. "Thank you for sharing your special day with me, Lucy."

Lucy hugged her. "This just made it even more special."

"Stop you guys!" I said. "I swear to god I'll start crying again."

The band began playing "On the Street Where You Live." I looked up to see The Waiter walking towards me with the cutest grin on his face.

"They're playing our song, Red."

"I thought 'Super Freak' was our song."

"Well, you are a very kinky girl." He extended his hand. "Come on, dance with me, freak."

He led me out onto the dance floor and held me close. It was incredibly romantic.

"You look so handsome in this tux."

"And I can't keep my hands off of you in that dress."

"I'm sure Tom Ford would appreciate the stamp of approval."

"You know what it reminds me of?"

"What?"

"Our first date. You had on that halter top and long skirt. It was so sexy. I kept finding excuses to touch your back."

"You didn't need an excuse. Why do you think I wore it?"

I couldn't believe we had come so far from that day. Our very first date. Never in a million years would I have thought I'd be in his arms on New Year's Eve, in the middle of Times Square, in a Gucci dress. It all seemed too good to be true. And it scared the hell out of me.

"So your plan went off without a hitch," he said. "Katie had no idea Josh was going to propose."

"Nope! Not a clue."

"What would you have said if it were you?"

"I would have said, 'Josh, I know we're cousins from Georgia and people expect this of hillbillies, but no I won't marry you.'"

"You know what I meant." I did know what he meant, but I was deflecting because I didn't want to answer the question.

"You also know I'm not the marrying type," I replied.

"Well," he said. "I would marry you. If you were the marrying type."

"That was a total non-proposal," I said.

"Followed by a total non-acceptance," he replied. I laughed as we continued to dance cheek-to-cheek.

"Tell you what, Red. If you ever change your mind, you just let me know."

"Deal."

"Okay, I'm gonna dip you now," he said.

"I wouldn't do that unless you want my boobs to pop out of this dress in front of all these people."

"Right. We'll save that for later. I'll swing you instead."

"Don't make me puke!" I screamed as he swung me around. "Or pee!"

He laughed and put me down. Then he kissed me.

"Get a room,'" Josh said, as he and Katie joined us on the dance floor.

"We've got one," The Waiter replied.

"Oh, yeah," Josh said. "So do we! We've all got rooms."

"That's a good thing," Katie stated. "Because I'm already drunk."

"My fiancé's drunk!" Josh said.

"I'm a fiancé!" Katie yelled. Seeing her and Josh so happy made me all emotional again.

"Oh god," The Waiter said, handing me his handkerchief. "Here come the tears again."

"Dammit!" I wiped my eyes. "I can't be doing this at midnight! They say that whatever you're doing at midnight on New Year's Eve is what you'll be doing the whole year. I don't wanna be drunk and crying."

"Baby," The Waiter looked at me. "You'll be kissing me all year."

"I can live with that."

Around eleven-thirty, the wait-staff began handing out L2K (Lucy-2-Kyle) themed party favors - hats, crowns, horns, glasses, the works. By eleven-forty-five, the champagne was flowing and everyone had gathered at the windows to watch the ball drop. The DJ was playing the longest version of Prince's "1999" I'd ever heard, and everyone was dancing and singing along.

"I see Josh will still be doing the white man overbite in 2000," Kyle said.

"I do that too!" I screamed. "I'm doing it right now! It's totally hereditary!"

Everyone laughed as we continued to dance. To say that the crowd below us in Times Square was packed in like sardines would be an understatement. It was so tight that you couldn't even make out individual bodies. Just a sea of people pulsating as one gigantic wave. They wore multicolored shaggy wigs and waved long wiener-shaped balloons frantically above their heads.

"Hello peasants," Josh said as he stood in the window and waved down below.

"What if all the lights in Times Square go out at midnight because of Y2K?" Simon asked, prompting a swift punch in the shoulder from Dana.

"Really, Simon?" she said. "Why don't you just go up to the DJ booth, scratch the record and stop the music?"

At fifty-nine seconds, the crystal ball atop the New York Times Building began to move. And of course, I began to cry. By the time we hit the ten second countdown, it was so loud with everyone inside combined with the hundreds of thousands of people outside, that it literally sounded like the entire world was counting.

Ten. Nine. Eight. Seven. Six. Five. Four. Three. Two. One.

And then, insanity.

"Happy New Year!" everyone screamed. Balloons fell from the ceiling. The Waiter grabbed me and kissed me for what seemed like forever and yet still wasn't long enough. The sound of the confetti canons outside startled me, as did the fireworks going off from the top of the Times tower. I was so overcome with joy. And I could not stop crying.

"Welcome to the millennium, baby," The Waiter said, kissing my face and wiping the tears. "This is going to be our year."

"I love you," I said.

"I love you, Red."

"I'm crying. And drunk. At midnight," I said. "Dammit!"

He laughed.

"These are happy tears universe!" I screamed at the top of my lungs. "I want happy tears all year long!"

The band sang "Auld Lang Syne." Afterwards, they sang "New York, New York." The eight of us formed a circle by the windows and sang along, arm-in-arm.

I wanted time to stop. I wanted to stay like this forever. I had never been happier at any point in my life. And I was terrified that I would never be this happy again.

32. Good News, Bad News

Pat Kiernan lied.

My favorite news anchor warned me about the cold start to my morning commute. It was ten degrees. However, he failed to mention the bitch-slapping my face would endure as I waited for the train on the 125th Street platform. By the time I got to work, I couldn't feel my cheeks, my eyelids, or my lips, and the only thing warm on my body was the snot dripping from my nose.

It was the Tuesday after Martin Luther King Day and Jackie was back from a two-week vacation in Bermuda. The weather in New York could not have been more of a contrast. It was so cold over the long weekend that The Waiter and I never left the apartment. Daily deliveries from Kozmo sustained us with all the necessities - food, wine, DVD rentals, condoms, oatmeal raisin cookie dough, etc. I spent the entire weekend helping The Waiter prep for a meeting with a group of investors from California. They were flying out to see him and Nick this afternoon. I'd never seen him nervous before. I was equally nervous for him.

Jackie waltzed into the office with her usual bouquet of flowers and an enviable tan that made her look like Jennifer Aniston and me look like Snow Miser.

"Happy New Year, Sammy," she said as she passed my desk. "Why don't you grab a cappuccino and meet me in my office?"

"Will do."

"I already made you one," George said, handing me a cup. "You looked like you needed it."

"I've never been this cold in my life."

"It gets worse. You might want to invest in some La Mer. You're kinda pasty."

I laughed and hung up my coat. I opened my desk drawer to grab a legal pad and saw the holiday card I'd received from Dalton. He'd sent it to the office because he didn't know where I lived. Inside, he'd written a long apology. An apology that six months ago I would have thought heartfelt but now found hollow. I didn't throw it away because it said all the things I'd always wanted him to say. However, I did put two sticky notes on it - one on the outside saying "EVERYTHING IN HERE IS A LIE" and one on the inside saying "NEVER BELIEVE HIM AGAIN. SERIOUSLY SAM."

I grabbed my cappuccino, legal pad, and FranklinCovey day planner and headed to Jackie's office.

"Sit down, Sammy," she said. "I've got good news, bad news, and good news."

I immediately thought I was being fired. Of course, I had no reason to think Jackie wanted to fire me and I knew I'd been doing good work, but that was the first thing that came to mind.

"So, the good news is that we just got another substantial round of funding and everyone, including you, is getting a raise."

"That's definitely good news. But I'm bracing for the bad."

"The bad news is that no additional headcount was approved. The board wants us to keep our team small but grow big. We're going to have to increase the number of articles we're publishing and attract more advertisers."

"You're going to pay me more to write more? That doesn't sound so bad."

"It's a lot of work, Sam. A lot of deadlines. I want you to hire more freelance writers. In fact, I want you to take on a much bigger editorial role."

"I can do that."

"I know you can," she replied, arranging her flowers in a vase. "That's why I'm promoting you to Editor-in-Chief."

"What?"

"As of today, you are officially the Editor-in-Chief of e-Styled.com."

"I think I'm going to faint."

Jackie laughed.

"So I'm like, the Anna Wintour of our website?"

"Not just the website. We're going to launch a quarterly print magazine later this year. You'll be in charge of that as well."

"I am going to faint."

"Sam, it's a tremendous responsibility and a ton of work. I know you can handle it, but if you start to get overwhelmed, you have to tell me. Deal?"

"Absolute deal! Jackie, thank you so much. I can't tell you how much this means to me."

She got up and hugged me. "I'm proud of you. And I'm really proud of the work you're doing. The work all of us are doing. We're having a staff meeting in the morning to discuss our plans for the upcoming year. I'll make the formal announcement then."

"Great!" I left Jackie's office and walked back to my desk. I wanted to call The Waiter immediately and tell him the good news, but I didn't want to interrupt his and Nick's meeting prep. Plus, I would have had to go out of the building and call him on my cell phone so that nobody else would hear, and I had no intention of going back out into the tundra. Instead, I made a note in my calendar that said, "Remember this day!" with a big smiley-face. And then I got to work.

At lunchtime, pizza arrived for the entire office and Jackie had us all gather in the conference room.

"Something's missing," Jackie said, looking around. She got up and walked out.

"I ordered garlic bread, too!" George yelled after

her.

She returned a few minutes later with a couple of bottles of champagne.

"Today we are celebrating. Not only my triumphant return from Bermuda," she laughed, "but the fact that we just got another round of funding. A substantial round of funding."

Everybody cheered.

"Wait!" Jackie yelled. "Hold your cheers. Because in addition, you're all getting raises!"

The cheers turned into screams.

"I'm so proud of all of you, and we've got a lot of hard work ahead. But today, we celebrate. Tomorrow we'll discuss details. And I promise to host a more formal celebration soon."

"I'll go get champagne glasses!" George said.

"I'll help." I followed him to the kitchen.

"I hope my raise is enough for me to get an apartment in Manhattan," he said.

"I thought you had practically moved in with Jeffery. I love you guys together."

"Me too. But his apartment is minuscule and we're on top of each other. And when we're not on top of each other, we're on top of each other."

I laughed.

"Are there any apartments available in your building?"

"I don't know. I can check."

"I want one on your floor. Right next door. So I can see your hunky man every day."

"I'll see what I can do."

Around four o'clock, The Waiter called with more good news.

"They bought it baby. We got a deal."

"Are you serious? That's incredible!"

"Yeah," he replied. The tone of his voice was less than chipper.

"You don't sound very excited."

"I am, babe. I'm just in shock."

"I need details."

"Um, why don't you meet me at Jake's after work. Nick and I are here drinking."

"I'll be there. I have some news worth celebrating as well."

"Are we having a baby?" he asked jokingly.

"That's not even funny. I'll see you around five-thirty."

I hung up the phone and looked down at my calendar. I drew another happy face under my "remember this day" entry. I couldn't believe it. On this random, bitterly cold Tuesday, my life had dramatically changed for the better. Twice. I had never been so certain or felt more validated of my decision to move to New York. I shuddered to think of what my life would like if I were still in Atlanta. Still with Dalton. The thought made me shiver more than my morning commute.

At five o'clock on the dot, I packed up, layered up, and headed out. I knew this would probably be the last day in a very long time I'd be leaving the office at five. And I was perfectly okay with that. I knew The Waiter would be okay with it, too. He'd be busy making his dream happen, and I'd be busy succeeding in my new role as Editor-in-Chief.

I flagged down a cab in front of the building. "Amsterdam between 80th and 81st."

When I walked in the door at Jake's Dilemma, The Waiter was sitting at the bar by himself. He looked exhausted. I walked over and hugged him. "I am so incredibly proud of you. You did it, baby."

"Thanks, Red," he replied. I ordered an apple martini. He ordered another bourbon. From the looks of it, he'd already had quite a few.

"Where's Nick?"

"Oh, he's doing some kind of personal training thing tonight."

"Well, he won't have to do that much longer."

"So," The Waiter asked. "What's your good news?"

"I just got a big raise and a big promotion. Your girlfriend is now the Editor-in-Chief of e-Styled.com."

"Oh my god, baby!" He hugged me. "That's incredible!"

"I know, right? We just got another round of funding. Everybody is getting raises, and a few of us, yours truly included, are getting promotions."

"I'm so proud of you," he said. "Are they planning on expanding to other locations?"

"I don't think so. Not now anyway. But we are launching a quarterly print magazine in the fall. I'm so excited. It's going to be huge."

"I'm so happy for you, Red."

"I'm so happy for both of us! You know, I totally thought this day was going to suck because it was so cold and I was in a bad mood this morning, but now look at us! Talk about a New York minute!"

The Waiter's smile looked pained. I couldn't begin to imagine the amount of stress he was under now, and the shock that came along with having your dream idea green-lighted over lunch. We got our drinks and headed to the back of the bar where there was a fireplace and comfy couches.

"Tell me everything," I said as I plopped down on one of the sofas. "Like, where's the gym gonna be? Did they talk about a location?"

"They've already got one," he said as he sat down next to me.

"Oh my god! Where?"

He hesitated. And in that moment, I knew something was wrong. Very wrong. He couldn't make eye contact with me.

"It's in Los Angeles, Red."

The brick walls of the back room seemed to close in on me. I was hoping that what he'd just said didn't mean what I thought it meant.

"Wait. The gym is going to be in L.A., but you'll still be here in New York, right?"

He shook his head. "They want us to move to California."

"You and Nick?"

"Of course, me and Nick. But when I said 'us,' I meant me and you."

I sat my drink down on the coffee table and buried my face in my hands. I could not have formed a cohesive thought at that moment if you'd offered me a million dollars to do so. The Waiter scooted over closer and put his arms around my waist, his head resting gently on my back.

"I know I have absolutely no right to do this," he said, "but I love you and I'm doing it anyway. I'm moving to California, Red. And I'm asking you to come with me."

33. The Icing

It was the first time I'd ever been inside Madison Square Garden. It was packed. And loud. If I weren't still in shock from yesterday's news, I would have found it very exciting. Plus, I'd been up since five this morning and was exhausted, both physically and emotionally.

Josh's boss at Ernst & Young had reserved the company's luxury suite for the New York Rangers' game but was unable to attend at the last minute. He gave the tickets to Josh, who, of course, invited all of us. The suite was stocked with plenty of gourmet food and thankfully, plenty of top-shelf alcohol.

"You can't leave New York," Katie said. "You just got here." She, Lucy and I were sitting on a leather sofa in the back of the suite while Josh, Kyle and The Waiter sat up front, completely engrossed in the game.

"You don't have to leave," Lucy said, taking a sip

of her martini. "You'll just be bi-coastal. Being bi-coastal is the ultimate dream of every New Yorker."

"Does this mean you consider me a New Yorker now?"

"Girl, you were a New Yorker the night you walked into the Bubble Lounge in that Ralph Lauren dress."

"I don't wanna leave," I said. "But I don't want him to leave either. Everything was just starting to fall into place. I'm madly in love, I just landed my dream job, and Dalton's leaving New York soon. Why the fuck did this have to happen now?"

"Wait, Dalton's leaving?" Katie asked.

"His assignment is up at the end of March. At least, that's what he said in the card."

"Is he going back to Atlanta?"

"I don't know. I guess so. Or wherever his next gig is."

"What else did the card say?"

"The usual bullshit. That he was sorry. That he wasn't seeing Rhonda anymore. He missed me. Blah, blah, blah."

"I'm glad he's leaving New York," Katie said.

"Me too."

"And when is he leaving?" Lucy asked, referring to The Waiter.

"Don't know yet. Sometime next month, I think."

I looked over at him. He and Josh were in deep conversation. I assumed they were talking about the California deal. That fucking deal that was taking him thousands of miles away from me. Of course I was happy for him. This was a once-in-a-lifetime opportunity. But so was my new role as Editor-in-Chief.

"Sam," Lucy said, putting her hand on my knee reassuringly. "I know you love him, but under no circumstances should you consider quitting your job."

"I agree," Katie said. "I mean, I know I'm being selfish, but I don't want you to move to California. You have to be here to help me plan the wedding."

"He will not be in L.A. forever," Lucy said. "Just do the long-distance relationship thing. You'll make it work."

"That's what Dana said," I replied. I'd gone into the office early this morning because I wanted to get a jumpstart on all my new responsibilities. I called Dana as soon as I got there.

"First off, you can't quit your job," she said.

"I don't want to quit my job. I love it here. But I love him, too."

"I know you do. And if he loves you the same way, he'll understand. You guys will just have to make it work."

"And if it doesn't?"

"Sam, if it doesn't, it doesn't."

I immediately started crying. She had just articulated my greatest fear. *If I didn't move to California, I'd probably end up losing him.* But I was already losing. I'd come into work early for a specific reason and yet here I sat, crying and unable to focus on anything but The Waiter. This is not how I wanted to spend my first day as Editor-in-Chief.

"I'm crying, Dana," I said. "At work. I'm sitting at my desk at six o'clock in the morning crying. See? I told you when I was crying on New Year's Eve that I'd be doing that all year long."

"Those were happy tears, Sam. These are not."

"Well, apparently the universe can't distinguish between the two."

"Okay, you need to calm down and focus. Throw yourself into your work and trust that everything will work out the way it's supposed to. And trust me, Sam, it will."

"God, I wished you lived here."

"Find me a dream job up there and I'll move tomorrow. Now, get your shit together and call me later."

After Dana's pep talk, I did manage to get my shit together before anyone else showed up at the office. I downed my Starbucks Venti White Chocolate Mocha and got to work brainstorming two pages worth of article ideas and reviewing portfolios for two freelance writers I was hiring. By the time Eric from IT arrived at seven, I was fully caffeinated and frantically flipping through the February fashion magazines. That was another perk I loved about my job. Every month, the office would receive advanced copies of all the major fashion publications from around the world. Part of my job was to review all of them and write a monthly "round-up" of trends. I was actually getting paid to do what

I loved. Read fashion magazines. How could I ever consider giving that up?

"I don't get hockey," Katie said, looking up at the television monitor in the suite. "I can't keep up with the puck."

"Yeah, it's a low score game," Lucy said. "But hockey players are the hottest."

"Yes, they are," I said, looking over at The Waiter.

"How come he never went pro?" Lucy asked.

"Well, he says he was good. But not that good. I'm kinda glad. He probably wouldn't have that perfect face if he'd gone pro."

"Or all his teeth," Katie said. I think it was the first time I'd laughed all day. And I was feeling a bit more hopeful about being bi-coastal.

After the first period ended, the guys came back to the lounge area and joined us. Actually, I think they just came back to refill their booze.

"Your man knows everything there is to know about hockey," Kyle said.

"He should," I replied. "You guys should see the tapes of him playing in college."

"When did you watch those?" The Waiter asked.

"Oh, I watch them sometimes when you're not home."

"What she's trying to say is that she reserves them for the spank tank," Lucy said matter-of-factly.

"I'm not even gonna deny that," I said.

"Girls have spank tanks?" Josh asked.

"Big ones," Lucy replied. Katie and I nodded in

agreement.

The Waiter laughed. "We have to get you a Rangers jersey before we leave."

"Why can't I just have that one?" I asked, referring to the one he was wearing. The one with the name "Messier" emblazoned on the back.

"Because this, my love, is as valuable to me as that Chanel bag is to you. I got it six years ago when we won the Stanley Cup." He grabbed a beer and sat down next to me.

"I'm going to get some more food," Lucy said. "You want anything?"

I shook my head.

Katie got up and followed her. "I'll go with you. I need more cheese."

"How was your day, Red?" The Waiter asked. "You left really early this morning."

"Yeah. I had a lot of work to do. How was yours? Did you find out when they want you in L.A.?"

"I did actually," he replied.

"Well?"

"You're not gonna be happy."

"Just tell me," I said. "I'm already miserable."

"Monday," he replied. I just looked at him.

"You're moving to L.A. Monday? Like in five days, Monday?"

"No! Not moving yet. Just going out for a couple of weeks to see the space. They already have corporate apartments for us and everything."

"I think I'm going to be sick."

"Baby, why don't you fly out next weekend and

just check it out?"

"I can't take any time off right now."

"So fly out on Friday after work and come back on Sunday. Just a couple of days."

"That's a long ass flight for a couple of days."

"You can write on the plane. And it's really warm and sunny out there. Please?"

He was practically begging. I could see that the whole situation was just as hard for him as it was for me. And as much as I hated the idea of him moving to California - for any period of time - I wanted him to succeed. And I certainly could use some warm weather.

"Okay," I said. "I'll go."

"I love you, Red."

"I love you," I replied. "But I fucking hate L.A."

I'd been to Los Angeles once, with Dalton. A friend of his was getting married in Vegas, and Dalton was a groomsman. The wedding was beautiful. The trip was ugly. I didn't know anyone at the reception besides Dalton, and aside from the bride and groom, Dalton neglected to introduce me to anyone. I'd worn this beautiful scarlet red chiffon dress with a matching long, flowing scarf, but I may as well have worn a scarlet letter. I spent most of the evening sitting at a table by myself watching Dalton work the room, catching up with his friends while leaving me to fend for myself. At one point, the quite handsome brother-of-the-bride sat down next to me and began chatting me up. Like magic, Dalton suddenly appeared and wanted to dance with me. It was the last dance of the evening. The wedding photographer snapped a photo of us. I looked happy. Dalton looked annoyed.

The next day, we drove out to Los Angeles. After doing the usual tourist attractions, I pretended to take a nap in our hotel room while I listened to Dalton on the phone, talking negatively about our relationship to one of his ex-girlfriends. An ex-girlfriend who just happened to live in Los Angeles. An ex-girlfriend that we ended up meeting for dinner that night. She had huge tits. I've hated L.A. ever since.

"Come watch the game with me baby," The Waiter said, taking me by the hand. "I'll teach you all about hockey." The fifteen-minute intermission was up and the Rangers were back on the ice.

"Okay," I smiled. "And then we can watch one of your games when we get home. And you can teach me more."

"If that means what I think it means, then I'm down."

"Oh, you'll be down alright," I replied.

He laughed. There was that sexy, knowing smile that I loved. That same smile I'd seen in the back of the cab the night we'd left *De La Guarda* and were headed uptown to my hotel. That was the first night we slept together. And now we sleep together every night. We don't have sex every single night, of course. But I was getting laid on a regular basis. That was about to end. And it wasn't even the sex that I was going to miss the most. I mean, the sex was incredible. But falling asleep in his arms, waking up with him spooning me, hell, even brushing our teeth together in the morning...those were the moments I was already missing. And he wasn't even gone.

I sat down on one of the chairs at the suite's high-top table overlooking the rink. The Waiter stood behind me with his arms around my shoulders, leaning in close and explaining everything that was happening on the ice. There were fights and power plays and something called icing that had nothing to do with a cake. It was exciting and exhilarating, and for an hour or so, I forgot about California. Tonight was all New York.

When we left The Garden, the Rangers had won. But I couldn't shake the feeling that I had lost.

34. *Fuck Los Angeles*

My Friday night flight landed at LAX at ten, which was one in the morning for me. I was exhausted, but I quickly got my second wind when I exited the jetway and saw The Waiter standing there.

"You have a tan!" I said hugging him.

"It's L.A., Red. What did you expect?" He kissed me. "God, I've missed these lips."

"I missed you too. Where's Nick?"

"He's out with some of his L.A. friends tonight. You'll see him tomorrow." He took my carry-on from me and we headed out of the terminal, hand-in-hand. "How was the flight?"

"Long."

"Were you able to get any work done?"

"A ton, actually."

I spent the entire five-hour flight writing and editing a series of articles that would post on the e-Styled website in March. I was way ahead of schedule as far my editorial calendar was concerned, and that felt great. After The Waiter left for California on Sunday, I focused completely on work, staying late at the office every night except Wednesday, when Lucy and Katie insisted I meet them for dinner at Tortilla Flats. I'm pretty sure they were just performing a wellness check to make sure I wasn't suicidal.

"How's California treating you?" I asked The Waiter.

"Good. Wait 'til you see my view."

He'd called me on Sunday and told me about the corporate apartments they had set up for him and Nick in Santa Monica. Apparently, his new place was three times the size of our apartment and had a large balcony with a view of the Pacific Ocean. Our apartment in Manhattan had a fire escape with a view of the elevated subway.

"In addition to the view, I also have a bottle of wine with your name on it," he said.

"This is the best airport pickup ever!" When we stepped outside of the terminal, I stepped out of my coat. "I guess I won't be needing this for the rest of the weekend."

"No you won't," The Waiter replied as he escorted me to his rental car. "It's gonna be in the sixties. I hope you brought some non-New York clothes."

All I had were New York clothes. I did manage to pack some sleeveless dresses and sandals, but they were still very New York. It was twenty-three degrees when I left the office for the airport today, so I arrived in L.A. in black leather pants, a black cashmere turtleneck, and a black wool coat. Oh, and black boots. I looked like Johnny Cash.

"Welcome to Los Angeles," the sign said as we drove out of the airport. *Fuck Los Angeles.* She was trying to steal my man, with her warm sunny weather and big apartments with balconies and ocean views. Though I have to admit, when we arrived at his apartment and I stood on that balcony, glass of wine in-hand, I was impressed. The sound of the waves crashing onto the shore. The moonlight shining down on the ocean. The warm breeze that felt amazing now that I'd changed into one of my little black dresses. The Waiter had his arms around my waist and his lips on my neck as I stared out at the ocean. I could definitely picture a life here with him. A much more laid-back, less stressful life than what I had in New York.

"It really is beautiful here," I said.

"You're beautiful here. You're beautiful everywhere."

God, I loved this man.

"Come on." I took him by the hand and led him back inside towards the bedroom. "We've got a week to make up for."

Sex with The Waiter was always intense, but tonight was even more so. I was trying to hold on to every single touch, every single kiss, every single second. Even though I had one more night with him before I flew back to New York, I knew that it might be awhile before I saw him again. Like a Buddhist monk, I was living in the moment. Of course, I realize that Buddhist monks aren't having sex and trying to mentally record every detail. But I was.

The next morning, I woke up cradled in The Waiter's arms. I looked at the clock on the nightstand. It was only six-thirty. But I was still on New York time. I snuck out of bed and into the bathroom. I grabbed The Waiter's robe from the back of the door and put it on. Then I went into the kitchen and started the coffeemaker. It was still dark outside. We had plans to meet Nick for lunch and then take a tour of the new gym. I was both looking forward to and dreading it at the same time. I had to pretend to be happy for them even though this whole deal was tearing me apart.

I made myself a cup of coffee and went outside on the balcony. I stared out at the ocean as the sun began to rise, weighing my options. Actually, my options were weighing on me. It was a no-win situation. *Heads.* I give up my job and my friends in New York and move to California. I lose. *Tails.* I stay in New York and The Waiter and I attempt the long-distance relationship thing. I still lose. Over time, and over this much distance, our relationship would eventually fade away. I didn't want that either. And I definitely didn't want The Waiter to give up his dream for me. The only logical choice would be for us to break up and go our separate ways. All that logic went out the window when The Waiter walked out wearing nothing but his underwear.

"Damn, you look good in a tan," I said, looking him up and down.

"And you look good in my robe." He hugged me. Then we stood there looking out at the ocean. "Tell me you couldn't get used to these sunrises."

"Of course I could."

"Are you hungry?" he asked. "I can make you breakfast."

"Not really. You?"

"I want you for breakfast," he said.

"Well, I can't say no to that tan. Or those abs. You'll probably end up on a Calvin Klein billboard in Hollywood soon."

We spent the entire morning in bed. Afterwards, we got dressed and drove up the Pacific Coast Highway to meet Nick at Gladstone's in Malibu. The drive alone was enough to make me reconsider moving out here. It was just as beautiful as it was in the movies. Even more so. Sitting on the deck at Gladstone's overlooking the beach had me wondering if Jackie would ever think about opening an office here. California was reeling me in.

"There she is!" Nick yelled as he approached our table. I stood up and hugged him. He picked me up and swung me around. "How are you gorgeous?"

"I'm good, Nick. How are you?"

"Great," he replied. "How you like this weather?"

"It's incredible. I think it's like thirty-two degrees in New York today."

"So you could get used to this?"

"I could totally get used to this."

"Good. Because this guy's missed you like crazy," he said, referring to The Waiter. I looked over and smiled at him. There he and Nick sat, wearing their Aviator sunglasses and looking very Hollywood. "I'm gonna have to start calling you guys Ponch and John," I said laughing. They looked like characters from the 1980s hit television show *C.H.I.P.S.*

"I get to be Ponch," Nick said.

The three of us sat out on the deck, eating and drinking for two hours. I listened to them discuss their plans for the gym and what they had to do over the next several weeks. I couldn't help but be excited for them. And after a second appletini, I started to wonder what my life would like if I did move out here. Now I was more confused than ever. Or maybe I was just drunk. At three o'clock in the afternoon.

"I'll be right back, babe," The Waiter said, leaning down to kiss me and then disappearing towards the bathroom.

"He's crazy about you," Nick said.

"I'm pretty crazy about him too."

"You know he's not going to do this deal if you don't move out here."

"What?" His statement hit me like a line drive to the face. Whatever buzz I had from my martini times two suddenly vanished.

"He said he's not doing it without you. That if you didn't move out here, he wasn't moving either. He said I'd have to find another partner."

"Oh god, Nick."

"He loves you, Sam. He loves you more than he loves this business."

"Nick, I promise you, you will not have to find another partner. Don't even worry about it."

"So you're gonna move?"

"I don't know yet. But I swear to you I won't let him give this up. Under any circumstances."

"Don't tell him I told you."

"Of course not. And Nick, I appreciate you telling me."

We left Gladstone's and drove back to Santa Monica to tour the space, which was just off Wilshire Boulevard. The building was enormous. It had two stories with a loft-like atmosphere, a gorgeous view of the ocean, and rooftop access. We walked through the space, as Nick and The Waiter pointed out where everything would go. There was a retractable part of the ceiling that would allow climbers on the rock wall to access the roof but could be closed when it rained, which apparently it never did in California. There was enough room to have four full-sized boxing rings - two on the main floor and two upstairs. And the aerialist training area was right by the front windows so that anyone walking or driving by would be able to see people inside dangling from the ceiling.

"This place is perfect," I said to them as we stood on top of the roof. "It's absolutely perfect." After my conversation with Nick, I wanted to make sure that everything I said and everything I did from now on would encourage The Waiter to stay. Plus, just being here and watching him talk about it, seeing how excited he was about the whole thing, further cemented my decision that he had to do this.

Later that night, The Waiter and I went down to the Santa Monica pier and rode the Ferris wheel. I didn't stop smiling all night. And it was genuine. I decided to let go of all the "what ifs" and just try to enjoy whatever moments we had together, for however long we would have them.

When the Ferris wheel began stopping to let people off, we were perched at the very top. You could see for miles. The twinkling lights of Los Angeles in the distance seemed to be winking at me, as if they knew something I didn't. I leaned over and kissed The Waiter passionately, like it was our last kiss on earth.

At that moment, I still didn't know if I wanted to move to L.A. But I knew he had to.

35. California Girls

"**D**id you spend the entire weekend having sex? Because you don't have even the slightest hint of a tan."

It was the first thing Lucy said when I sat down at the table. I promised to meet her and Katie at Gramercy Tavern on Monday for dinner and a debriefing.

"You guys know I can't tan," I replied, taking off my coat. "But yes, I did have all of the sex this weekend."

"So, how was it?"

"The sex?"

"No, silly. California."

"Warm. And sunny. And perfect."

"Oh god," Katie said. "You're leaving us, aren't you?"

"No, I'm not. When I said perfect, I meant perfect for their business. After I saw the space, I totally got why they're opening there. Right location. Right market."

"But not right for you," Lucy said.

"Totally not right for me."

"So, what does this mean?" Katie asked.

"It means I'm going to have to get used to being bi-coastal."

"See?" Lucy said. "I told you that's what you should do. It's the best decision for both of you."

"I agree. But now I just have to convince him of that. He told Nick that he would give up the deal if I didn't move out there with him."

"Seriously?" Lucy asked. I nodded.

"I'm not gonna let him give this up. He'd end up resenting me. And I'm not gonna give up my job and my life here either. I'd end up resenting him. It's the only logical solution."

"Have you told him this?"

"Not yet. He'll be home on the twelfth for two weeks. I'll tell him then."

"Aw, he'll be here for Valentine's Day," Katie said.

"Yeah. And then two weeks later, he'll be moving to California. Without me."

"You'll get through this. You guys will make it work. I know you will."

"I just feel terrible because I spent the weekend acting like I loved California and that everything was perfect. I intentionally gave him the impression that I was going to move out there."

"Did you actually say that?"

"No. He asked if I could picture a life out there with him and I said yes to that. But what I was picturing were long weekend visits. Not me moving there."

"So, how did you leave it with him?"

"I told him exactly what you just said. That we would make it work. And guys, I really want it to work. But it has to work for both of us."

"Sam," Lucy said. "I know this is going to be hard on you, but you made the right decision. You can't leave New York."

"You can't leave us is what she meant to say," Katie added. "Besides, Josh would die."

"Speaking of Josh, what are we doing for his birthday next month? Are we still planning a surprise party?"

"We can't surprise him," Katie replied. "He's already told me he wants a karaoke party. Karaoke with a twist."

"What does that mean?"

"He has this idea of having a karaoke-requests-themed party. Like, we all write down songs we want him to sing on a piece of paper and put them in a jar or something. And then throughout the night, he'll pick a song out of the jar and sing it."

"Oh my god! That is so Josh!" I said. "That will be hysterical."

"Where are we having it?" Lucy asked.

"Well, since the twenty-fifth falls on a Saturday, I was thinking we could reserve the upstairs lounge at Pageant."

"Where's Pageant?"

"It's on Ninth Street," Katie replied. "Between

Third and Fourth."

"I like that place," Lucy said. "Yeah, let's do it there."

"Wait," Katie said. "Sam, you're not going to be in L.A. that weekend, are you?"

"Of course not. I wouldn't miss Josh's birthday for the world."

"Maybe that should be a weekend when your man comes to New York," Lucy stated.

"Or I'll just be the only one at Josh's party without a date."

"Don't tell Darryl that," Katie said.

"Oh, I love Darryl."

"You don't love Darryl the way Darryl wishes you loved Darryl," Lucy replied.

"No, but I still love him."

"Because he punched Dalton?" Katie asked.

"I smile every time I think about it," I replied.

"Me too," Lucy agreed. "So, is Nick leaving *De La Guarda*?"

"He already has. An understudy took over for him. You should see him out in L.A. He's had no problem adjusting to that scene."

"I'm sure the ladies out there will have no problem adjusting to Nick either," Katie said. I felt Lucy kick her hard under the table. "Oh, shit. I can't believe I just said that."

"No, Katie, it's okay," I said. "I'm certain the ladies will be all over both of them."

"That man would never cheat on you, Sam." Lucy said. "He's not Dalton."

"I know he's not, but my god, the women out there."

"What?" Katie asked.

"They're gorgeous. They're all perfect. They're all tanned."

"You're gorgeous," Katie said. "You're perfect. Okay, you're not tan, but nobody who lives in New York is tan in January."

"I just know I'm gonna be obsessing about it. Like every day, I'm going to be wondering if some girl is flirting with him. Or worse. Because you know they're gonna be flirting with him."

"Sam," Katie said, "don't you trust him?"

"Of course I trust him. I don't trust other women. Except for you two. And Dana. And my sisters. And my mom. And that's it."

"Did you ever stop to consider that he's thinking the same thing about you?" Lucy asked.

"What do you mean?"

"I mean, other guys flirt with you all the time. And that's gonna drive him crazy too. Unless..."

"Unless what?"

"Don't ask, don't tell."

"Don't ask what? Don't tell what?"

"You guys could have an arrangement. When you're together, you're together. When you're not, you see other people. But you have a rule that you don't talk about it."

"You mean like *Fight Club*?"

"Yeah, something like that."

"I don't know if I can do that."

"I guarantee you he won't be able to do that," Katie said.

"Well," Lucy continued, "you should both think about it. That could be the key to your sanity. And to making this long-distance relationship thing work."

She had a point. My biggest fear was that he would cheat on me. If we had an arrangement, then I wouldn't have to worry about him cheating. If we were seeing other people, there could be no "cheating." I mean, I still hated the thought of him being with someone else. But the thought of him doing it behind my back was even worse. What I'd been through with Dalton had scarred me for life. Not just because I found out about him and Rhonda, but because I had always suspected that he was cheating on me the whole time we were dating.

When Dalton and I first got together, one of my friends from college was working as a dancer at the club in Atlanta where he was a bouncer. She wasn't a stripper. It was a club that played techno-dance music, and it had a catwalk high above the dance floor. Dancers - both male and female - were hired to dance there on the weekends. She told me that Dalton hit on her and that she turned him down because she knew we were together. I never confronted him about it because I was so in love with him at the time and was terrified of losing him.

A few years ago, Dalton was on a six-month assignment in Phoenix. I was at his apartment and needed to look something up on the internet. When

I sat down at his computer, I noticed a pop-up advertisement for a dating site that said, "Still looking for women in Phoenix?" That time, I did confront him. I almost broke up with him over it. But he managed to convince me that the pop-up only happened because he had booked a hotel in Phoenix and that the dating site used an ad-software that targeted anybody making reservations in the area. He swore to me he hadn't actively been looking for a hookup. And I was stupid enough to believe him.

Of course, The Waiter was no Dalton. Lucy was right about that. But I knew there might come a time that he would be tempted. And I might be tempted, too. I had just moved to New York and had gone from one serious relationship right into another. And even though I loved The Waiter with all my heart, I didn't want to put my life on hold. The only other alternative would be for us to just break up and go our separate ways. The more I thought about it on the cab ride home from dinner, the more I convinced myself that the "don't ask, don't tell" policy might be our only chance at making it work.

The next morning at the office, I had some very exciting news to share with George.

"So," I said to him as we were getting off the elevator. "Are you still looking for an apartment in Manhattan?"

"God, yes! Did you find one in your building? Please tell me you found one in your building."

"Well, not in my building. In the Ansonia. Broadway and 74th."

"The building your man used to live in?"

"The apartment my man used to live in."

"Are you serious? When? How?"

"Nick is moving out to California in a couple of weeks, so the apartment is available for sublease."

"I'll take it. I don't even have to see it first. Tell him I'll take it. Did your man happen to leave any of his stuff there? Like any clothes? Clothes that still smell like him?"

"Um, no George. Those clothes are now at my apartment, but I could ask Nick to leave something behind."

"Yeah, Nick's hot. That would work. Damn, I bet that place has sexy karma."

"You'll love it. The apartment is small, but the view is amazing."

"Well, it can't be as good as the view you wake up next to every morning."

"Yeah, I'm not gonna have that view much longer."

"Oh my god? Did you guys break up?"

"No, we're not breaking up. But he is moving to California for a while."

"What? For how long?"

"I'm not sure. As long as it takes to get their business off the ground."

"Oh, Ginger Spice," he said, hugging me. "This news makes me so sad. Are you okay?"

"No, I'm not. But I will be. I'm just gonna have to get used to the long-distance relationship thing."

"So you'll be bi-coastal. And maybe he could just

be 'bi.'"

"In your dreams, George."

"Yes, he is. Quite often."

I laughed and walked over to my desk. I sat down and opened my planner.

11 Days.

I'd started a daily countdown on my calendar. In eleven days, The Waiter would be back in New York for two weeks. And then he would be gone for months. Possibly even years. I had no idea how I was going to be able to handle this. Or how I was going to break the news that I wasn't going to California with him. But I had eleven days to figure it out.

36. It's a Date

The Waiter's flight was scheduled to land at four. I took the M60 bus to La Guardia to meet him. I enjoyed riding the bus. It gave me a chance to see different parts of the city and watch my fellow New Yorkers going about their daily business. The city was like a pulsating heart and the people were its blood supply, flowing back and forth, keeping it alive.

By the time I got to the airport, I was starving. I'd only had coffee for breakfast and had spent my entire morning and most of the afternoon writing a roundup of fashion week that would be published on Monday. I left my home office desk littered with notes, lookbooks, an entire weeks' worth of *Women's Wear Daily*, and a Sony Mavica camera packed with digital images of models, designers, accessories, and even a few of Lucy and me in the tents at Bryant Park. Of course, Lucy and *Vogue* had much better seats at all of the shows than I did, but she used her clout to get me bumped up to the second row for Michael Kors, where I coveted every single piece that appeared on the runway (sans the fur.) I also got to see Sarah Jessica Parker and Kristen Davis in person. I still could not believe this was my life. That I was actually getting paid to write about fashion and more specifically, *New York Fashion Week.*

Even though the previous week had exposed me to super-tall models and super-skinny starlets, making me feel a little bit short and a whole lotta stout, I couldn't stop myself from ordering a Cinnabon as soon as I got to the airport. By the time The Waiter arrived, the Cinnabon was gone.

"Hey, Red." He dropped his backpack and gave me a long kiss. "Wow, you taste like cinnamon."

"The two things I can't say no to. Cinnabon and you."

"How long have you been here?"

"About eight-hundred calories long. And long enough for my fingers to get very sticky."

He kissed my fingers. "Good enough to eat."

"That's exactly what I said to the Cinnabon!"

We made our way to baggage claim, and once his suitcase rolled around, we rolled out into the taxi line.

"Wow, I have totally forgotten what cold weather feels like."

"You want in my coat?" I opened it up and offered to snuggle him inside.

He looked down at me and grinned. "I want inside all of that."

Twenty minutes later, we were making out in the back of a cab headed west on the Grand Central Parkway. I felt bad for the poor driver.

"I'm sure he's seen worse," The Waiter said. Then he pulled out his wallet and handed a crisp fifty-dollar bill to the driver.

"My man. I apologize for making out in the back of your cab, but I haven't seen my girlfriend in two weeks, so could you please just take this tip and pretend like we're not here?"

"No problem, thank you my friend."

The sun was just starting to set over Manhattan as we crossed the Triborough Bridge. I was staring out the window while The Waiter kissed my neck. I had never felt more in love before, with him or with the city.

"Have you ever seen anything more beautiful?" I asked.

"I'm looking at it." He kissed me again. I wanted the moment to last forever. But of course, it didn't. Coming off the bridge into Harlem, we hit a pothole that violently thrusted me back into reality. Soon we would be back at the apartment and I would have to break the news to The Waiter that I wasn't moving to California. And I was dreading it.

"Are you hungry?" I asked him.

"Starving. Can we just order from Peking Garden and stay in tonight?"

"That sounds amazing."

When we got home, The Waiter paid the cab driver and gave him another generous tip. As soon as we got inside the apartment, I grabbed the menu for Peking Garden.

"You want your usual?"

"Yes. Go ahead and call. I have to pee."

He disappeared into the bathroom while I placed the order. The lady on the phone asked for my address. Then she asked if I wanted the usual, which for us was Vegetable Fried Rice, Beef & Broccoli, and an order of steamed veggie dumplings. I loved the fact that we had a usual. It pained me to think that soon, my regular order would be missing the Beef & Broccoli. And I'd be missing The Waiter.

When he came out of the bathroom, he plopped himself down on the bed and motioned for me to join him.

"Man, it's good to be home. Why don't you slip out of that dress and those boots and come over here and join me?"

"I can't be naked when the delivery guy shows up."

"Why not?" he laughed.

"You want some wine?" I was in the process of pouring myself a full glass in anticipation of the conversation I didn't want to have.

"Definitely." He got up and walked into the living room. He glanced over at my messy desk.

"I've never seen your desk this junkified."

"That's Fashion Week." I handed him a glass of Cabernet. He picked up the digital camera and began scrolling through the photos.

"These are great babe. Did you take them?"

"No. Justin, one of our staff photographers did."

He stopped on one of the photos of Lucy and me at the Michael Kors show.

"Wow. Look at you guys." Then he paused. "You look so happy."

It was the perfect opening. What I wanted to say was *I am happy and I love my job and I love you too but I can't leave New York and I have to let you go and oh god I hope you understand and I hope we can find a way to make it work.* But I couldn't. I couldn't say any of that. I just looked at him.

"I know you're not moving to California, Red."

It turns out, I didn't have to say anything. I stood there, shocked. And heartbroken.

"It's okay," he continued. "I get it. I should have never asked you to do it in the first place. But I don't wanna do this without you."

"You have to. You can't give up your dream for me. And I can't give up mine. We'd end up hating each other."

"Are you breaking up with me, Red?"

"Not completely."

"But you are breaking up with me."

The downstairs buzzer rang. The Chinese food that neither of us now had the appetite for was here. I reached over and pressed the button to let the delivery guy in. The Waiter was just standing there looking at me with those soulful brown eyes I'd fallen in love with five short months ago.

"Do you not love me anymore?" he asked. I placed my hand on his cheek.

296

"I'm doing this because I love you. I'm letting you go because I love you." And then I started crying. He hugged me.

"What if I don't want to be let go?"

The delivery guy knocked. I grabbed the money from my desk and opened the door.

"Hi, thank you." I handed him the cash. "Keep the change."

I closed the door and put the food down on the table. Then I took The Waiter by the hand.

"Come," I said, leading him to the bed. "Sit."

We sat down.

"Here's the deal. I still want us to see each other whenever we can. But long-distance relationships are hard. And we're both gonna be tempted because we're both gonna get lonely."

"You wanna see other people?"

"Not particularly. But I would rather have an agreement that it's okay to see other people than to worry about you cheating on me. If we're seeing other people, that can never happen."

"I would never cheat on you."

"You say that now, but you have no idea what's going to happen when you're in L.A. And I have no idea what's gonna happen here. The way I look at, we have two logical choices. We break up or we just take a step back and see how thing go."

"Meaning?"

"You said you weren't going to be in L.A. forever, right? That eventually you guys would open a gym here in Manhattan and you'd be back."

"Yeah, that's been my plan all along."

"So, baby. Go do your thing. Make it happen. And we'll just do the best we can until you're back."

"Fuck!" he yelled as he laid back on the bed. "This is not what I want. I know you're right, but this is so not what I wanted for us."

"I have something for you." I got up and walked over to my desk in the living room. I walked back into the bedroom and handed him an envelope.

"What's this?" He sat up on the bed.

"An early Valentine's Day present." He opened the envelope. It contained six round-trip tickets from New York to Los Angeles. I had gone ahead and booked myself a monthly weekend trip to California for the next six months. He looked up at me and smiled.

"See?" I said as he reached over and wrapped his arms around me. "We're still going to see each other. At least once a month for the next six months."

"I love you so much," he said.

"I love you too."

The Chinese food would have to wait, because we spent the next two hours in bed. Lying in his arms afterwards, I actually felt more relieved than sad. I knew I'd made the right decision. And I think, deep down, he knew it too.

"Can we eat now?" I asked.

"I just did," he replied, laughing. I smiled at him.

"And can we stay in and do this for the rest of weekend?"

"Yes, my love. We can."

I was hoping we could parlay the "staying in" trend for Valentine's Day too, but The Waiter was not about to let that happen.

Monday night, he'd made arrangements for us to have a private romantic dinner at Pomodoro. He wanted to say goodbye to all the people he'd been working with and he knew we'd get the royal treatment, which we did.

When I arrived at Pomodoro after work and sat down at the table, he handed me an envelope.

"I matched you," he said. Inside the envelope were six round-trip tickets he had booked for himself. "Now we'll be seeing each other at least twice a month for the next six months."

I got up and went over to hug him. He pulled me into his lap. "We'll figure this thing out, Red. I promise." Then he kissed me.

Alfred, the manager of Pomodoro, came over to our table with a bottle of champagne. "I see we're already celebrating."

"We are," The Waiter replied.

"Sammy, why are you letting him move to California? You know he's my best waiter."

"I do know that, Alfred. But he'll be back." I winked at The Waiter.

"Yeah, but he won't be a waiter," Alfred said. "He'll end up buying the restaurant."

"That's actually not a bad idea," The Waiter said. Alfred popped the champagne and poured us both a glass.

"Cheers to you two. Happy Valentine's Day."

As he walked away, I got up from The Waiter's lap and returned to my seat.

"A toast," he said, holding up his glass of champagne. "And a plan."

"A plan?"

"Look," he said. "I know things are about to change between us. But no matter what, next year, Valentine's Day, you and me, right here. This restaurant. This table. What do you say, Red?"

I smiled across the table at him. "I say it's a date."

37. Swan Song

The night before The Waiter officially moved to California, we all gathered for dinner at Rancho. Surprisingly, I was in a pretty upbeat mood. I was also on my second frozen mango margarita, which probably had something to do with it. Tonight was both a celebration for The Waiter and a coming together of my support system. My support system was drunk.

"You know you're not leaving without singing karaoke tonight," Lucy said to The Waiter. "You've never done it before."

"There's a reason for that."

"I can't believe you're leaving tomorrow," Katie said.

"Stop!" I yelled. "I'll start crying right here! Right now!"

"Babe, you're gonna see me in like five days."

It was true. I was flying out to Los Angeles on Friday for the weekend. But something about tonight just felt so final.

"I know. But still. It's New Year's Eve all over again."

"Oh god. Here she goes with the New Year's Eve thing."

"It's true! What was I doing at midnight on New Year's Eve?"

"You were drunk and crying," everyone at the table said in unison.

"See? And I'm gonna be drunk and crying tonight, and I'm gonna be drunk and crying all fucking year. I told you guys."

"You are so freaking cute," The Waiter said, leaning over again and kissing me. "You know what else you were doing at midnight?"

"What?"

"Kissing me."

"Yeah."

"And what are you doing right now?"

"Kissing you."

"Exactly."

After dinner, we gathered for a group photo. Josh climbed up on Rancho's signature saddle stool at the bar and struck a cowboy pose with his hand high in the air.

"Bull riding," The Waiter said. "That should be your next hobby if you get tired of karaoke."

Josh laughed.

"Man, I'm sorry I'm not gonna be in town the weekend of your birthday. I've got a trade show in San Francisco."

"I know," Josh said. "Sam told me. You'll be missed. Especially by this one." He motioned towards me.

One of the waitresses snapped a few photos of our group as we all gathered around Josh. I smiled, even though I knew that every time I looked at this photo in the future it would remind me of The Waiter's last night in town. And every time, it would break my fucking heart.

We left Rancho and walked down to The Gin Mill. As soon as we got there, Katie, Lucy and I made a beeline downstairs to the bathroom while the guys worked their way through the crowd to the bar.

"So," Katie said as we waited on line in the tiny narrow hallway, "what are you guys doing tomorrow?"

"Going to the GreenFlea. His flight leaves at three, so tomorrow morning, we're going to get H&H bagels and then going back to the spot where we had our first date."

"That's so poetic," Lucy said. "Now I think I'm going to cry."

"Don't you dare."

"You're not going to the airport with him?" Katie asked.

"No, I couldn't bear it. And he couldn't bear it either."

"Then you'll be meeting us for brunch tomorrow," Lucy said. "How about The Heights?"

"I don't think I'll be in the mood for brunch."

"You'll be in the mood for alcohol," she replied.

"Well, that's true."

By the time we got back upstairs, The Waiter was at the front of the bar. And he wasn't alone. A very tall, very blonde woman was chatting him up as he paid for our drinks. He looked completely uninterested. But I knew that wouldn't always be the case.

"Sam, don't even go there," Lucy said.

"Too late. Now I have a very clear visual of what the man I'm madly in love with will be subject to for the next year or so."

The Waiter turned around and made eye contact with me. I smiled. He smiled. A few minutes later he delivered my apple martini.

"Here you go, babe."

I glanced over at the blonde who was still at the bar. She had already moved on to flirting with somebody else.

"You think I don't think about it?" The Waiter asked.

"Think about what?"

"Other guys hitting on you. At bars. At work. On the subway. Everywhere."

Once again, I realized that this was just as hard for him as it was me.

"Well, they're not you," I replied.

He kissed me on the forehead.

"And nobody will ever be you," he said.

We stayed at The Gin Mill long enough to watch the Rangers lose to the Senators. Then we headed out to The Parlour.

"Darryl's meeting us," Josh said as we left the bar. "He's bringing his new girlfriend."

"Oh, I can't wait to meet her."

"Yes, you can. Trust me."

"What's she like?"

"Insane," Katie said immediately. "She's from Texas. And she's like insane."

"You'll see," Kyle said.

"You guys met her?"

"Once," Lucy replied. "That was enough."

"She's like a younger, shorter version of Joey's agent on *Friends*," Josh added.

"Well this should be interesting."

The six of us walked up Amsterdam. Lucy and Kyle held hands in front of us. Josh was giving Katie a piggyback ride because her high heels were hurting her feet. The Waiter and I were arm-in-arm. It was freakishly warm for February and I would have been content to just walk the city all night. I thought about all the times our little group had walked the streets of Manhattan over the last several months. Bar hopping. Going to dinner. The night we all went to *De La Guarda*. Soon, it would only be five of us. I'd be the odd man out.

"I can't believe it's this warm," The Waiter said as we turned onto 86th Street. "It's only going up to sixty this weekend in L.A."

"Can we go back to Gladstone's on Saturday?"

"Of course we can. Anything you want."

"I love that place."

"It can be 'our' place," he said. "Our West Coast

place."

Hearing him say that made me feel like everything was going to be okay. We would be a successful bi-coastal couple. We'd be together every other weekend on our home turfs, and I'd get a nice dose of California sunshine every month. When we were together, we'd be together. When we weren't, I would keep myself busy with work and not think about all the tall, tan California girls flirting with him. At least that's what I was going to keep telling myself.

When we got to The Parlour, there was a sign outside advertising tonight's drink specials and karaoke contest.

"Hey look! They're doing cock blocks," Josh said.

"You mean rock blocks?" I asked.

"What did I say?"

"Cock blocks, Josh," Katie answered. "You said cock blocks."

"Well, I'm sure there's plenty of that happening, too."

The Parlour had been doing Rock Block Karaoke since the night before Thanksgiving. The same night Daryl had famously impersonated Axl Rose for several songs before infamously punching Dalton in the face. When we walked in, they had just started a Bon Jovi block and someone was singing "Living on a Prayer." Technically, the entire bar was singing "Living on a Prayer." We said hello to Jimmy who was working the door and then made our way inside.

From across the bar, I saw Darryl waving his hands above his head, frantically motioning us over.

I looked for his new girlfriend but didn't see her. That is until we got closer. She was that short. Barely pushing five feet, I'd say. What she lacked in height, she made up for in volume. Both in her hair, and in her voice.

"Yay!" she screamed as we approached. "Darryl told me I was gonna get to meet y'all tonight!"

"Hi!" I extended my hand to greet her. "I'm Sammy."

"I'm Molly!" She reached up to hug me and all I could think was *please don't let her cigarette catch my hair on fire.*

"You're so pretty!" she screamed in my ear. "Is that your real hair or a wig?"

"Um, it's my real hair. Not my real hair color, but my real hair.

"This is not my real hair color either!" That was pretty obvious. She had bleached blonde, heavily teased hair straight out of a Whitesnake video. I was guessing she'd stuck with this hairstyle since the eighties because she needed the extra height.

I introduced her to The Waiter.

"You're so fucking tall! And I thought we grew 'em big in Texas. Where you from?"

"Brooklyn!" He squeezed my arm and began pulling me backwards. "We're gonna grab some drinks," he said to Darryl and Molly. "You guys good?"

"Yeah, we're good," Darryl responded.

"What the hell was that?" The Waiter said as we joined the others at the bar.

"Did I tell you?" Lucy asked. "Did I not tell you?"

"She's a little loud, but sweet. Where in the world did Darryl meet her?"

"Off the Wagon," Katie replied.

"'Off his rocker,'" Josh added.

"What does she do?"

"She's a kindergarten teacher."

"Get the fuck out," The Waiter said.

"Actually, that kinda makes sense," I added, looking over at them. "Darryl seems pretty happy."

"He's getting laid," Josh said. "Of course he's happy. Here. I ordered shots for all of us." He motioned for Darryl and Molly to come join us and began handing out Kamikazes.

Josh held up his shot glass and looked at The Waiter. "To your success in Los Angeles, and to you and Sam officially becoming bi-coastal."

"To Sam becoming bi!" Darryl yelled.

"Hear hear!" Everyone laughed and drank.

"And now, if you guys will excuse me," Josh said, "it's time to get my Bon Jovi on." He walked over to the karaoke host who handed him a list of songs.

"Man, Josh is like royalty in here," The Waiter said.

"Well, he is the karaoke king," Katie replied.

"Oh my god!" I said. "Now I know what I'm getting him for his birthday."

"A crown?" Katie asked.

"We should probably get him one of those too."

The sing-along continued as Josh started belting out "You Give Love a Bad Name." Molly and Darryl were right in front of him, head-banging and singing at the top of their lungs.

"Jesus, it's fucking Sid and Nancy," Kyle said, causing The Waiter to laugh hard enough to spit out his beer.

"Damn, I'm gonna miss this," he said.

"Don't! Don't start that! I am not crying again tonight."

"Okay, it's time for you to sing!" Lucy pointed at The Waiter.

"I think I'm just drunk enough to do it," he said. I grabbed his hand as he started to walk over to the karaoke book.

"If you sing 'Never Say Goodbye,' I swear to god I will slit my wrist and bleed out right here at the bar."

He laughed. "I'll try to choose something a little more upbeat." He kissed me and walked away. I watched as he ran his finger down the list of songs and then stop. He showed it to the host who nodded.

As soon as Josh finished, he handed the microphone off to The Waiter. The music started. "Born to be My Baby" blared from the speakers and the entire bar started singing the opening chorus. The Waiter smiled at me and I nodded my approval as he sang the first verse.

"Oh my god! He can sing!" Lucy shouted.

"Yes, he can. He's fucking perfect!"

She and Katie put their arms around me as we all sang together and cheered The Waiter on. He sang the entire song looking directly at me as I mouthed the words along with him, smiling through my tears. Tears that were thankfully interspersed with bursts of manic laughter watching Darryl and Molly dance spastically in front of him.

Nobody in the bar, aside from our core little group, had any idea the significance of the moment. It wasn't just another Bon Jovi song sang at a karaoke bar on a random Saturday night. It was my swan song.

The Waiter was leaving tomorrow. And I was dying inside.

38. The Moments in Between

The next morning, The Waiter and I were strolling 77th Street and reminiscing our first date. We'd just picked up bagels at H&H and planned on washing them down with ice cold grape juice at the GreenFlea. We were denied.

"What happened to the grape juice dude?" The Waiter asked as we stood in front of the stand, which was now offering hot cider.

"He's seasonal," the cider-man said. "We share the space."

"We'll have two ciders then." The Waiter handed him some cash and he handed us two cups. Then we began browsing the market. We stopped to say hello to John and Adriana. The Waiter started flipping through their latest collection of vintage albums.

"Oh Red, you have to have this one." He held up a copy of The Mama's and The Papa's *If You Can Believe Your Eyes and Ears*. "It's got 'California Dreamin' on it."

I smiled at him as he paid John for the album while I made small talk with Adriana. We waved goodbye to them as we left.

"Wanna go for a walk?" he asked. "Over to the park?"

"You asked me that on our first date."

"Yes, I did."

"I'd love to go for a walk with you." And off to the park we went, hand-in-hand.

"You know, I was really nervous the first day I met you here," I said. "Walking past those brownstones back there, I couldn't stop my hands from shaking."

"Really? I didn't think you were gonna show up."

"Why not?"

"I don't know. I thought you might think it was weird that some random waiter dude asked you out the second he met you. That you might think I was psycho."

"I thought you were hot," I replied. He laughed.

"I just couldn't believe you were the girl I'd seen in the park that morning. I'd been thinking about you all day."

"Get the fuck out!"

"No, I'm serious. We made eye contact, remember?"

"Of course I do. Josh told me to stop leering at you."

"Did you know that wasn't even my section you guys were sitting in at the restaurant?"

"I did not know that."

"When I saw you walk in, I made one of the other guys switch with me so I could talk to you."

"How come you never told me this before?" By this time, we'd made it into Central Park and over to our bench.

"I don't know. I didn't want you to think I was some kind of freak. And I didn't wanna jinx it, ya know? Like what are the odds?"

"That was my first authentic New York moment. And look at us now. Right back here. On our bench."

"This is our bench," he replied. "You can't sit on this bench with anyone else but me. Okay?"

"Okay."

"Look, Sam. I know we talked about seeing other people and I get it. I don't like it, but I get it. I just need to know that other people doesn't include him."

I knew he was referring to Dalton.

"I hate the thought of him being here and me not," he said. "I hate the thought of him, period."

"He's leaving New York. His gig is up at the end of March."

"How do you know that? I thought you weren't talking to him."

"I haven't talked to him. And I don't plan to. He sent me a holiday card back in December. Well, he sent it to the office."

"So he's moving back to Atlanta?"

"I guess. The card didn't say. He just said his gig was up and that he'd be moving on to his next assignment."

"That's not all it said," The Waiter said know-ingly.

"That's all that mattered." I took his arm and put it around me. Then I leaned back into his chest and stretched my legs out on the bench.

"Can we just sit here until you have to leave? We don't even have to talk. We can just be."

He pulled me in closer.

"Yeah, Red. We can just be."

We sat there for almost an hour. People walked past us. Bicyclists sped by. I pet every single dog that would allow it. And then it was time for him to go. We started walking back.

"Are you gonna grab the subway uptown?" I asked. The Waiter was taking the M60 bus to the air-port. He'd already shipped out most of his things to L.A., so all he had with him was his backpack.

"No, I'm gonna catch the M7 up to the gym first. I have to cancel my membership before I go."

We continued walking. Past The Museum of Nat-ural History. Past the GreenFlea. Just like we did on our first date. The whole time, I kept repeating over and over in my head, *you'll see him in five days, you'll see him in five days*. It was the only thing keeping me from having a full-on breakdown. Before we knew it, we were back at the corner of Amsterdam and 77th.

"This is where you first kissed me."

"I remember," he smiled. "You were leaving me. Going back to Hotlanta."

"Now look who's leaving," I said. In the distance,

we could see the M7 bus. The tears began to well. There was no stopping them. I didn't even bother.

"Oh god baby. Please don't cry." He leaned down and kissed my entire face, as if he were trying desperately to make the tears disappear.

"I can't help it," I blubbered. He put his arms around me and held on tight, his chin resting on top of my head. I sobbed uncontrollably into his chest.

"I love you, Red," he said. I cried even harder. I could hear the bus approaching. "This is not the end of anything. You know I'm gonna end up back in New York. And I'm gonna see you in five days. Five days, okay?"

"I love you, too. But you have to go or I am going to die right here on this corner."

He leaned down and kissed me. When he let go, it felt like someone had punched a hole in my chest and all the air in my lungs was escaping. I just stood there on the corner, gasping for air.

I watched him walk away from me, just like I did the first time. The joy I'd felt that day was replaced with a heartache I'd probably never recover from. But I knew I'd made the right decision to let him go.

He stood there across the street, waiting to get on the bus. I yelled out to him.

"Hey Dominic!"

He turned around and looked at me.

"I'll see you in five days," I said, holding up five fingers while attempting a smile. He smiled back and blew a kiss right before he stepped onto the bus. And then he was gone.

I watched the bus pull away. Then I waited for the light to change so I could cross over Amsterdam. I looked across the street and saw Lucy and Katie standing on the corner. When the light changed, I ran towards them. They sandwiched me with bear hugs while I cried uncontrollably. They cried with me.

"We got you," Katie said.

"Yeah, we do," Lucy agreed.

"How did you guys know I was here?"

"We've been stalking you," Lucy said. "From a distance, of course. Come on. Let's get you wasted."

"I look like shit."

"So do we now," Katie said.

The three of us walked arm-in-arm toward Broadway.

"I'm not sure I'm up for brunch. Can I just go home and die already?"

"Sure," Lucy said. "Right after brunch."

"Do you know how many broken hearts in this city have been soothed by bottomless mimosas?" Katie asked.

Lucy stepped out into the street and hailed a cab. We climbed into the back seat. "Broadway and 111th," she informed the driver.

I laid my head in Lucy's lap and cried some more. She stroked my hair. "It's gonna be okay, Sam. I promise."

We arrived at The Heights and the three of us climbed the stairs to the second-floor entrance. As soon as I walked in, I noticed a familiar face sitting in the corner. It was Dana.

"We called for backup," Lucy said. I immediately bursts into tears and ran into Dana's open arms.

"How are you here?" I said, sobbing on her shoulder.

"How could I not be here? Come, sit. I have a pitcher of mimosas ready and waiting.

I sat down and tried to wipe my eyes as Dana hugged Lucy and Katie.

Dana looked at me. "How are you, babe?"

"Dead inside. Other than that, I'm pretty good."

The three of them smiled at me.

"It just sucks, guys," I said. "This just sucks so much!"

"Yeah, it does," Dana agreed. "There's no denying the suck factor."

The waitress came over and took our order. I wanted blueberry pancakes.

"Dana, how long are you in town?" I asked.

"Until Wednesday. I actually have a job interview tomorrow."

"Oh my god!" I squealed. "Are you serious?"

"Well, it's not really a formal interview. It's just a meeting with a person who could potentially give me a job."

"Where?"

"*Time Out New York*."

"I read that every day!" Katie said. "It's like the Bible for what's happening in the city. And oh my god, if you worked there, you would get free tickets to everything."

"Well, my boss in Atlanta is friends with one of the editors, and when I told her I might be thinking about moving, she mentioned *Time Out*."

"Wait," Lucy said. "Your boss is trying to help you find another job?"

"She's moving to Chicago in a couple of months. I love her. She's my mentor."

"If you moved here, my life would be complete," I said.

"Well, apparently *Time Out* is always looking for really good PR people. And there are no PR people as good as me, so there's that."

"What about Simon?" Katie asked.

"Simon would move to New York in a fucking heartbeat. Are you kidding?"

"My life is made," I said. "My life is made right now."

A little while later, the waitress was back with our food. She put the plate of blueberry pancakes with fresh whipped cream down in front of me. They smelled like heaven. And I felt like I'd just had a divine intervention. The fact that Dana was sitting next to me and the thought of her and Simon moving to the city was a bright spot in a dark day.

"Where are you staying?" I asked her.

"With you, of course," she laughed.

"My stuff is at Josh and Katie's. Josh met me at the airport this morning."

"How long did you guys have this planned?"

"A couple of weeks," Lucy responded. "We knew this day was going to be tough for you."

"I love you guys so much." I started crying again. "I assure you, these are happy, grateful tears."

"Well, I think Mr. Obvious over there would be happy to come over and wipe those tears," Dana said, motioning over to the bar. "That guy's been staring at you ever since you walked in."

I looked over at the bar. There was a relatively attractive man sitting there, and he was indeed staring at me.

"Not interested," I said. I then proceeded to stuff a huge forkful of pancakes into my mouth.

"Yeah, he's totally not your type," Katie said.

"My only type is Dominic," I replied, speaking with my mouth full.

"Remember when you thought your only type was Dalton?" Dana asked.

"I'm eating here, Dana. Don't make me puke blueberries on you."

"Well," Lucy said, "eventually, you're going to see other people."

"I'm seeing other people right now. I see you and I see Katie and I see Dana. See?"

"Very funny," Lucy laughed. "It'll take some time, but someday you'll be ready."

"Ready for what?"

"For all those firsts. The first look. The first date. The first kiss. I mean, I love my husband more than anything in the world. But sometimes it makes me sad that we won't get to experience our first kiss again."

"I want my first kiss with Dominic to be my last

first kiss."

"You say that now," Dana said, "But believe me. One day, some really cute, really sexy guy is going to smile at you, just like Dominic did, and you'll smile back. You won't be able to help yourself."

"And then what?"

"Then it goes wherever the universe wants it to go. I think eventually you and Dominic will be back together here in New York."

"You do?"

"Yeah, I do. But here's the thing, Sam. There are a lot of exciting moments to be had between now and eventually. Do you really want to miss out on all the moments in between?"

I thought about it for a second.

"No, I don't."

"Of course you don't," she said. "I'm just saying, give yourself time to heal, but then you need to go out there and grab those moments."

Katie held up her mimosa.

"To grabbing the moments in between."

The four of us clinked our glasses together. *To the moments in between.*

39. Checkmate

T hree weeks after Dominic moved to California, I was home on a Saturday afternoon, doing what I always do on Saturday afternoons. Cleaning my apartment. In two days, it would be the first official day of Spring and I felt the need to spruce things up a bit.

A lot of his things were still in the apartment, and I found that comforting. At any moment, I could open "his" closet and climb inside one of his coats, sweaters, or his Mark Messier jersey. He'd also left the big television in the living room along with a fancy stereo system. His new apartment already had both. I made him leave a bottle of his Aveda hair gel because it smelled like him. It was on my bedside table.

We'd fallen into a new routine. He would call me in the morning when he woke up, which was usually around ten my time. I'd call him in the evening before I went to bed, which was usually around eight his time. And there were always random ICQ chats and funny messages throughout the day. He would be back for a visit at the end of the month. This would be the longest period of time we'd gone without seeing each other. Four weeks. I was doing everything possible to keep myself busy.

I went down to the basement and started a load of laundry. I stopped and picked up my mail in the lobby on the way back up. There was a thank-you card from George. He had an apartment-warming party last weekend and I'd gotten him an antique mirror from the GreenFlea. It looked exactly like the one the queen from *Cinderella* used to ask who was the fairest of them all. He loved it. I also gave him a framed photo of all of us from the night we went to Potion and danced to Prince. I think he liked that even more because Dominic was in the photo looking all sexy, which was the way Dominic normally looked. Being back in Dominic's apartment, even though George had completely redecorated, made me miss him so much I could barely breathe. Jackie was there, and she noticed.

"Sam," she said to me that night. "I know that was a hard decision to make. But it was the right one. You can never give up your career for a man, no matter how much you love him. Trust me, I know. And the fact that you wouldn't let him give up his career for you, really shows how much you love him."

"Thanks, Jackie."

"And you know, there's a lot of fashion happening in L.A. We should probably be covering more of it. I might have to send you out there from time to time. If you don't mind that long-ass flight."

I smiled at her. "Jackie, you're the best boss I've ever had. I mean that."

"And you're the best Editor-in-Chief I've ever had," she replied, hugging me. "Of course, you're the only Editor-in-Chief I've ever had, but still."

I put George's thank-you card on the refrigerator with a calendar magnet from Peking Garden. My mobile phone rang. It was an "out of area" number. I answered, thinking it must be Dominic again. I'd already talked to him earlier this morning.

"Hey stranger." Hearing Dalton's voice on the other end of the phone startled me.

"How did you get my number?"

"I have ways." That startled me even more. I'd gotten a new cell phone and a New York number shortly after I left Dalton. And now he had it.

"What do you want?"

"To say goodbye, Sam. I'm starting my new job on April third."

"Oh."

"Meet me for dinner tonight, so I can say goodbye in person."

"Not a good idea, Dalton."

"Why? You got plans with pretty boy?"

If he only knew how much I wished I had plans with Dominic tonight.

"Just not a good idea."

"Come on, Sam. We both need closure. There are

a lot of things I need to say to you. And I need to say them in person."

"Fine. For closure. And for drinks. Not dinner."

"Fine. Eight o'clock. Atlantic Grill."

"Ugh," I said. "How convenient for you."

The Atlantic Grill was right around the corner from his apartment on the East Side. The apartment I had snuck out of five months ago. I hadn't been back to the neighborhood since. But I certainly didn't want him coming over to my side of the park.

"I thought you liked Atlantic Grill," he said.

"It's fine. I'll see you at eight."

I hung up the phone, knowing full well I'd just made a huge mistake. Sure, I wanted closure. But what I really wanted was revenge. I wanted to sit across from Dalton looking sexier than I'd ever looked before and watch it happen. To see the look on his face when he finally realizes that after all the lies, all the cheating, all the emotional bludgeoning I'd put up with for the last decade, I'm over him. One-hundred percent completely and totally over him. I was glad he was leaving New York. I would never have to worry about running into him again.

I spent the rest of the afternoon cleaning the apartment and finishing up my laundry. At seven-thirty, I was in a cab headed to the East Side. I was wearing a black and white zebra-print Diane von Furstenberg wrap dress with my black Kenneth Cole boots and a bright green wool coat. And of course, my Chanel bag. When I got to the restaurant, Dalton wasn't there. *How typical.*

I grabbed a stool at the bar and ordered my usual. As soon as the bartender sat my martini down in front of me, someone sat down right next to me.

"Any chance I could buy that drink for you?"

I turned, expecting to see Dalton, but it wasn't. It was just some guy I'd never seen before.

"Thanks," I replied, "but I'm good."

"You're good alright. You're fucking gorgeous. Excuse my French."

"Fuck isn't French," I replied. "But thank you."

"Hi," he said, extending his hand. "I'm John."

"I'm Sam," I replied, shaking his hand. "And I'm kinda meeting someone here."

"Well, can I keep you company until he gets here?"

"He is here actually." Dalton was standing right behind John, towering over him and smiling down at me. John turned around and looked up at Dalton.

"Oh, sorry man," he said as he slithered off the barstool. "I was just keeping your girlfriend company here."

"I'm not his girlfriend," I said, taking a sip of my martini.

"Well then, that's definitely his loss," John said before disappearing into the crowd.

Dalton plopped down on the barstool, shaking his head and laughing. He leaned over and kissed me on the cheek.

"Hi baby," he said.

"I'm not your baby either. And isn't it about time you tried a new cologne? That Eternity shit is nauseating."

"You used to think it was sexy."

"I used to think you were sexy."

He smiled at me. *Motherfucker*. He was still sexy. He'd always be sexy. But it didn't matter anymore. I still felt nothing. Except annoyed. And, based on the way he was looking at me, vindicated.

"You look incredible, Sam."

"Thanks." I took another sip. "Aren't you drinking?"

"Yeah, sure." He ordered a scotch. "Remember the last time we were here?"

"Yeah. We sat right over there. And we were fighting. We'd been fighting all day."

"Had we?"

"Yep. I remember thinking that you and I should never go out to dinner in Manhattan because we were always fighting, and I was always too upset to finish eating my really expensive meal. Seemed like such a waste."

He smirked.

"How are things with you and pretty boy?"

"He has a name, Dalton. It's Dominic."

"That's a pussy name."

"Speaking of pussy. How are things with you and Rhonda?"

"Over."

"Oh, that's a shame." It came out as a hiss. Exactly the way it was intended.

"Look, Sam, I'm sorry I did that to you. I'm sorry I brought her to The Parlour and I'm sorry I cheated on you."

"Which time?"

"All of them." I was stunned that he had given me an honest answer. And speechless. For the first time since I'd known him, he actually looked uncomfortable. He quickly changed the subject.

"So, did you get the flowers I sent you last month?"

"I did. They were beautiful. But you shouldn't have sent them."

On Valentine's Day, I had gotten flowers from both Dominic and Dalton. Around ten o'clock that morning, George came walking over to my desk carrying the biggest bouquet of red roses I'd ever seen. The card said, *Red for my Red. I love you more than anything.* An hour later, George returned with a somewhat smaller bouquet of white roses with a card that simply said, *I'm still a dick. I'm still sorry. And I still love you.*

"These are actually for you," I'd said to George as I tossed Dalton's card into the garbage. I knew George had already read the card. He knew they were from Dalton. I took out a post-it note and wrote a little love note: *To George, you complete me.* Then I stuck it on the vase and handed the flowers back to him.

"Thanks, Ginger Spice," George said as he walked back to his desk, carrying the white roses like he was a pageant winner. I never told Dominic about that.

I ordered another martini.

"How's Dana?" Dalton asked.

"She's great! She just got a job at *Time Out New York* and she and Simon are moving up here on Friday."

"Seriously?"

"Yeah! Her mom is totally going to kill me."

"What about Simon? Does he have a job up here?"

"Not yet. But he's a really good graphic designer. He'll land something in no time."

"Where are they going to live?"

"Downtown. In the financial district. They found a one-bedroom near Battery Park."

"And where are you living?"

"That's none of your business."

"Why? Are you living with him?"

"Yes, as a matter of fact, I am." It was kind of the truth. There was no way I was going to tell him about mine and Dominic's bi-coastal status. If Dalton sensed any kind of weakness in the relationship, he'd move in for the kill.

"How long have you been living with him?"

"Also none of your business."

I could see him getting agitated.

"You ran right to him that night, didn't you?"

"Does it even matter, Dalton? We're done. And you're leaving. What's the point?"

He sat there, staring at his drink.

"Can we just talk about something else? Tell me about your next gig. Do you have a new assignment or are you going back to Atlanta for a while?"

"No, they already gave me my new assignment.

It's for twelve months. I start Monday, April third."

"Wow, your new assignment is for a year?"

"Yeah."

"Where is it?"

"Hoboken," he said. And then he smiled.

I felt like someone had just jammed a needle full of adrenaline into my chest, like that scene from *Pulp Fiction*.

"Hoboken? New Jersey? Like, right across the Hudson River Hoboken?"

"Yes, Sam, that Hoboken."

"So, you're not leaving New York?"

"I'm not even leaving my apartment," he said, taking a swig of his Scotch. "I kinda like this neighborhood. I'll just take the PATH train to work every day."

I had nothing. No response. I just sat there on the barstool shaking my head, thinking about the fact that Central Park was the only thing separating Dalton and me for the next year. I looked at him. He smiled at me and downed his drink.

Dalton had just checkmated me. And he fucking knew it.

40. I'll Have a Manhattan

"**R**eservation for nine," Katie said. We had just arrived at Pageant, a popular Irish pub and restaurant on Ninth Street in NoHo known for its Shepherd's Pie and stout drinks. It was the night of Josh's birthday. We were all having dinner downstairs before taking over the upstairs lounge for his karaoke party.

I'd talked to Dominic earlier while he and Nick were at the trade show in San Francisco. It was loud and I could barely hear him, but he wanted me to wish Josh a happy birthday for him and to take lots of pictures.

"Hey Red, I'll see you in five days!" he yelled into the phone before hanging up.

I couldn't wait to see him. I was sad that he wasn't here tonight, but I was so proud of him. The gym was set to open at the end of April, and I was flying out to California to celebrate with him.

But tonight, we were celebrating Josh. We were

also celebrating Dana and Simon's status as the newest New Yorkers. They had just moved into their apartment on West Street and Morris. I spent the entire day helping them unpack. I took the little black dress I was wearing tonight with me so I could change there. I wouldn't have time to come all the way back to the Upper West Side. Their apartment was way downtown. Way further than Dana wanted to be, considering that her new office was in Times Square. But the rent was much cheaper down here. Plus, they had a large balcony with an amazing view.

"I plan on spending a lot of time out here," I said to Dana. We stood there, staring out at the top of the Woolworth Building, sipping wine as the sun set over Lower Manhattan before heading out to Pageant.

"I'm so fucking glad you're here," I said, hugging her.

"The adventure continues." She clinked my glass with hers.

She, Simon and I arrived at Pageant the same time as Josh and Katie. Lucy had called and said that she and Kyle were on their way. Josh wasn't sure if Darryl and Molly were meeting us for dinner or just coming to the party. We all hoped it was just the party. We could handle Darryl by himself, but the combination of him and Molly together was too much. We did our best to tolerate her because we loved Darryl.

The hostess walked us to our table, which was

right in the center of the restaurant. Josh sat down at the head of the table with Katie next to him. I sat next to Katie and Dana sat next to me with Simon beside her. Then Lucy and Kyle arrived and Lucy sat directly across from me.

"Oh god," she suddenly realized. "I guess this means I'm sitting next to Molly."

"Simon," Dana said, "be a doll and go sit on the other side of Lucy across from me." Of course Simon, being the doll that he is, did so.

"Who's Molly?" he asked as he greeted Kyle and then sat down beside Lucy.

"Oh, you're about to find out," Lucy replied.

"I think they're just coming to the party," Josh said. The waitress came around and took our drink orders.

"You guys all moved in?" Kyle asked Dana and Simon.

"Yep," Dana replied. "We have a few more things being delivered this week, but we're in for the most part."

"Wait until you guys see the view from their balcony," I said.

"When's the housewarming party?" Katie asked.

"I don't know," Dana replied. "How about next weekend?"

"Yes! Yes!" I screamed. "Dominic will be here!"

"Speaking of Dominic," Lucy said. "Are you going to tell him about Dalton?"

"I have to. Eventually, we're gonna run into him. Dalton's probably plotting to make that happen right now."

"Dominic's not going to be happy about that," Dana said.

"No, he isn't. I wish this fell into the don't ask, don't tell category."

"Yeah," Katie said. "It doesn't."

"Speaking of don't ask, don't tell," Dana said, "Sam is convinced that Dominic is already seeing other people."

"What?" Katie was shocked. "Why?"

"The more important question," Lucy said, "is why wouldn't he be? And why aren't you? Wasn't that your agreement?"

"Yeah, I know. But still."

"What makes you think he's seeing someone?" Katie asked.

"Intuition. And you guys know, my intuition is spot on."

"Sam, baby," Lucy said, "you knew this was going to happen. Hell, you planned for this to happen."

"I know. But I thought by agreeing to see other people, I wouldn't obsess about him cheating on me. Now I'm obsessing about him seeing other people. I'm fucked."

"Well," Lucy replied, "you could unfuck yourself by seeing other people too."

"I agree," Dana said. "You need to do it soon. And you know why." I knew she was talking about Dalton.

"There is not a snowball's chance in hell of that happening again."

"That man is like a heat-seeking missile when you're vulnerable. And you know it."

"Don't you get lonely sometimes?" Katie asked.

"How could I get lonely? I have you guys!"

The three of them looked at me.

"Of course I do. But I just want Dominic. And I definitely don't want Dalton."

"Well, somewhere between Dominic and Dalton is where you need to get to," Dana said. "For your own sanity."

"And ours," Lucy added. The four of us laughed.

"What are you bitches laughing at?"

Molly and Darryl had arrived with a bang. She made her way around the entire table, hugging everyone like we were long-lost family, including Simon, who had a pained look on his face that caused me to immediately snap a photo with my digital camera. Molly was friendly. Maybe a bit too friendly at times. But she was funny, and like Darryl, she had a tendency to grow on you. She was just so loud! And she wreaked of cigarettes.

"Have we done birthday shots yet?" she yelled out. I felt sorry for the people around us.

"Not yet," I replied. "We were going to wait until the party."

"Hell no!" She flagged the waitress down. "Buttery Nipples for the whole table!"

I avoided making eye contact with Lucy while Dana grabbed my hand under the table. I quickly realized the best way to keep Molly from causing more of a scene was to engage her in conversation, which I did throughout dinner. Turns out she, just like me, had moved to the city to pursue her dream. She wanted to open a cleaning services company. Currently, she was a part-time kindergarten teacher, and the rest of the time she cleaned apartments. And made incredible money doing so.

"I figured, there are just so many rich folks here in this damn city," she said. "And rich folks don't like to clean. I actually like to clean."

"I like to clean too," I said, finding a little common ground.

"You should come work with me," she replied immediately.

"I already have a job. But thank you."

"What do you do?"

"I'm the Editor-in-Chief for e-Styled. It's a fashion startup."

"I knew you had to be involved in fashion! You're always so fancy. So put-together."

"Thanks."

"Do you like it? Your job?"

"Yeah," I smiled at her. "I absolutely love it."

After dinner, we all went upstairs for the big party. Katie had done an excellent job planning it and we all split the costs. The DJ she'd hired as the karaoke host had timed Stevie Wonder's "Happy Birthday" song perfectly for Josh's entrance. He followed that up with "Boogie on Reggae Woman," which had Darryl and Molly already on the dance floor, doing their thing.

"I just love reggae music!" Molly shouted, causing Dana and I to look at each other and shake our heads. Molly was definitely entertaining. You had to give her that.

The upstairs space was small and cozy and filled with birthday balloons. There was a long bar along the back wall and a VIP area by the stairs. It was filled with cushy banquettes and a table where we placed all of Josh's gifts next to a gigantic birthday cake. We were all VIPs tonight because we'd reserved the entire space. We even had our own waitress. And the biggest VIP of all was about to sing his first song.

The karaoke stage was set up over in the left corner by the bar. There was a large glass fishbowl with small slips of paper and pens beside it. We were all instructed to write down our requests and place them in the fishbowl. Next to the fishbowl was one of those bells you ring at a front desk. We all grabbed slips of paper and pens and sat down at the VIP table and began writing down songs, trying to think of the funniest and most obscure tunes for Josh to sing.

"Okay, while you guys are doing that," Josh spoke into the microphone, "I'm gonna get this party started with the song that started it all. This one's for Katie."

He proceeded to sing "Never Gonna Give You Up." It took me right back to the first night he sang it at The Parlour. He was just about to meet Katie. I was just about to meet Dominic. If I hadn't come to the city that very weekend, none of us would be here right now.

When he was finished, it was time for him to open one of his presents.

"You have to open Sam's first," Katie said, handing him three wrapped boxes that were stacked on top of each other, small, medium, and large.

"You have to open them in order," I said.

As he began to open the smallest box, the waitress took our drink order.

"I'm actually in the mood for a margarita."

"I'll have a Manhattan," Dana said. "Cuz I live in Manhattan, now."

From the first box, Josh pulled out a black t-shirt with gold lettering on it that said "Karaoke King." He immediately took off the shirt he was wearing and put the t-shirt on as we all laughed.

The second box contained a matching crown, robe, and bejeweled microphone with his name on it.

"This is so fucking awesome!" He tied the robe around his neck and placed the gaudy crown on his head.

"You look like a pimp," Kyle said.

In the last box was a large framed and matted photo of him down on one knee, proposing to Katie on New Year's Eve. For a second, I thought he was going to cry, which was something I'd never seen Josh do. Katie started crying the second she saw it. Josh just looked over at me and nodded. Then he gave me the thumbs up.

"Well done, cuz."

"What is it?" Lucy asked.

Katie turned the photo around so everyone could see. It was a black-and-white photo of Katie with both of her hands on her face, obviously shocked at Josh's proposal, while the rest of us - Lucy and Kyle, Dana and Simon, and Dominic and me, looked on with huge smiles and happy tears.

"Oh wow!" Lucy said. "Now I'm gonna cry."

"This is a ploy!" Kyle shouted out. "This is Sam's New Year's Eve ploy to have us all drunk and crying with her."

Everybody laughed out loud as the waitress returned with our drinks.

"To friends," Josh said, holding up his glass. "And to family."

"To Josh!" everybody yelled. "Happy Birthday!"

I took a sip of my drink. It was the best margarita I'd ever tasted in my life, and I'd certainly had my share of tastings over the years.

"Oh my god. Dana, you have to try this." I slid my glass over to her.

"Oh wow," she said after taking a sip. "That bartender is good."

We both glanced over at the bar.

"That bartender is hot," I said.

"Oh so hot," Dana confirmed as we both stared at him.

Molly began ringing the service bell. Time for Josh to do a request. He ran over to the fishbowl in his full-on king regalia and pulled out a piece of paper. He handed it to the DJ, who just shook his head and laughed.

The music started, and the words flashed onto the screen. It was Cher's "Believe." And Josh was nailing it. He was doing his full-on Cher voice while the rest of us jumped up and down and danced around like lunatics, giving Darryl and Molly a run for their money. When he hit the chorus, I lost it.

"I think I just peed a little," I screamed to Dana.

I was laughing so hard that tears were streaming down my face. And they were definitely happy tears.

I had no idea what the future held for Dominic and me. Our happily ever after was yet to be determined. But I had finally managed to extricate myself from Dalton. Not geographically as I'd planned, but emotionally, which was all that mattered. Sometimes you have to let go of someone you love for your own good. And theirs. I'd done that with both of them.

And now maybe, just maybe, I was ready for the moments in between. I looked over at The Bartender. He smiled at me. I smiled back.

Thank You

I cannot thank you enough for reading
my debut novel, *The Waiter.*

If you have any questions about the book
or my writing process or just want to
chat, I'd love to hear from you.

You can contact me on my website at
bradleighcollins.com, where you can also sign
up for my email list, see my "dream cast" if
this book were ever made into a movie, and
download a playlist to go along with the book.

Thanks again for reading *The Waiter.*
I truly appreciate you.

About The Author

Bradleigh Collins

 Bradleigh Collins is a freelance writer and blogger living and working in New York.

She decided to use the extra time she suddenly found herself having during the pandemic of 2020 to finally finish her first novel, The Waiter.

Originally from Atlanta, Bradleigh moved to Manhattan in 1999 and never looked back. To this day, the city - specifically the Upper West Side - remains her one true love.

For more information and to get the scoop on upcoming releases, please visit bradleighcollins.com.